THE

SURINAME JOB

A Case Lee Novel

Vince Milam

Published internationally by Vince Milam Books

WANT TO RECEIVE MY NEWSLETTER? Simply copy the link below and paste into your browser:
http://eepurl.com/cWP0iz

Other books by Vince Milam:
The New Guinea Job: A Case Lee Novel

The Unknown Element: Challenged World Volume I
Pretty Little Creatures: Challenged World Volume II
Gather the Seekers: Challenged World Volume III

Acknowledgments:
    Editor – David Antrobus https://bewritethere.com/

    Cover Design by Rick Holland at Vision Press - *myvisionpress.com*. Front cover photo by Ian Mackenzie (madmack66) at flickr.com. Back cover photo by Maarten van der Bent at flickr.com.

    Story Consultant – Robert Ford

We sleep soundly in our beds because rough men stand ready in the night to visit violence on those who would do us harm.

Chapter 1

I carried a price on my head. A million bucks. The source of the bounty unknown. A Yemeni sheik, perhaps. Somali warlord, Malaccan pirate, Taliban mullah—all possibilities. I'd trade my situation in a heartbeat for more mundane burdens. A failed marriage. Money issues. But that wasn't my reality. I toted early retirement for the conductor of my violent demise.

A quick scan of the small bar—a clockwork affectation to identify threats—ensured the cast of patrons hadn't changed. The older couple at a corner table. He rubbed her back, absorbed. Her eyes bright, telling a tale. Both still in love. The man at the end of the bar opposite me in a gimme T-shirt. He rolled his own smokes and sipped his drink, stretching it. A bum hip caused him to adjust on the barstool. A middle-aged woman, divorced—no ring evident—sat with her grown son, having a beer. She radiated pride and love as only a mother could do as he talked of a new job, full of excitement. She bathed in his youthful exuberance, smiled, nodded. She lived in the moment and set aside life's knocks she'd encountered. Knocks and bumps and disasters guaranteed to strike her son, and all of us. A cluster of young people in a corner, laughing and arguing. A solid cast. Good people. No bounty hunters.

"Another one, Case?" Jonas asked. I'd known the bar owner for several years. He met all my expectations for a good barkeep. Served legitimate drinks, did a flyby when my glass showed lonely, and otherwise kept to himself.

"You bet." Jonas poured stiff four-dollar drinks with good booze—Grey Goose, in my case.

The lone bar in Joiner, North Carolina, sat on the banks of the Intracoastal Waterway. Its small dock offered a regular stop for my boat, the *Ace of Spades*. A quiet bar, where a man could hole up and find a small crevice of peace and protection.

The corner argument's volume, distant from my position, increased. I gave a wide berth to public involvement, and when the exchange between a large, muscular young man and a maybe-twenty woman kicked off, it entered my closed world as white noise—an irritant best ignored.

"Not an option, Jessica," yelled the young man. He had the knot-chord muscles of a shrimper and the volume of someone who had started the party early. "Not an option. You said we'd meet and go out. Well, here I am. Right here, Jessica. Right here."

Fine, kid. There you are. Alert the press. I captured a quick glance of the little vignette under lowered eyebrows, both hands on my head, elbows on the bar. The vodka rocks under my chin held dregs, awaiting Jonas's ministrations. A shifted gaze to the mirror behind the bar reflected back a man this side of forty who appeared to be praying over the small glass. In a sense, I was. I'd made a decision to take the gig offered by my client in Zurich. The money was too good to pass up. So off to Suriname, South America. Off for another day at the office, knife between my teeth.

"You're drunk, Billy," Jessica replied, tears welling. "We agreed to get dressed up and hit the town. You being drunk as Cooter Brown wasn't part of the deal."

Jessica wore clean tight jeans, a red silk blouse, and too much makeup. A local, she'd vacillate for several years between staying in her current environs or striking out for the big city. Charlotte. Raleigh. Greensboro. The Kendra Scott earrings spoke to the bright-lights allure. She stamped her foot to emphasize her point with Billy.

Why pretty young women thought their looks improved through the application of makeup with a putty knife was beyond me. Social pressures, sure, because they're taught to hide every perceived flaw. Interested men wouldn't care about those slight imperfections. Most would find them endearing. But makeup aside, the foot-stamping addition was cute as hell.

Jonas reached inside my huddled position, removed the dead soldier, and placed a fresh Grey Goose under my nose. The bar top held the remnant aroma of lemon polish. Jonas ran a tight ship. The hand that delivered my drink was missing the small finger. I'd asked about it several years earlier. Jonas had replied, "Accident," and left it at that. Fair enough. A man after my own heart.

Early evening choruses—insects and animals and the resident creaking of tied-up boats—filtered through the open windows and doors. The fall weather cut the sticky heat, and if Billy and Jessica would shut the hell up, the evening would take on a near-perfect patina.

"Not an option, dammit!" Billy had become more adamant. "We're going." Overloaded with youthful testosterone and Jim Beam, the strapping young fellow began to display behavior I wasn't going to abide. The kid had started to get mean.

I shifted focus from under my two-hands-on-head position and checked the *Ace of Spades* through one of the open windows. Tied close to a handful of shrimp boats, she bobbed sedately, a single barge and tug having left a slight wake as they passed. She could have used minor repairs and new paint. But she got me from *A* to *Z* every time, and appearance took a back seat to reliability.

Jonas had commented years before that she looked like the *African Queen* from the old Bogart/Hepburn film. Not true. I ran diesel instead of steam, and I had more deck space—essential for both my old recliner and a row of heirloom tomato plants. The former perched as a forlorn throne under the blue foredeck tarp. The latter lined the railing to accept sunshine. Capable of a sedate twelve knots cruising speed, the *Ace of Spades* was home.

The *Ace* and I lived on the Intracoastal Waterway. Permanent watery residents affectionately call it "the Ditch." Stretches of the Ditch crossed saltwater bays and natural inlets, but most of it consisted of dug canals. Quiet, with sparse recreational and barge traffic, it offered an eight-hundred-mile north–south living channel from Virginia to Florida.

"Don't!" Jessica yelped as Billy grabbed her arm. She twisted and aimed a kick at his leg. Good for her, for the effort. But poorly aimed. She should have kicked him in the nuts. Big Billy laughed and started to drag her to the door. "Stop it, damn it! Billy!"

The other patrons, peaceful citizens enjoying the evening, remained still. So the curtain rose on act one. I stepped from the wing and moved center stage. Damn. The smell of greasepaint and the roar of the crowd hadn't been on the evening's agenda. My lay-low spot in the world wished this had happened another night without my presence, but my gut called, "Fix this."

Not permanently—I knew the ensuing actions wouldn't alter Billy's character. But maybe, just maybe, Billy would think next time, and hesitate. Hesitation provided the Jessicas of the world a moment, a collection point, and perhaps an exit strategy. Besides, I couldn't abide bullies.

"Let her go, son." Hands still on head, my body relaxed, no hackles or fireworks. The statement wasn't meant for resolution. It meant to draw his attention toward me—an activity I was well trained to avoid. But this was Joiner, not El Salvador or Syria.

Billy's testosterone flowed—uncontrolled and ugly and washed with too much bourbon. He may not have been a bad-to-the-core kid—hell, I wasn't exactly Mahatma Gandhi—but signs pointed to a bully who had yet to have his ass kicked. That would soon change.

He released Jessica's arm, approached, and received a simple admonition from Jonas. "Don't, Billy. You won't want to mess with him."

The kid stopped to ask, "Why not?" with an eye toward me and a ham fist resting on the bar top. Billy's role had expanded, a star was born, and he smiled a surly lip and waited for me to respond.

Jonas had provided Billy this little informational tidbit about me due to a past altercation, years before. It had involved five tough men, visitors to Joiner. Three ambulances had hauled them off. Afterward, Jonas had asked me just what kind of person *was* Case Lee?

I didn't get into the Delta Force background but did explain, as he poured me a post-encounter drink on the house, that I possessed certain skills. Special skills.

"No shit," was his reply and last mention of the incident. The perfect barkeep.

"Well?" Billy challenged, waiting for my response. The blood and bourbon rose in his now-mean countenance, and his neck swelled—a bull pawing the ground. His left earlobe displayed a small barb earring—a member of the commercial fisherman tribe.

I felt no joy and more than a little angst knowing this kid would soon be floor-bound. I stayed hunched over my vodka. All other bar conversation had stopped.

This would have been a prime opportunity for Jessica to haul ass or call the cops. But the dynamics had changed, Case Lee introduced. My opening soliloquy to let her go had been delivered—short and sweet. The curtain had lifted, and everyone likes a good show, so Jessica wasn't about to depart.

Act two started. A slight head twist allowed for an eye lock with Billy. "Think about it, Billy. There's always—and I mean *always*—someone out there who can kick your ass."

"Like you?" he snorted, mocking.

"I'm not saying it's me. But it could be."

The Jim Beam replied. "Then let's find out, asshole."

Act three approached, ugly and unnecessary. Act four would consist of yelps, pain, trauma—all avoidable.

He turned the corner of the bar and entered my sanctuary, fists clenched. He reached back to throw a punch. I shot a fingertip into his right eye.

"Shit!" His forward progress stopped, hand to the afflicted eyeball.

A lightning jab to the throat, fingertips driving like a wedge into a tree stump. It partially collapsed his trachea, shut down his ability to breathe. He struggled to inhale, lost his focus on me. Big mistake.

A brutal grip up his nostrils and a quick violent twist. The muted pop of a broken nose spread through the room. Billy dropped to his knees, struggled to inhale. Blood flowed from both nostrils. I wiped two fingers clean on his ball cap, took a sip of vodka.

His bruised throat began to allow sips of air. Then he vomited. I've always disliked the vomit part. The smell forced a move away from whatever cozy corner I occupied, back against the wall.

A bit of smug affirmation, I'll admit. Only my left hand had left the top of my head. Not joy or exultation. Satisfaction. Satisfaction with a skill set still well honed. The same hand now lifted the Grey Goose and saluted the sprawled Billy. Bravo, kid, bravo. And so the curtain dropped on Thursday's Joiner community theater.

An empty corner table offered refuge. One of Billy's buddies helped him stand. Jessica retreated to a tight knot of friends across the room and replayed the scene, embellished as needed. The table chair squeaked on the wooden floor as it scooted position and offered me a view of the cypress-lined Ditch and the *Ace of Spades*. A shrimper on one of the fishing boats cussed as he struggled with an unseen piece of equipment. The sun hid below the treetops, and puffs of red and orange littered the horizon—a backdrop for shore and land birds as they moved to roost. The evening courtship calls of frogs accompanied the settled scene.

Reflections, unwanted, drifted in. Rae. My wife. Gone four years now. Murdered. Dead and gone because of me, my past. The memory, the realization was like a cast net descending, ever-present. Early on, I'd fought to dodge the remembrances. Over time I learned to let them settle and cover me. Live with it. The past's enveloping touch was now light, faded. Except for those melancholia moments, blessedly rare, when events and decisions sat wet and heavy. When past actions dripped remorse and guilt. I'd learned to reduce those times. Battle the memories back into an amorphous state. It took concerted effort.

"Need another drink?" Jonas asked. He'd edged over after demanding Billy's buddies clean up the blood and vomit. They'd moved to comply. Jonas wasn't someone you'd want to mess with, either.

"I'm good. Thanks."

He wandered off to supervise the cleanup.

My shot at normalcy gone, killed. So another overseas trip loomed, vacuous, bereft of any purpose other than to pad the bank account. It filled time, utilized practiced skills, allowed escape. Then a return to Ditch life, wandering, figuring it out. It wore, grinded, and the hole in my heart remained.

The bar patrons continued to point in my direction and speak with hushed tones. The seat of attention spelled bad news for a man with a bounty on his head. The Grey Goose downed, I slapped a ten on the table, nodded to Jonas, and said, "See you in a few." Ditch talk for a few days, weeks, or months.

"Watch your back, Case."

I returned an "Always," and walked home.

Chapter 2

Jessica's light snores snapped me awake at irregular intervals. I'd ensconced her in the aft bunk but kept the small door open to my forward bed. Not with any expectations. I'm a better man than that. The door was kept open because it wouldn't do for her to wander the *Ace* unsupervised. Sensitive electronics, private items, and enough firepower to start a coup left far too many opportunities for curious young fingers.

Earlier, the light footfalls on the wooden dock had pulled me from a front-deck recliner reverie. Jonas had closed the bar, and Ditch life had reverted to nature's call. The Glock pistol was aimed with well-practiced surety as the sound approached, on low alert. The steps indicated a woman, young, moving with hesitation.

"Hello?" Soft and questioning, a cookies-and-milk voice.

Jessica stood waiflike alongside the *Ace*, seeking shelter and succor and God knows what else.

I hid the Glock and replied, "Hi, Jessica. What's up?"

She scooted off the dock and came on board, uninvited. The *Ace* reacted and leaned into her body weight. "I need a place to stay."

I moved from the shadow of the wheelhouse to give her a moonlit perspective of my position. No point scaring the kid. "Nope."

She twisted a toe into the deck and talked to her feet. "The deal is, Madeline dropped me off, and I was supposed to, you know, spend the night with, well, *him*."

I remained silent. She continued to pull levers.

"And Madeline isn't answering her cell phone, and she's my roommate, and I don't have a ride back to my place and, well . . ." Jessica swept her arm toward Joiner, dark and still. "So I'm kinda screwed."

"You don't have someone else you can call?"

"No. No, not really."

A young-lady lie, for whatever reason, but I couldn't turn away a lost puppy. First, the ground rules. "There's an extra bunk downstairs. You *will not*, and I repeat, *will not* touch anything. You leave at first light. I have an appointment."

It was against my practice to open the door for her type of request. But a "You had a hand in this, Case" twinge jabbed at me hard, and I couldn't push it away.

Jessica smiled, nodded, and perked up. Ready for her next little micro adventure. I showed her the bunk and the head, in case she needed it during the night.

"Thanks for letting me stay. And thanks for taking care of the deal with Billy."

"I didn't take care of it. He's not going to change."

She shot me a quick quizzical look, dismissed my statement, and turned to seek something. I lived alone, and it took me a moment to grasp that she sought privacy. So I doused the overhead light, threw the bunk rooms into deepest black, and started up the steps to the top deck.

"Thanks." Shoes clomped on the floor. She shimmied out of her jeans and top and slid between the sheets. "Jonas said your name is Case. Case what?"

"Doesn't matter." I took the final step, stood on the deck, and scanned the perimeter. The Glock remained tucked in my back waistband.

Her voice rose from the dark of the lower bunk rooms. "Well, anyway, thanks again. You going to bed?"

"Later. Good night, Jessica." It was hard to discern if an invitation came with her question, but it didn't matter. I eased back to the front-deck throne and planned tomorrow's mission. Within two minutes, light snores drifted from the secure internal warmth of the *Ace* as Jessica slept.

A four-hour run to Chesapeake, Virginia, just south of Norfolk. Dive the dark web, and shoot Jules a message, requesting a Clubhouse appointment around noon. My satellite cell phone had the best encryption money could buy, but Jules remained prickly about voice-to-voice communication. She lived down deep. The dark web existed on overlay networks within the public Internet. It required specific software, configurations, and authorizations to access. Search engines like Google didn't index the dark web. It offered a murky and brackish hiding place for people who sought anonymity.

With this new assignment in Suriname, Jules would sell me her available information on that place. This assumed she'd agree to meet at her Chesapeake Clubhouse—a small, windowless, steel-walled room above a Filipino dry cleaner. Infamous, a woman of indeterminate middle age and origin, Jules met by appointment only. Close to Norfolk and DC, she plied her trade as an information broker, and the Clubhouse received visitors from clandestine civilian and military services. If you wanted information, she'd provide it—for a price.

While she did communicate to set up appointments through dark-web encrypted means, she conducted business face-to-face and with hard copy—specifically, plain index cards with written contacts, descriptions, and actionable information. She also bought information, as long as you provided such on an index card, a task I'd perform during the run north.

Interactions with Jules resembled a poker game, and I had a few jacks, queens, and kings. It kept her price down. She calculated the balance of the information dollars with the clack of an abacus. Jules of the Clubhouse—what a piece of work. But underneath her unfathomable facade, she always indicated a soft spot toward me. Go figure.

Jessica's light snores joined the Ditch nightlife chorus—frogs, the occasional swirl of a fish surfacing, and the death-knell call of a rabbit or other small creature as it succumbed to the night hunters. The old recliner protested with a creak as I shifted to survey the dock area. Once I was downstairs, the early alarm system on the *Ace* would alert me to any intruders. But now, exposed on the foredeck and surveying my kingdom, the standing orders were to move swift and be ready to kill.

I considered a silent trip belowdecks. Retrieve a bottle. I dismissed the thought and invited another. Rae Ellen Bonham. My wife. A Memphis girl, graduate of the University of Tennessee, majoring in graphic design. She'd worked at a Savannah design company when I'd met her. The connection had been instant.

I'd retired from Delta Force, along with my other team members. Delta was a young man's endeavor. We'd all left that chronological category. A hard decision, and I'd missed the focus on mission, team, doing good. Taking out the bad guys. Somalia, Syria, El Salvador. Malaysia, Iraq, Yemen. Insert, take care of business, pull out. A known place in the world, spear point for the good guys.

Once retired, I'd drifted, sought meaning, and wandered my hometown of Savannah. Then I'd met Rae. She had anchored me. Pulled me into a new world, a different picture. Stable and fulfilling in its own way. We'd dated, I'd gotten a job at the Port of Savannah, and we'd married. Delta Force faded, left behind.

I'd long heard speculation of a bounty. Rumor had it our tight team of Marcus, Bo, Angel, Catch, and I all had prices on our heads. Somewhere, we'd stomped on a hornet's nest with deep pockets. But it was human nature to shove bad thoughts aside, coupled with the hope that inactive duty would remove the alleged reward for our deaths. I was a civilian now, far removed from the intensity of special operations.

Life in Savannah settled into a satisfying tempo. We talked of starting a family. There was work, lazy walks, and Trivial Pursuit night with friends. Rae excelled at the entertainment, art, and literature categories of the game. Geography and history for me. We made a great team across a wide range of endeavors. My mate, my lover.

Neither of us had felt like cooking that night, so I'd gone to get takeout. Chinese. I returned; the front door of our small bungalow was ajar. The internal warning sounded, shrill. Leaving the food on the sidewalk, I circled to the back. The kitchen door remained quiet when opened. A strange man, pistol with silencer at his side, stood over Rae. Blood pooled around her head.

An explosion filled me, a flash of pure animalistic fury, the kill switch on. He didn't hear my approach across the linoleum floor but sensed me, too late. I snapped his neck.

He turned out to be Lebanese. A run-of-the-mill bounty hunter.

I moved my mom and sister to Charleston, away from our home base, and swept our tracks. And I bought the *Ace of Spades*, starting a low-key, lost life. Through backdoor contacts, wealthy business clients communicated with me. They asked for my services. Former Delta Force members were in global demand.

Somewhere in the muck and haze, a personal formulation developed. A line drawn, lived. I'd find answers for clients but wouldn't murder. A moral framework, a road map. Something that helped define this next phase of life. Kill to protect myself and my loved ones, but never murder.

A splash off the bow drew my attention. A fish, feeding. It surfaced again, the circular ripple visible in the moonlight. Stars cast great swaths across the sky, the distance impenetrable, unfathomable. The universe, with my sorry ass a minuscule pinpoint on the blue ball called Earth. That universal force—God or cosmic energy or an interwoven power—knew me, acknowledged me. Had to. I felt it, sensed it. Absorbed it among the life all around me, the emotions, the efforts. And among the brutality of what we called nature. But my ability to reciprocate, to communicate, had been slapped, thwarted. I tried, reached, but couldn't formulate that connectivity.

I caught myself starting to doze, and sack time called. Ditch night sounds diminished as I set alarms and trip wires and then made my way to the forward bunk. Jessica slept, the *Ace* cradled us both, and violent dreams came easy.

Chapter 3

The still of morning greeted me with its usual muted manner. I padded past the sleeping girl to grab bacon and eggs from the fridge, emerged on the top deck, and scanned the area. Barefoot, shirtless, and dressed in green Walmart running shorts—my Glock tucked in a pocket—I shivered awake in the morning cool. The topside propane grill accommodated a coffeepot and griddle. The two-burner setup also offered heat. A busy day ahead, and the aches and twinges said nothing, but it's great to be alive, and here we go again. I shook off last night's musings and acknowledged the inarguable fact that millions this morning were doing a lot worse than me. A flock of ducks splashed nearby, the sky cloudless, and I huddled over the propane burners, rubbing my hands.

I'd make sure Bo watered the tomatoes. Plenty of grocery stores lined the Ditch at irregular intervals, and their fresh produce was more than sufficient, except for the tomatoes. You couldn't buy a decent tomato anywhere except for the occasional farmers' market. I loved the heirloom varieties not found in commerce. The lineup of black plastic pots held a Caspian Pink, a Cherokee Purple, a Yellow Brandywine, and an Aunt Ginny's Purple. Four heirloom plants filled with promise.

Bo Dickerson would tend them well. He took such things seriously. Bo was one of four true friends. Our Delta Force team. Our former team leader ranched in Montana. Another lived and worked near Portland, Oregon. The fourth resided parts unknown.

Bo called the Great Dismal Swamp home, a couple of hours south of Chesapeake via its own canal. His boat, unnamed and unregistered and tucked back in a swamp slough, made the *Ace of Spades* look like the *Queen Mary*. Bo kept a pickup at an abandoned house he owned off Highway 17. This conveyance would rumble me to the Norfolk airport for the flight to Suriname. The *Ace* would stay with him.

My buddy had kept the scraggly beard and long hair from his Delta Force days—bright-red hair, hence easier to identify for those who wished to kill him. He'd once told me, "I want them to know it's me, Case. I want them to know exactly who it is that's canceling their birth certificate."

Bo Dickerson might have been semi-batshit-crazy, but he'd found a weird sort of peace—a behavioral attribute I envied. Besides, I'd die for him, and him for me. Those types of friends are hard to come by.

Sounds of life drifted up from below.

Jessica decided to emerge, either due to the smell of coffee and bacon or my poorly hummed rendition of Willie Nelson's "Angel Flying Too Close to the Ground." She climbed to the deck with a large, loud yawn. "I used your bathroom."

"Good. Hungry?"

She had washed her face and hand-combed her hair and now stood as the child she was—wrapped in a bed blanket, vulnerable, curious, and blinking. "I guess. Aren't you cold?"

"Bacon and eggs okay? Coffee's ready soon."

She wandered over, ran a hand along the deck rail, and stood next to me—pretending to stare into the distance. She cast glances in my direction while facing the Ditch. "Cool tat."

The tattoo comment danced around her real question, but she'd arrive there soon enough. The early light, prior to the sun's direct rays, accentuated my scars from bullets, knives, and shrapnel.

"Thanks." She had referred to my sole tattoo: a small passion cross on my left shoulder. A remnant from a wandering relationship.

I poured coffee into two thick ceramic cups. She accepted hers and took a deep inhale. "Man, this smells good. So, what's with all the scars?"

That discussion wasn't going to happen, but I had to smile at her youthful directness. The coffee did smell good, and the bacon began to pop. "Altercations of one type or the other. I've got to leave after breakfast. You'll be okay. The town's waking up."

She drifted toward the bow, plopped on the throne, and pulled her feet beneath her. The blanket stayed wrapped as a large shawl. "Sure. You coming back here to Joiner soon?"

"Eventually. Scrambled okay?"

"Sure."

We ate, her in the throne while I leaned against the wooden rail. The morning coolness faded, vehicle sounds drifted over from Joiner, and a small tug pushed down the Ditch. She spoke about Billy and attempted to confirm my assessment. "Basically, you think I can do better."

"I think you can do different. That boy has a mean streak. It might help if you acknowledge it." I'd spoken my piece and had no intention of a Dr. Phil moment, so I added, "How do you spend your days, Jessica?" I held up a bottle of Cholula hot sauce as an offering.

"No, thanks. And I get to go first, and I'll bet anything whatever you do is related to those scars. You some kind of badass spy? Did you get those in foreign countries? I want to travel."

The circular statements back to Jessica, center of the universe at her age, were normal and smile-inducing.

"Simple private investigator. That's it. How about you?"

She attended community college and worked part-time at a supply store. Once unleashed, she flew the conversational gamut from home to work to boys and back again. She appeared young and fresh without all the makeup. A pleasant scene with a nice young lady to start the day, but the time to be underway approached.

"So Mom thinks office skills—you know, Microsoft Excel and Word and PowerPoint and stuff—but graphic design is a lot cooler, but Mom doesn't think the jobs are there, you know? But then she sent off for these stupid commemorative plates, which makes no sense. So I'm not sure she's in a position to offer great advice. Good eggs and bacon. Thanks. And I'll do the dishes."

She did, while I checked the mechanical status of the *Ace*, shoved memories of a lost graphic designer aside, and fired the lone diesel. A quick check of the satellite phone and laptop confirmed connectivity to a geostationary big bird in the sky. Jessica climbed the steps from below as I headed down to find index cards to populate with handwritten notes for Jules. A quick glance showed that Jessica had done a more than adequate job of cleaning up. "Thanks for doing the dishes."

"No problem."

I retreated and let her exit. She threw one leg over the *Ace*'s rail and prepared to step on the dock when she reversed the process, came over, hugged me, and kissed my cheek. I reciprocated with gentle back pats. Then off again as she climbed onto the dock and turned to say, "Thanks again for putting me up. You're cool, Case."

She shuffled along the dock toward Joiner central while I untied, settled among the clutter of the wheelhouse, and turned north. The old navigation charts, empty booze bottles, and various paper receipts and notes shifted with the breeze coming through the wheelhouse windows. The Glock was used as a paperweight. Busy day ahead. We plowed along the Ditch, fish broke the placid surface, and fragile watery vegetation bobbed and weaved in the *Ace*'s wake.

Chapter 4

The Intracoastal Waterway emptied into Currituck Sound and allowed me to switch the *Ace of Spades* to autopilot. Currituck offered a ten-mile passage across open water, straddling the North Carolina–Virginia border. The breeze off the Atlantic generated a slight chop, which the *Ace* handled with aplomb. The old diesel engine belowdecks sounded its soothing blue-collar rumble, the air thick with the primal smell of estuarial saltwater.

A stack of empty index cards represented potential trading currency, so I got to work. Contact information for a Yemeni arms trader made for a good start, followed by a Colombian smuggler for hire. Southeast Asia was always in-demand currency, so I added several cards with contact details pertaining to arms dealers and pirates. I added some foreign-consulate staffers who could be transformed into conduits of information with a few Benjamins. In short order, I'd compiled a dozen trading cards.

The Clubhouse meeting request had been left on the dark web for Jules. Confirmation was always iffy—Jules had her own peculiar set of rules and moods. More than once she'd disappeared for weeks, throwing the clandestine community from DC to Norfolk into a rumor mill of kidnapping, a defection to the Russians or Chinese, or an early retirement either through her personal decision or a violent death. Then she would return, refuse to talk about the disappearance, and move forward with her usual insouciance.

Cruising the Currituck and waiting for a response from Jules afforded an opportunity to catch lunch and catch up with Mom and CC. I put an earbud in the phone and speed-dialed prior to rigging a simple hook-and-sinker combination on my fishing rod. Mom answered after two rings.

"What's shaking, Mary Lola Wilson?" I asked. Mom and my mentally challenged sister lived in Charleston, South Carolina. Mom had taken back her maiden name after Dad had died of cancer. Moving her to Charleston after Rae's murder had worked out well. If any headhunters of the deadly serious kind swept through my hometown of Savannah, sniffing my trail, they'd come up empty. Mom's name and location change offered a degree of safety for the two of them, and I never lingered long when visiting. Just in case I had been trailed.

"Case, Case. Before you get wrapped around the nearest axle, just know Ginger Hendrik's daughter is both a lovely intelligent girl *and* available. That's all I'm saying, and next time you do one of your flybys in your rickety boat, it wouldn't hurt one little bit to go have coffee with the girl. That's all I'm saying."

She could always make me smile. Her voice and the fine day lifted me. "Does she tango, Mom? I like a girl who knows how to tango."

"Hush and tell me where you are and what you're doing."

I baited the hook with a piece of squid and tossed the line forward of the *Ace*. I intended to catch a few small croakers. Given the *Ace*'s mellow speed, the bait would stay on the bottom for twenty or thirty seconds before it began to drag behind. I'd reel back in and repeat.

"Cruising north of you. I'm going to be out of touch for a week or so."

"Oh, honey." I heard a slurp of coffee as she fueled up for another admonition. "You are a fine young man with vast potential, child of mine. It's time to settle down, stop traipsing around the world, and find a nice girl." Mom declined to qualify it—*another* nice girl—and I appreciated it.

"Well, given my sterling attributes as per Mary Lola, it's probably best to wait until that president of the United States gig opens up."

"I'm serious, and when you get back from your trip to what I'm sure is some godforsaken place, I fully expect you to visit. And have coffee with that lovely girl. And CC misses you."

CC, eight years my junior, never responded to her given name of Celice. She had been born with what the docs called an intellectual disability. She required considerable support from Mom, but she had learned simple health and safety skills and participated in activities.

She was my polestar. Despite my failings and flailing and path-seeking, CC never ceased to fill me with joy and appreciation of life's small wonders. She lived in the immediate and observed and digested the events I passed off as mundane. CC painted verbal pictures with vibrancy and amazement and fed them back to me, wondrous.

"And I miss her. And you. Is CC handy?"

Mom put her on the phone. "Case! You cannot believe. I mean it," CC said.

Focused intent and awe of the world came over the line. I reeled in and cast the bait again. "What, my love? What?"

"Roses. Miss Johnson next door. You know her?"

"I do."

"Roses. Red and white. Some with red and white on one flower. Together! On one flower!"

"I bet they are beautiful."

"So beautiful. Miss Johnson said she would cut me one of the red ones, for me, but I told her no. No because a flower belongs in the ground where they grow. That's why."

"Of course, you're right. Are you taking care of Mom?" A hit on the fishing rod and a quick reel-in produced a half-pound croaker.

"Mom and Tinker Juarez."

Mom had rescued Tinker Juarez from the pound a year ago. CC named him. Mom and I had no clue where she came up with Tinker Juarez, but there it was. A mutt of indeterminate lineage, he fit right in the family, his black and brown smiling face a constant companion of CC's.

"How is Tinker Juarez?" I tossed the croaker in the fish bucket and re-baited.

"A dog."

"A good dog?"

"Very good dog. You know."

"I know."

"Tinker Juarez had breakfast. He's happy."

"Are you happy?"

"Mom makes me happy. Tinker Juarez makes me happy."

"Good. I want you to be happy."

"You make me happy. Breakfast makes me happy."

I laughed while a second croaker hit the bait and soon thereafter landed in the fish bucket. Sufficient for lunch. "I'll visit you soon. Do you remember the one big thing?"

"That you love me. More than the sun."

"And?"

"And more than the moon."

"And?"

"And more than the stars. That's a lot!"

"And all true, my love. Every bit of it true."

She handed the phone to Mom, and I let her know of my expected arrival back in the States and when a Charleston stop was likely.

"Love you, honey," she said. "Be careful, although I know you always are, but it doesn't stop me from worrying. Can't wait to see you."

"Love you too, and I'll drift your way in a couple of weeks. Kiss CC for me."

I scanned the horizon for boat traffic and fired the grill. The wheelhouse laptop indicated a message received, and after encryptions and passwords I read, *One o'clock.*

Jules had replied in her usual succinct manner. The Clubhouse meeting set, I sliced poblano peppers and onions, tossed them into the cast-iron pan with olive oil, and filleted the croakers. Al Green sang "Love and Happiness" through the foredeck speakers, and I moved to the music while cooking. A longing for family and convention tempered the otherwise fine day.

I left Currituck Sound and headed up the North Landing River, part of the Intracoastal network of canals, rivers, and sounds. We plowed a sedate path as barge and boat traffic increased. Two hours later, a cut-through canal had the *Ace* cruising the Elizabeth River and into Chesapeake, Virginia. The usual tie-up spot, a simple two-boat pier, was empty. With bumpers over the side, I secured my home. Alarms and security measures set, I wandered up the steep hill to the convenience store perched above the small pier and bought a bag of pork rinds. I slid a twenty across the counter to the old man I'd dealt with numerous times before. "Keep the change. And keep an eye on the *Ace.*" As always, he pocketed the money and nodded.

A run-down section of town greeted me during the six-block walk to the Filipino dry cleaners. A door-handle bell rang as I entered and nodded to the woman behind the counter. She returned a noncommittal stare. Our eyes remained locked. I produced the Glock and placed it on the counter. She covered it with a few unlaundered items. You didn't bring weapons into the Clubhouse.

A nondescript door to the left of the counter led to dark stairs. They creaked with each step. A small window at the top of the stairs provided the sole light. A door, steel with a simple welded handle, waited. It was one minute after one o'clock.

Two door taps brought an electronic buzz, and the door unlocked with a metallic click. I swung it open and entered to stare down the usual twin barrels of a sawed-off shotgun.

"Enter my parlor, said the spider to the fly. Close the door, dear."

I did. Jules sat behind the old wooden desk, both elbows on top. Her left hand held the forward part of the weapon, and her right rested on the trigger. She smiled, cheek pressed against the shotgun's stock.

"You appear in fine fettle. Turn around, dear."

A pirouette assured her I wasn't armed, at least not in a manner allowing quick access.

"Empty your pockets. Still angst-ridden about life, Montague? How be the family?"

"Fine." Instant alarms. Her reference to my family put a marker on the table—one I didn't like.

After I emptied my pockets and showed her a money clip and a stack of index cards, Jules signaled with the weapon's barrel where to sit. The room, windowless, was paneled with sheet steel, the walls devoid of decoration except for an old *Casablanca* movie poster with Bogart and Bergman. The poster might have hidden something, but I'd never know. An air conditioner hummed, but I couldn't discern any vents unless they resided under her desk. Two large steel cabinets added to the decor, possible storage for her electronics. A lone overhead naked lightbulb with a pull-chain switch and a small desk lamp provided yellow-hued illumination.

Jules hadn't changed. An itinerant sheep shearer appeared to have cut her hair, with the band of the eyepatch over her left eye lost amid the tangle. All ten fingers were tipped with small latex covers to prevent the spread of fingerprints. A KA-BAR knife remained embedded in the old wooden desktop. Her ancient abacus awaited transactions.

The wooden chair I occupied squeaked, and she lowered the shotgun, although it remained within quick reach.

"How you doing, Jules?"

"Comme ci, comme ça." A quick, violent convulsion overtook her. A held-in sneeze and a regular occurrence. I'd never asked her why she didn't take allergy medication. Too personal. The dangerous downside of her pent-up sneezes manifested with her immediate reaching for weaponry. Just in case the split second of physiological weakness had afforded her guest an opportunity to attack.

"About my family."

She lowered the shotgun again. Few people knew of Mom and CC's existence or their whereabouts. Jules's mention of them staked a flag far out-of-bounds and required elaboration.

She produced a long, thin cigar from a desk drawer and spun one end against the embedded knife blade, trimming the tip. The sealed end of the cigar fell to the desktop, and she fished a kitchen match from her shirt pocket and fired it on the wooden armrest of her chair. Her one eye never left me during the process. She puffed sufficiently to light the cigar and send acrid smoke around her face.

"Simple bonhomie, Case. Do not construe a deeper meaning."

An insufficient answer, and my silence would trigger further clarification. I liked Jules, as far as it went, but she'd exposed a raw nerve.

"This misunderstood creature before you is but a simple and honest broker of information," she continued. "That said, I admit to preferences. I prefer you over many others with whom I have dealings. A tender locale within my beating heart."

She smiled again. It indicated nothing.

"Thanks. I appreciate it. The thing is, I have a price on my head."

"I'm well aware of that."

"So any information about my family is out-of-bounds. They're vulnerable."

"Well put, and acknowledged." She paused to puff and blow smoke toward the ceiling. I shifted position, the chair creaked, and she continued. "During the course of my career, there have been numerous bits of personal information that will follow me to my grave. Familial connections, in your case, is one of those bits."

How she knew of Mom and CC would remain her secret, but the reality of her knowledge still sat uneasy. Jules, tough and strange and honest, had plucked a loose thread of danger. Danger to my family.

My silence remained and Jules, to her credit, expressed a rare conversational gambit outside her usual stick-to-business facade. "Allow us to mull this over from a species perspective, dear. Are you familiar with the habits and peculiarities of *Sus scrofa domesticus*?"

"I'll take the fifth."

"Pigs. Domestic pigs. Amazing creatures. I shall pardon your ignorance. Chalk it up to a failure of your educational experiences. Be that as it may, a somewhat large herd is maintained not far from here by the Filipino community in our little burg."

"I suppose that's good news."

"Indeed! Below us, at this moment, is a hardworking family of Filipinos operating a profitable dry-cleaning establishment."

"I've noticed."

"Then you may also wish to note they pay no rent." She puffed on the cigar.

"Do tell."

"A rent-free operation. Due to the fact they occasionally moonlight, as it were, for me—the owner of this building. Indeed, they do."

"Moonlight."

"You see, dear. The position you now occupy, situated across from me, is from time to time occupied by someone whose inquiries offend the tender mercies in my less-than-ample breast. In short, they ask the wrong questions."

"Is this about pigs, Jules?"

She puffed the cigar and sent a thin stream of smoke above our heads.

"Ah. You sit with bated breath. Fair enough. You see, when the wrong person asks the wrong questions, I am forced, through a litany of tortured emotions, to use this."

She hefted the shotgun with a grim look. "An effective tool, which, most unfortunately, tends to make quite the mess."

I turned to inspect the steel door and its adjoining steel walls. The telltale smear of lead pellets and small peppered indentations showed in several spots. "I imagine it would be messy."

"Quite so. On the rare occasion such a little scenario occurs, I request moonlighting expertise from my Filipino compatriots downstairs."

"A cleaning crew."

"So to speak. An element of quid pro quo. They arrive with a large stout waterproof bag, a bottle of Clorox, and innumerable rags." She paused to take another puff and continued. "One can only hope the rags are not remnants of some poor woman's dropped-off Christian Dior."

Her chair protested as she leaned back and inspected the ash of the cigar. "Lickety-split—and how I do love that expression for such an activity—the Clubhouse is cleaned, and the offending party removed. Removed where, you might ask?"

"Pigs. The Filipino community."

"Give this dashing man a gold star! For pigs will consume everything. Bones, toenails—I shall not elaborate further. Suffice it to say, evidence of the offending party is digested."

"Back to my family."

"This little narrative has been all *about* your family, dear. Any knowledge I might have is safe."

"Safe."

"You see, anyone asking the wrong questions about the same is simply, well, digested."

My protective alarms ratcheted down several notches. Jules's candor was welcomed, but her interest still grated. "I appreciate it. But why me and my family? Why even go there and ask me about them?"

Her body relaxed, draped over the desktop. She placed the cigar on the edge of the desk. The creak of her chair filled the dead silence. Jules's eye showed, for the first time, true empathy. She addressed me from the heart.

"Some are born with less than full alacrity in the intellectual realm. The wiring, not quite right. Mentally challenged is, I believe, the current vernacular." She leaned back and held out her hands, palms up. "They are most special. I have personal experience with such matters. And that, Case Lee, is the last we shall ever speak of this."

Chapter 5

The atmosphere changed to one of connection and comfort. But the jaundiced portion of my personality, combined with past experience, cued a possible Jules strategy to soften my outlook prior to negotiations. A hell of a way to live, and unwelcome.

"Got a gig in Suriname."

"Yes, you do, dear." She pulled open a desk drawer and produced a stack of index cards. How Jules knew of my assignment from the Swiss firm Global Resolutions would remain unbroached.

"A coup. Fighting over who knows what, but aluminum concerns rank high," I said.

"Aluminum concerns." She plucked her cigar from the desktop and tapped more ash on the floor.

"Several bauxite mines in Suriname."

"Hmmm."

"Hop down there, ascertain the landscape, report back. On the surface, a cut-and-dried assignment." Beneath the surface, something else brewed. I'd been in the business too long not to feel it. Now Jules had copped an attitude, confirming the "something else."

"A peculiar place," she said.

She had that right. Formerly Dutch Guiana, it nestled on the northeast corner of South America between British Guiana—now just Guyana—and French Guiana. The official language was Dutch, although most residents of that strange little country also spoke Sranan Tongo—a fusion of English, Dutch, Portuguese, and West African. Hindustani and Javanese were also widely spoken. With half a million residents, Suriname held the distinction of being the smallest South American country. Ninety-five percent of the population lived along the Atlantic coast, the interior wild and jungle-covered.

"Spoken exchange?" I asked. Prior to the brass tacks of index-card information, the Clubhouse offered the option of oral information transfer. The pricing of such, as always, fell to Jules's discretion.

"Fine." She laid her index cards down and cast a hard eyeball toward the end of her cigar. A few hard puffs ensured it remained lit.

"Something about this assignment sticks in my craw." Suriname had a history of revolutions and insurrections. But bauxite mining had continued through it all, uninterrupted. This smelled of something larger than the average coup of the month.

"The economic considerations—the bauxite mines for aluminum production—may not constitute your client's major concern," Jules said. Her cigar hand flicked two large black balls among the many on the abacus. The wooden clicks committed a payment, the amount of which I had no clue. Jules would let me know the bill at the end of our talk.

"How so?"

"Geopolitics. Establishment of a presence in South America." A single black ball scooted down one of the abacus's wooden posts.

"Chinese? Russian? Middle Eastern? Drug cartels?" The FBI had recently busted the son of Suriname's current president-for-life and convicted him of offering material support to Hezbollah. His offer to help them establish a permanent base in Suriname demonstrated the wild nature of my destination. I wished my clients, the gnomes of Zurich, would offer assignments to more tranquil parts of the world.

"Undetermined." The abacus remained quiet. She didn't charge for murky answers.

Jules's oral information was gold. To spin my wheels focused on economic aspects—bauxite mining—would mean wasted effort. Good to know. But geopolitical intrigue had a downside. It increased the challenge of information collection. And it damn sure increased the danger factor.

"All right. Let's talk players." The time had come to spill some of those brass tacks.

She lifted the deck of index cards at my statement and popped them once on the desktop as a fresh deck of cards.

"Clandestine players?" she asked.

It wouldn't hurt to know the CIA element stationed in Suriname, so I nodded. She flipped through her cards, produced one, and slid it across the table. Two balls clicked on the abacus. The name—Fletcher Hines—didn't ring a bell. His official title was agricultural liaison for the US embassy. What crap. Couldn't they come up with something a little more inventive than *agricultural liaison?*

"Special interests?" If available, Jules would provide any personal insights such as sexual tendencies, drug addictions, etc.

"None." The abacus remained silent. So this Fletcher Hines was a straight shooter. He'd be less than enthused at my presence on his dance floor.

"Dutch," I said. Knowledge of any key players with strong Dutch ties and therefore deep knowledge of local history and current events would make for a legitimate anchor point. Jules slid another index card across the desk, and I digested the information. The abacus clicked.

"No special interests," she said preemptively.

"Suriname government or military," I said.

"Little or no difference between the two," Jules stated, slid another card, and waited for the inevitable.

"Special interests?"

"Cocaine." The abacus clicked. "He likes money to pay for his habit."

Nothing unusual about a government functionary with a drug habit, although it made for distasteful exchanges. But I'd travel with a large wad of American dollars, and Global Resolutions always reimbursed me for such expenses. Still, slime-covered stuff.

"Out-of-country insertions." Foreign spy networks and associated players provided sound informational footing prior to entering an operational theater. I would have been surprised if Jules didn't know of these assets.

"One of ours. A merc." She slid the card, I digested the name, the abacus clicked. I riffled through my mental Rolodex, remembered this guy. An American mercenary by the name of Bishop. Have helicopter, will travel.

"Others?"

"Rumors."

"I'll take it."

"A woman. Unknown origin. Unknown paymaster. Nothing concrete." The abacus remained silent. The well showed dry on that front, so I moved to more personal matters.

"Firearm." There was little point smuggling a weapon into most foreign countries. Local black markets offered a wide selection of weaponry.

"Heavy or light?" Jules asked.

"Light." A semiautomatic pistol would suffice for my endeavors.

She slid another card across the table, clacked a couple of abacus balls, puffed her cigar. I memorized the information on the cards she'd handed me. I wasn't going to leave with them. None of Jules's hard-copy information left the Clubhouse, ever. Sixty seconds later, the information absorbed, her cards were returned. She collected them, added them to her stack, and placed the deck back in a desk drawer.

"Let's talk about what you've brought me, dear."

It was time to provide discounts to the cost of my information bill. "Yemeni arms trader."

She wafted a dismissive hand. A bit of a surprise given the hotbed of activity in that part of the world, but she may well have been inundated with such information.

"Colombian smuggler. Member of FARC." The terrorist group FARC, long established in Colombia, knew every back road and mountainous trail.

"Could be handy, although the Mexicans have usurped the need for a great number of Colombian dealings. That said, I'll accept."

I slid the index card to her; she clacked a few abacus balls—my discount.

"Southeast Asia pirate."

"Straits of Malacca?" she asked. The narrow 500-mile stretch of water between Malaysia and the Indonesian island of Sumatra had been a pirate haven for centuries. Insider information on the pirate bands proved notoriously difficult to come by. They were as clannish as the Mafia.

"Yes."

"Recent?" She wanted to ascertain the freshness of the information.

"Three months."

"How nice, dear. Yes, that would be wonderful to have."

I passed the card, and the abacus clicked. I ran through my other index cards, and she dismissed all but one.

"Chinese embassy staffer in Brazil. Loves drugs and girls. Lots of both. Benjamins speak loudly with this gentleman." Much of the world's sordid low-level activities revolved around $100 bills.

"How less than inscrutable. I'll accept."

Her fingers flew across the abacus, adding and subtracting. "Three thousand, five hundred."

Neither I nor anyone else allowed access to the Clubhouse had the foggiest notion whether the abacus clacks were bullshit or real. It didn't matter. Three and a half large for Suriname insights and contacts was cheap. I unfolded the $100 bills and handed them to Jules.

"One last thing," she said as the dollars disappeared into another drawer. "The unknown out-of-country insertion suspected to be female? Watch your back with that one."

"Okay."

"Whatever is going down in Suriname smells of high stakes. Very high stakes, dear. Do not get sucked into the mundane—economics, corporate interests, or any other such folderol."

"Okay, again."

The AC hummed. She cast a hard, hooded eye.

"Head down, nose to the wind, my boy. And do be prepared to run like hell."

"Always am. Thanks, Jules. Sincerely."

"No, you're not. Running is not in your nature."

I stood and shrugged.

"I do so wish you were more prone to graceful, albeit hasty, exits. But you're not. Be extra cautious. Whatever is happening in that unfortunate place is most certainly not worth dying for."

I turned to the door, and she pressed a hidden button to unlock it. Prior to my exit, I added, "Nine lives, Jules. Nine lives."

"And you've used up eight of them, dear."

Chapter 6

A poisonous cottonmouth snake swam an *S* shape through the water, head raised, seeking. The *Ace* sent it diving as we edged a cautious path through the bald cypress trees in three feet of water. The Dismal Swamp—gloomy even on such a bright day—offered few viable routes for watery navigation.

I'd contacted Bo Dickerson after leaving the Clubhouse. He, too, had a satellite phone. He answered after two rings.

"Amos and Sons."

Code speak—known to fewer than five people—allowed Bo to filter any misplaced communications.

"You still squatting on federal land?" I asked. The Great Dismal Swamp consisted of several hundred thousand acres of wildlife refuge and protected wetlands.

"Squatting is precisely correct, cracker boy. A bowel movement. A moment of quiet and solitude, interrupted by a sorry-ass Georgian calling me. How you, Case?"

His voice bridged memories good and bad, based on a foundation of trust and brotherhood. As former members of Delta Force, we shared a rich past. Narrow misses with death, covering each other's backs. Leaps into stacked-odds situations with absolute assuredness we'd each give our life for the other. A rare bond; precious.

"I'm tight and fine. The question before us is whether you can multitask. Your current activity plus a phone conversation. I know how you like to focus on the effort at hand. Should I call back?"

"No. This borders on pleasant. I may squat longer than intended."

"I'm heading your way. ETA three hours. You all right with that?"

Any friendly incursion into someone's home required approval. It made for common courtesy, even if home consisted of many square miles of swamp. Approval was especially important for a visit to Bo. There would be trip wires and booby traps around his current anchorage in the middle of the Dismal Swamp.

"Area B. Arrive before dark so you can avoid unpleasantness. I'll burn some venison steaks, and we'll sing of love lost."

Bo had three swamp hiding spots—A, B, and T. The illogical alphabetic progression made sense only if you knew Bo. The unpleasantness he referred to were explosive traps, triggered with near-invisible fishing line. I knew the location of his three anchorages, but not the whereabouts of his security explosives. He tended to move those with regularity.

"Venison? Must be deer season already." Bo didn't have refrigeration, so dinner would be fresh meat.

"This concept of a defined deer-hunting season. One established for less than expansive minds."

I explained my travel plans and asked to borrow his truck the following day, leaving it at the Norfolk Airport for a week or so.

"No worries. Hasten onward, you cretinous goober. I await. Ciao, au revoir, vaya con Dios."

I continued to steer with caution and reminisced on our time together in Special Forces. Delta Force did not officially exist. The US government didn't acknowledge the organization. Unlike Seal Team Six, who carried positive publicity, Delta worked the shadows. The men of Delta rarely even used the name, designating their collection of warriors as *the Unit*. We referred to each other as operators. Sent in hard and fast, we took care of business and left. Every insertion was considered a hot-fire situation, and operators accomplished the Unit's missions with deadly efficiency. Then back to the obscure, the shadows.

The Unit's operators were masters at the covert art of counterterrorism, excelled at hostage rescue, the elimination of terrorist forces, and intelligence gathering of terrorist threats. Experts at close-quarters combat, sniping, covert entry, and explosives. Our enemies recognized, and feared, Seal Team Six. But they feared us as much, if not more. The most skilled warriors on the planet, operating in obscurity.

The individuals in our Delta Force team had specific roles, duties, and strengths. Marcus Johnson, team leader, established the mission, the plan. He stayed in the middle of the action, directing. Angel kept to the edges, covered our flanks. Catch eliminated surprise threats, the unforeseen. I was charged with ensuring tactical goals were accomplished, and followed the lead warrior.

Bo Dickerson—lead warrior. The first to engage. Occupy the enemy's focus, draw their firepower, become the target of their ire. He'd go after them in unexpected ways, utilizing surprise and a touch of insanity. There were none better.

***

A mission in Yemen had personified Bo's approach to battle. The city of Al Mukalla, a seaport on the coast of Yemen, served as Al Qaeda's headquarters for the region. The terrorist group had carried out the 2000 bombing of the *USS Cole*, the 2008 American embassy attack in Yemen, and several attacks against foreign tourists. They had expanded operations and struck in other parts of Yemen as well as Djibouti and Somalia, spreading terror, horror. Suicide bombings, mass killing, the capture and rape of women.

Western intelligence sources had identified a small building as their prime gathering spot. But these guys were smart, and the two-story structure nestled against a hospital on one side and an orphanage on the other. Drone strikes were ruled out as collateral damage was guaranteed. Hello, Delta Force.

The key to success was on-the-ground intelligence to alert us when the leaders were assembled. So the reliable, ancient, tried-and-true tactic of bribery kicked in. Money, paid to a taxi driver in Al Mukalla, initiated by me. I spoke Arabic, and it didn't take long after a night insertion via inflatable motorized raft to find an amenable partner. In addition to money, the taxi driver was handed a small radio for communications. Then the five of us operators waited on a US Navy LCS—littoral combat ship—off the coast.

Six days of standby, and the consensus grew of a taxi driver laughing all the way to the bank. Then the radio call. An assembly of Al Qaeda leaders, now, in the early evening. We boarded our combat raiding craft, a small inflatable boat equipped with a muffled 55 HP outboard engine. We headed for a landing spot several miles outside of the city. There was a risk of being spotted, a risk of word relayed to Al Qaeda fighters. And a risk of being attacked before we reached our objective. It didn't matter. We were going in.

The taxi driver met us with a borrowed van and drove our team through the darkening streets of Al Mukalla. It could have been a setup, a drive to our demise. Marcus held a pistol to the neck of our driver while I explained our concern to him. He understood.

The driver pulled into an abandoned cinder-block garage, got out—accompanied by Marcus—and closed the double doors. He covered his own butt and delivered us out of sight. Understandable. Catch cracked open the back door and extended a handheld GPS. Ten seconds later, we knew exactly where we were. One block away from the Al Qaeda assembly building.

We'd studied the layout until blue in the face and understood we would be surrounded by Al Qaeda supporters, all armed. The mission: strike hard, fast, and take out the terrorist leaders. Then exit ASAP. A white-hot insertion and exit. Our escape plan abandoned the inflatable craft and entailed a mad dash for a nearby soccer field where a Pave Hawk helicopter, deployed from the offshore ship, would pick us up. All while being chased and shot at by Al Qaeda fighters. Another day at the office, Delta style. We lived for these opportunities.

We sprinted the city block to the target building, Bo in the lead. No hiding or sneaking. Full frontal, counting on speed, surprise, and ferocity. Bo ran down the narrow space between the two-story building and the orphanage, disappeared from sight. The rest of us took up positions, anticipated his engagement. Angel circled to the opposite side of the building, along the narrow alley separating it from the hospital. Catch stepped back to the middle of the street, bold as brass, prepared to take on interfering force. No one would mistake him for a street vendor. Marcus and I waited at the heavy front door. Salt air, aromas of food being prepared, dusty, ancient street smells. A mother called to her child, out of sight.

It didn't take long. In less than twenty seconds, the rattle of Bo's Heckler & Koch MP5 submachine gun sounded from the second floor. He'd clearly scaled the back wall to a second-floor window and unleashed hell. Marcus hand-signaled Catch that we were entering, and I'd begun to push through the front door when a hand grenade exploded in the entryway. The concussion slammed the thick door shut.

A second attempt to push the door open and enter was greeted by a quick glimpse of another grenade flying through the air toward the large entryway area. This time, I slammed the door shut and waited for the explosion. Bo's weapon continued to fire short bursts as screams and yells and return fire filled the interior of the building.

Marcus shot me a "Get your ass in there!" look, and I opened the front door for the third time. The entry area held several dead bodies and three men firing up the stairs. I entered, took the three out, then backed into Marcus as another grenade floated over the upstairs stone bannister and headed our way. Marcus and I made it to the doorway entrance and plastered against a protective wall as the grenade exploded.

Our crazy redheaded brother had clearly opted to take care of the whole rat's nest himself. Bo continued to fire controlled bursts from above while casually lobbing grenades downstairs at regular intervals.

"Wait for a flash-bang!" Marcus hissed, still pressed against the wall.

Up to this point, Bo had been tossing fragment grenades, meant to kill. He'd run out of those soon enough. Then he'd be reduced to tossing a stun grenade—flash-bang—in our direction. This device was used to temporarily disorient an enemy's senses. At least one of those wouldn't kill us.

It came quickly, and the concussive explosion filled the lower floor of the building. Our protective spot helped shield us, and in the aftermath of the explosion, Marcus and I rushed past the stairs and into the lower-floor rooms, all the while yelling, "Lower floor! Lower floor!" in the hope it would stem the tide of raining grenades. It did.

We encountered four more Al Qaeda leaders in lower-floor rooms. My H&K weapon barked and dispatched two of them. Marcus followed rapid suit, his fire deadly. A final round of submachine gunfire echoed from above. A short burst of fire from outside indicated either Angel or Catch had stopped an escaping Al Qaeda member. Exit time.

Marcus and I ran toward the front door, yelling, "Clear! Clear!" to let the team know this little soiree was officially over. A movement on the wide stairs caught my eye, and I brought my weapon to aim, finger squeezing the trigger.

Bo Dickerson, wearing a big smile and splatters of blood on his face, slid down the bannister toward us. Slid. Down the bannister. "Ho, ho, ho!" his entry cry. What a piece of work.

The Pave Hawk helicopter hovered outside of town, and we radioed for pickup. Catch cut loose on a half dozen AK-47-wielding fighters who had rushed our direction. Time to haul ass.

Our sixty-second dash to the soccer field coincided with the chopper's touchdown, waiting for us to scramble on board. A large neighborhood greeting committee had assembled by then, and AK-47 bullets whined past us as we dove into the chopper and lifted off.

"Anyone hit?" Marcus yelled.

"Good," came back four times. The entire hot-fire operation, from exiting the garage to entering the helicopter, had taken less than six minutes.

On the helicopter ride back to the naval vessel, Bo leaned into my face and asked, "You ever read Camus?"

"No."

"Man is the only creature that refuses to be what he is."

"Okay, Bo. Okay."

What a piece of work.

***

Bo hailed from Tulsa, Oklahoma. His mom had worked at a tire store until breast cancer took her. His dad, a master welder, had worked the oil fields until his death in a car accident. No siblings. Fellow operators were his family. When we'd all retired from the Unit, Marcus first, it was Bo we worried about most. It was an unfounded concern—he'd picked a zone in the universe where happiness resided. A mental, physical, spiritual place unique to him.

I'd left Chesapeake, cruised west along Deep Creek for several miles, and entered the old lock at the head of the Great Dismal Swamp canal. One other boat waited—a large fiberglass cruiser—and I joined stern-to-bow until the lock operator closed the gate, lifted both vessels, and sent us on our way south down the forty-mile canal.

George Washington had been a lead instigator of the canal's creation to provide a route between Chesapeake Bay and North Carolina's Albemarle Sound. Thick cypress, tupelo, maple, and pine hid Highway 17 to the east. To the west: miles of cypress swamp inhabited by birds, black bear, deer. Alligators, otters, snakes. And Bo Dickerson.

It was illegal to live there, but enforcement was nonexistent as no one in his right mind would consider it. A valid assertion and applicable to my wild friend.

I let the large expensive cruiser pull away and ensured no traffic of any sort would see the *Ace* as we made a sharp right turn into the swamp, meandering between cypress trees and islands of dry land. The speed cut to a sedate walking pace, I maneuvered with caution. The *Ace* drew two and a half feet of water, leaving little room for error and lots of opportunities for a cypress knee to damage the hull. After an hour of vigilant travel, a subtle rock cairn on a hummock of dry land marked a sharp turn to the right.

Alligators viewed my passage with periscope eyes, performing a languid descent when the *Ace* passed too close. An animal crashed through brush on a sliver of island, and the air was redolent with the thick decay of an ancient swamp. Several minutes later, I threw the *Ace* into reverse and brought us to a dead stop. The late day's rays peeked through the thick trees and glinted off a thin string of fishing line stretched across my watery path. An act of the explosive kind would have been triggered if we'd pushed against the near-invisible line.

"Scaramouch! Scaramouch!"

The singsongy voice came from the right. I cut the engine and left the small wheelhouse. He was perched on a large cypress stump twenty yards away. The low sun highlighted wild strands of red hair as a halo around his head, a wide smile and crazed eyes aimed my way.

"I'd have damn sure done the fandango if we'd tripped that wire. Claymore?" The business end of the booby trap had either a claymore mine or plastic explosive or a flash-bang grenade—each dependent upon whether Bo wished to kill, maim, or scare.

"A mystery, old son, and one best left alone." His smile widened. Man, it was good to see him again. "Back your tub and squeeze between those two trees." He pointed toward safe passage.

Bo leaped on board as I maneuvered. He came into the open-window wheelhouse to hug me from behind and bumped his forehead against the back of my head several times. His untrimmed beard scratched the back of my neck. He smelled of swamp and pine and rich, dark earth. A half dozen light rabbit punches to my lower back had me squirming and laughing and delivering declarations of an imminent ass whipping if he didn't stop. Bo placed a hand on my head as if to bless me.

"An auspicious return, prodigal son. Timing solid and right."

"How's that?"

"Part of the plan. Ebb and flow," he said, and left the wheelhouse to position himself in the foredeck recliner and provide navigational directions. Life presented few sureties, but one indisputable fact sat before me—they'd broken the mold after Bo Dickerson's creation.

"You're looking fit and happy, Bo. I'm not surprised."

"A reason for that, my brother. Weave left. There. Now right."

The *Ace* maneuvered at a sedate pace through the tight passages, the low rumble of the diesel an intrusion, alien. Bo inspected the big toe on a bare foot.

"My condition rests on having not opted to burden myself with the weight of the world," he said to his foot. "A release mechanism. One you should develop."

"No argument here."

A final turn, and his wooden houseboat came into view. Here and there, remnants of paint, evidence that once upon a time it had been white. A gray canvas tarp extended over parts of the deck, and Christmas lights wound around the small midmast that served no purpose other than to fly the Jolly Roger. Numerous solar panels hung from the boat's side, along with tails of old rope and an extended-over-the-water wind chime. A ratty Kermit the Frog stuffed toy was tied around one of the guardrail stanchions.

"No excitement since last time?" I asked. Last time—ten weeks earlier—I'd paid a visit, and bad things had happened. Things of the killing variety.

Chapter 7

On that day two and a half months ago, Bo had met me at the edge of his turf. A battered aluminum canoe poked into the Dismal Canal, and Bo stood alongside, waist deep and bathing. Hot, sticky air and the buzzing of insects marked deep summer. His long hair dripped and his wide smile flashed as the *Ace* chugged closer. The scene was unusual, peculiar. He hadn't met me at the edge before. Canoe tossed on the stern deck, he guided me past trip wires toward his home.

"Kinda wished you put on some clothes," I said as we maneuvered.

"It's hot."

"How 'bout a loincloth, Tarzan?"

He moved on, other interests drawing his attention. He pulled his satellite phone from a rucksack, scanned the screen, and mumbled something indiscernible. He twisted around, locked eyes, and extended three fingers. "We ain't fakin'. Whole lotta shakin' goin' on." An event had taken place in Bo's vast swamp. He'd reveal the details at his own pace.

We tied to the stern of his unnamed vessel next to a hummock of land, and Bo scrambled onto his home. "Movement and ill intent, Mr. Lee. Movement and ill intent," he called over his shoulder as he disappeared down the steps. I clambered on board his boat, and the tinkle of wind chimes voiced my presence as his vessel shifted. They hadn't sounded with Bo's movements.

I meandered to the front deck and sidestepped a few T-shirts drying on a short piece of line. A bucket of wild greens occupied a spot near a hung wild-pig carcass. An old Weber charcoal grill, two of its three legs replaced with twisted cypress limbs, was poised at an angle and ready for the next meal. Three large pots held marijuana plants, thick and bushy. There were several old Clorox jugs, sealed and shoved toward the front of the deck. Each with fishing line and a large catfish hook attached. Trotlines. A once brightly colored hammock of South American origin stretched between two canopy posts.

Bo hummed from below and carried on a personal discussion with himself. His voice mixed with metallic clatter—clear indications of weaponry preparation. He called to me and raised his voice to clarify.

"They arrived sometime over the last few days. Now they stumble, foolish, toward my location. And their demise." A mass of red hair and a smile painted with mirth and wildness poked up from belowdecks. "Three of them. Bounty hunters." Declaration delivered, his head disappeared back into the lower cabin.

Damn. It had been a while, and the yearning thought of resolution and a world moved on had taken firm root within my mental makeup. Son of a bitch.

"Coming for me, old son. Excellent timing on your part," he called.

"You sure?" False hope, and I knew it. When it came to kill or be killed, Bo didn't make mistakes.

He climbed back on the deck—now dressed in fatigue pants and boots—armed with a scoped assault rifle and a semiauto pistol, silencer attached. His Bundeswehr combat knife, sheathed, hung from a belt loop on his jeans. He thrust the rifle in my direction. "You are writ large on the same hit list, Mr. Lee. Let us winnow the field." His smile was matter-of-fact and calm.

I took the rifle. "Mind providing a few details?"

Bo pulled his satellite phone and wafted it before me. "I've got wild-game cameras set all over this place. Many miles. Hey, not a bad name for a jazz-rock band, is it? Many Miles."

Long experience had shown it best to let him ramble. Bo Dickerson seldom squeezed into conversational boxes. He raised a finger to his lips and indicated it was time to lower the volume.

"Solar powered. Images taken, uploaded via satellite, and dropped into this little pretty." He waggled the phone at me again. "Movement triggers the cameras. So I get lots of cool wildlife shots. Deer. Black bear. Bobcat. The occasional gator that crawls up on these slivers of land."

"Great. Then get a Nature Channel gig. Meanwhile, kindly focus on the bounty hunters." I checked the weapon he'd handed me—.223 caliber, semiautomatic, 4X scope with night-vision capabilities. I didn't need to ask if it had been sighted for accuracy.

"Passing boats in these little sloughs also trigger the cameras. The rare kayaker or canoeist. I can't imagine wanting to wander through the Dismal, can you?"

"No, Bo."

"Yesterday a couple of cameras picked up a shallow draft skiff. Outboard motor. With three critters in camo. All well armed. Tourists, my son?"

"Probably not." Damn.

"They bashed about in the dark yesterday and now—most unfortunately for them—make their way in this direction. Three. *Tres Hombres.* Love that album."

Three men. Focused on finding and killing my friend. All for money. Their intel, acquired God knows how, had clearly been Bo Dickerson specific.

"We'll chalk three off the pursuit list, have a fine meal, and discuss the ways of the world," he continued. "Now, as to tactics."

Three dead men walking, or rather riding in their small boat. The filter—the mental shield to separate me from the killing—descended. I'd asked the cosmos often for inflicted death to quit its participation in my life. I'd done enough. But these situations were them or us, and it damn sure wasn't going to be us.

"All right. Tactics," I said. "Let's start with you not doing any crazy shit."

Bo tucked the silenced pistol into a front jeans pocket and waggled both arms in a loosening-up motion, rolled his head, stretched neck muscles. Then he leaned close, nose-to-nose. His breath smelled of ginger. "And what's my modus operandi, goober boy? What, pray tell, do I excel at?"

The sound of an outboard motor, distant, growled across the swampland, and I shifted my gaze to ascertain its relative position. A big sigh, and once more nose-to-nose with my blood brother. "Crazy shit, Bo. You excel at crazy shit."

Chapter 8

The skirmish environment lay still on that day—punctuated by random treetop breezes, cypress needles shifting. The air had turned thick. Evening approached. The witching hour.

Our two boats nestled against a narrow brush and tree-covered plot of land stretched south. Three more small islands curved left, forming the shape of a question mark. Our location marked the bottom of the punctuation. The islands held tangled vegetation, shadowed and dense and uninviting. Thirty feet of dark, tannin-laden swamp water separated each small island from the next.

The outboard motor stopped, followed by the distinct scraping of an aluminum hull edging onto dry land. A bird flushed from the farthest island at the curved tip of the question mark, disturbed.

Bo leaned into my ear. "Situate yourself on the island next to us. You'll have a ringside seat as affairs unfold." He winked.

I returned a tight nod and slipped off his vessel onto dry land. Bo eased into the swamp water, noiselessly. A feral smile and excited eyes disappeared underwater. Combat commenced. Three of the enemy. With Bo and I together, they should have brought thirty.

I crawled, silent, through thick brush—changing direction once. A fat copperhead snake lay curled underneath a palmetto bush. Two feet from my face, it puffed up, warning me. I acknowledged the message and crawled on. At the edge of my little island, a small opening in the vegetation provided a clear view of the operational area. Stretched flat, I raised the rifle and viewed events through the scope, safety off and finger on the trigger. Birds flapped, twittered, overhead. The moment held no emotion. Clinical focus, the kill switch on.

A single face, Central Asian, eased through the vegetation on the farthest island, fifty yards away. The assassin studied Bo's boat and the *Ace of Spades*, then withdrew. Slight movement farther into the brush indicated he met with his fellow bounty hunters and revealed his findings.

Without a ripple, Bo's head emerged from the water near their island. He slithered his way into the brush, unheard, unseen.

As I sighted through the scope, brushy holes allowed quick glimpses of three headhunters advancing toward the adjoining island, intent on closer proximity to our boats. Each armed with assault rifles and pistols. Each bearded with camo of the unprofessional variety, purchased off-the-shelf.

I sang. The selection and delivery of the song mattered little. The goal—keep them headed my way. "Hear—that lonesome—train go by." I sang into the ground, voice muted, still sighting through the riflescope. Loud enough to draw their attention. They couldn't pinpoint my location and would assume the off-key noise came from one of the boats. Their target, unconcerned, singing.

"You used—to love me—night and day." I was just some guy putzing around on his boat, singing off-key. But these killers weren't music critics.

The lead man again poked his head through the brush at the island's edge, checked our two boats, and entered the small stretch of water separating him from the next plot of dry land.

"Now—that love—is gone."

Waist deep, he pushed ahead—focused on the two boats and my singing. He created a wake. Splashed. Amateur hour. One of his fellow bounty hunters followed suit, weapon at the ready, eyes glued to the two vessels. The third never emerged from the brush.

One down, two to go.

"It tears me up—to see you—this way." My voice, directed toward the soil inches away, remained muted. The earth returned rich humus smells.

Several minutes passed. The two who had crossed, back inside the dense brush of the second island, waited for their third. A flock of wood ducks whistled among the swamp trees and splash-landed out of sight. I could discern a tight, quiet, and emphatic discussion from the remaining two. Perhaps they figured their partner had pulled back. Perhaps they knew of Bo Dickerson's unique talents and sensed a silent violation. A touch of doom.

"Coming at me—with vengeance—in your eye."

Vegetation shifted and indicated their movement toward the third island. Advancing toward our boats and my voice. I couldn't determine Bo's presence or location. No surprise there. Bo hunted, and the remaining two bounty hunters—if they had any sense—should have been scared witless.

A wake appeared in the tannic water separating the third island. With leathery back and tail, an alligator moved away from the vicinity. Something underwater had disturbed it. Bo. The most seasoned eye wouldn't have picked out any sign of him.

The first man peeked in my direction, crossed the watery gap, and waded onto the third island. Crouched, committed, his weapon aimed at the boats. His remaining partner followed, and waded the thirty-foot section backward, weapon trained on his trail. Halfway across, Bo slipped the water's surface at the second man's back, slapped a hand over his mouth, and drove his blade deep. They faded, slid back underwater without a ripple or sound. Bo had twisted the man's head so their eyes locked as the dark water covered them.

A blue heron parachuted on wide wings to nearby shallows and walked, one leg lifted and held suspended before the next step. It, too, hunted. Any remnant of bright daylight had passed. The grind of insect calls increased. Frogs joined the chorus. The Great Dismal Swamp began its shift toward primal nocturnal nature.

The final assassin, frozen deep in the brush, became sure of his circumstance and screamed for his comrades. The heron flapped, grabbed air, and flew off—soon lost among the deep dark of the cypress trees. Frogs fell silent. He howled in Tajik, frantic, alone. Silence answered.

He attacked, shrieked a battle cry, fired at random. The man from Tajikistan crashed through limbs and vegetation, toward the third water channel and my position. Fatalism, courage, insanity, or a mixture of traits—I never would understand—led him to the water's edge where he died. The single shot of my rifle rang and reverberated across the Dismal. Then silence, the quiet of death.

I pushed off the ground and stood.

"Dammit, Case!" Bo stomped out of the brush behind the dead man, waved his knife. "What the hell?"

He glared my way, then fished through the dead man's pockets. Wallet and papers pulled, he extracted similar soggy items from his pocket and added them together. He waved the bundle at me and bitched. "You were invited to the party as a freakin' observer. Not as an active damn participant!"

He paused and used his free hand to drag the body into the water. Alligator dinner. Then his body relaxed. "Although the singing was a nice touch. Good on ye, brother. Good on ye."

The internal Bo switch flipped back to his regular self, the irritated stone-cold man hunter shoved into the background. He waded toward his home, the papers and wallets held high. It pleased me to note he hadn't collected any body parts—at least none I could see.

Another one. Dead. I'd stopped counting years ago, but the number was too high. No adrenaline rush of battle, no great exultation of victory, no sense of satisfaction—and no remorse. A part of me, insulated and tucked away, had emerged, taken care of business, and retreated to dark corners. There to lurk, cold and callous. Years long gone, I'd tried to salve the emotion with rationalizations of "Fewer of them to worry about," and "Better him than me," but such musings had become shallow, disconnected. There would always be more. And my dark killer would emerge, efficient and final, again and again.

I climbed back on Bo's boat and met him on the foredeck. He tossed the bundle of documentation my way and stripped off his clothes. Buck naked, he went belowdecks for dry attire. The ordeal over, he'd moved on.

The wallets and papers, many of the latter too soaked to pull apart, confirmed the men as Tajik. Our Delta team had conducted operations around Kunduz, Afghanistan, against the Taliban—close to the Tajikistan border. Nothing unusual. Nothing to raise the ire of the Tajiks. Odds high, these men were simple bounty hunters, sent by an unidentified source. I'd let the papers dry on the *Ace* and pick through them the next day. Seek sponsorship. Funding. Kill the funding—the price on our heads—and perhaps the pursuit would stop. Maybe. Fanaticism didn't always need monetary fuel.

The papers revealed nothing. A dry hole. And out there, somewhere, they planned to come again.

Chapter 9

But this trip to the Dismal held no dangers. Only tales, laughter, brotherhood, and honest, heartfelt communication. Bo flicked on the Christmas lights wrapped around the midship mast. They provided us enough light for the evening. He fired up charcoal in the old Weber grill, proceeded to cut steaks from the backstrap of the gutted deer.

I wandered onto the *Ace*, grabbed a bottle of Grey Goose, and returned to occupy a duct-taped-together lawn chair. An upward cut of his knife removed one steak. He worked on the next.

"I note you're carving our dinner with a more than vaguely familiar instrument. Hope you cleaned it since I observed its previous use."

He turned and grinned. "Ritual and protocol. Let's not spoil the moment."

Bo slapped the venison steaks on the hot grill, balanced on his rock-hard belly across the top railing, and washed his hands in swamp water. He sat across from me, shifted position, and produced a pipe and lighter from his jeans. The pipe bowl, already stuffed with dried pot buds, flared. "Want some?" He lifted the pipe in my direction, his voice choked, smoke held.

I waved the vodka bottle back, took a long swig. Night fell, and we sat alone, singular. As warriors. As brothers.

"You heard from Tango Bravo Bravo?" Bo asked. Seared meat popped on the grill. He referred to Marcus Johnson, our former Delta team leader. Tango Bravo Bravo. Marcus's Delta Force call sign. It stood for *Tough Black Bastard*, an appropriate appellation. Tough as nails and an excellent leader.

"Still in Montana. Ranching. Fishing."

"Well, give the man credit. He's hardly hiding. There aren't a whole lot of black ranchers in his neck of the woods."

Marcus lived ten miles down a gravel road near the Absaroka-Beartooth Wilderness. I visited him with regularity and knew for a fact anyone after the bounty on his head would be seen from a long way away. Besides that defensive tactic, Marcus genuinely enjoyed the big skies and isolation of his ranch.

"Does it bother you?" I asked. "That little soiree a couple of months ago?"

He took another deep hit of pot, stretched. A shoulder popped. "You're asking about those three." A statement, tinged with mild resignation.

"Subject de jour."

"No, it's not."

The vodka swished, twirled, and burned hot on the way down. Bo jerked up, flipped the steaks.

"We killed three men, Bo."

"No." He took another hit of weed. "No, we didn't."

"And what world do you live in where three gator-bait Tajiks aren't dead?"

"They committed suicide."

The world according to Bo. I didn't live there, but part of me desired his address change.

"Hard to shovel it aside."

"Bullshit. Chapters or flow or random pings—it doesn't matter. Life. Move on."

He scuttled away and disappeared into the bowels of his boat. I didn't have his capacity to let go. Death mattered. A point, a flash in time, but there and real and deep. None of the circle of life horseshit resonated. Death and killing. One lives and one dies. Memories matter, past actions count, not to be dismissed as a damn speed bump.

Movement and clatter rose from below. He returned with a bottle of Virginian wine. A corkscrew tossed my way, he added, "Do the honors, s'il vous plaît."

Cork removed, the bottle placed on the deck between us, conversation moved to more neutral ground.

"Catch?" Bo asked.

Juan Antonio Diego Hernandez. "Catch." The fourth member of our Delta team. Fierce and sure with a cob-rough exterior.

"Still somewhere near Portland. Haven't seen him since you and I last visited. Since we killed those Tajiks."

"You're getting tedious, son."

"Yeah. Yeah, I know." I sighed and went back to our old Delta friends. "Wouldn't hurt you to contact Catch on occasion. Or Marcus."

He didn't reply and fished tin plates and forks from a large box container nearby. Away from the boat, deep in the swamp, shadows met water under the moonlight and extended across the still, reflective palette.

"Angel?" Bo asked, straightening up.

William Tecumseh Picket. Angel. The fifth and final of our retiree group. Battles, blood, and a bounty bound us together. Angel had said goodbye and disappeared several years ago. None of us knew his whereabouts.

"Nada. He'd mentioned Costa Rica, but who the hell knows?"

Bo took a deep hit on his pipe, spoke as he exhaled. "I miss him. And I don't see enough of you. Or Marcus. Or Catch."

"You'd have to leave this swamp to mingle with us."

He shrugged. "Glad you're here now."

"Me too."

"And I'll admit to some consternation. Just to make you happy."

"Over what?"

"Over involving you with those Tajiks. I know you want to walk away from all of it."

"And more."

"Can't help your mental angst, old son. You're flying solo on that one."

"Thanks."

His hand on my knee, firm, amplified his words. "I'd help if I could. You know that."

I appreciated Bo's comment and concern. "I want to put a full stop to all of this. Find a safe spot. Take care of Mom and CC, white picket fence—the whole bit."

"And sell the *Ace*?"

"You speak blasphemy, my redhead friend."

The aroma of grilled meat and marijuana filled our space. A large moth ruffled overhead and danced on the Christmas lights. We remained silent for several minutes, isolated, comfortable. Bo drew on his pipe.

"So where's your place? In all this?" Bo waved a hand at the emergent stars spread across the night sky, patches visible through the cypress tree openings.

"The stoned hippie has gone existential."

"I've found *my* place."

True enough. True enough, and good for him. "And I'm happy for you."

The steaks were done, and swamp noises became more active. A powerful swirl at the front of the boat indicated a gator. Several bats flicked and dodged at the edge of the Christmas lights, hunting airborne insects.

"A plan and a path. The universal force tempers the random nature of our space and time. Seek guidance," Bo said. "And pass the salt."

"I do seek. Nothing yet. Maybe I don't listen well enough."

"Don't listen. Feel, old son. You have to feel."

The venison was gamy, rare, and delicious. We'd each take a swig of wine, then return the bottle to the deck between us. No lights for miles, other than ours. The Great Dismal Swamp surrounded, blanketed. And this moment, an infinitesimal place in time, offered sanctuary. There was nothing I couldn't say to Bo, and the assurance he wouldn't pass judgment cast a calm over our tiny haven.

"I'd suggest you're seeking affirmation of your desires," Bo continued. "Stability. Family. The universe may have a different plan."

"You mean God, hippie boy. How did your sorry ass get so New Age squatting in swampy squalor?"

Bo laughed, grabbed the wine. "Semantics aside, the point remains. You wish and ponder and desire, but what does it get you?" He didn't wait for a response. "The whole situation is. Period. It is now, and here. Tomorrow dawns a new now and here. It unfolds. You're a part of the unfolding."

"Forget the Nature Channel. You'd best land a gig on spiritual TV."

"I'd shine."

"Sundays with Bo. Come have your butt enlightened."

We both laughed. But he'd found solace in the Bo Dickerson universal philosophy, and I envied it. I looked ahead, and did dream, and did yearn—when I didn't reminisce on the past. Bo truly let it unfold. Would he be in the Dismal Swamp next year? Five years? The rest of his life? I thought of such things. He didn't. Let it unfold. A release mechanism I didn't possess.

Perhaps poking at his philosophy or perhaps to seek help, I asked, "What about the killing? And I don't mean causes or reasons. Distill it down to the taking of another's life. You sanguine about that?"

"We're animals. Look around." He lifted his chin toward the dark swamp around us. "Violence and death. Every moment. The bat chomping an insect. The death throes of stars a billion miles away. It comes, and it goes. We're not separated from it."

"Yeah, we are, my friend. We have a conscience. We're different. Separate."

Bo placed his plate on the deck, settled back, belched, and tamped down remnants of his pot in the handmade pipe bowl. The lighter flared.

"A man should focus the mind on positive personal narratives," Bo said. "Love for others. You. Marcus. Angel and Catch. Rae. Allow the consciousness to flow. Segregate the death. The killing. Grind it down so the little pangs of guilt and questioning don't burr anymore."

I finished off the wine and slid the bottleneck over a stub on one of the Weber's cypress legs, then went and stood at the bow. A small bat whipped past my head, twisting, hunting.

"And she's still around, Case. Your heart, your head." He spoke of Rae. "Your consciousness. The essence. The love. Still there."

A deep sigh, a shake of the head. I had nothing to add.

If you had satellite imaging eyesight, and floated far above the Earth, you could have looked down into the miles and miles of Dismal Swamp and focused on the lone illumination, multicolored, and seen two blood brothers in isolation. Together, and with a bond so tight that it, too, glowed.

Chapter 10

Bo's old pickup started on the first try. The tires were bald, the gas gauge and passenger-side windshield wiper didn't work, and it smelled of mold and marijuana. I'd make it to Norfolk's airport with time to spare.

A drizzling, dank dawn had greeted us. Bo piloted the *Ace* while I'd packed and prepared. Casual attire—jeans and pressed shirts—would suffice for the lion's share of my Suriname mission. I'd also tossed in jungle wear and military boots. Rain forest would be the order of the day if I ventured out of the capital, Paramaribo. Everything fit in my travel rucksack. I sojourn light.

"Every other day, Bo. Tomatoes need water."

He guided the *Ace* toward the Dismal Canal. A short run down the canal, then a footpath on the east side that led to Highway 17 and Bo's abandoned house, barn, and pickup.

"Roger that," Bo replied as he focused on avoiding his swamp trip wires. He handled the *Ace* well as we zigzagged through cypress stumps and hummocks of land. "And I'll toss in a side note."

"Fine."   .

"Regarding your little foray to another foreign shithole."

"Yes?" Another admonition—locked, loaded, soon-to-be fired.

"There are other, less treacherous occupations. In case you didn't know."

"Thanks, Mom."

"Ways that don't include getting your ass shot at."

I poured another cup of coffee and topped off his mug. Bo made a sharp left, and water cascaded off the foredeck tarp. We moved through a liquid environment—swamp, rain, dripping trees, water-slick decks on the *Ace*.

"It's good money."

He grunted, having spoken his piece. There was no further discussion on that topic. We sipped coffee and emerged from the narrow swamp channels and into the Dismal Canal. No other boat traffic appeared.

"What did the Clubhouse have to say?" Bo asked. All US operators knew of the Clubhouse. He had concerns about my trip, and I appreciated it. But the die had been cast, and I was headed for South America. Twenty minutes to the drop-off point as the *Ace* rumbled its diesel growl.

"Something about the whole mess down there being bigger than economics. Cryptic, as usual."

"You want company?"

"No, thanks. But I appreciate the offer."

"You set on weaponry?"

"When I get there."

"You'll buy a pistol. Tuck it away. Mr. Incognito."

"Yep."

"Uncle Bo strongly recommends additional protection."

"I'm sure you do."

"Get a fully automatic weapon. Just in case."

"I'll think about it."

"Waves of lead, my brother. Waves of lead."

"I'll think about it."

The *Ace* edged against the east bank of the canal, and a little-used path showed through the trees and brush. I scrambled off the bow and onto dry land. Bo tossed me the travel rucksack.

"Your truck have gas?" I asked.

"Maybe."

"That's heartening."

The drizzle shifted into a steady light rain. A semi ground along Highway 17 several hundred yards away as I pulled the hood of my rain jacket over my head. Bo stood and stared, showed a wry smile and a touch of loneliness.

"Watch your ass. And other pertinent parts."

"See you in a few days, Bo. Take care of the *Ace*."

"Take care of Case Lee. Go with God."

I halted my first step on the path, turned, cast a quizzical look toward my friend. Mister Universal Power hadn't named a deity before in all the years I'd known him. He smiled, shrugged, and added, "Well, somebody had to say it." Bo turned and entered the wheelhouse. I headed up the trail.

***

The last leg of the Paramaribo flight landed at midnight. Tropical heat hit hard and fetid when the airliner opened its doors on the tarmac of Suriname's lone airport. Conditions didn't improve in the open-air terminal. One tired and desultory customs agent stamped the handful of travelers' passports. Mine read John Eliot Bolen.

"Reason for your visit?" the agent asked.

"Tourist."

He lifted tired, watery eyes, and we shared stares of acknowledged bullshit. He popped the stamp in my passport and signaled the next traveler.

I woke the driver of the nearest taxi and checked into Paramaribo's sole decent hotel after traveling quiet streets, lights few and far between. The hotel's native wood interior, dark and polished, smelled of linseed oil. The bar—open and empty. The bartender listened through earbuds to iPod music.

It was too late to visit the underground arms dealer and acquire personal protection of the semiautomatic variety. And too early for sleep given the catnaps on the flights. The blues came easy in these situations. Alone, in a strange country, and the lone patron at the lone hotel bar. The ice cubes clinked when I downed the last of the vodka and nodded at the bartender for another.

Bo, nestled in the Dismal, wrapped with personal surety of his place in the world. Mom and CC asleep; Tinker Juarez at CC's feet, protecting his pack. Marcus tucked away below the Absaroka and Beartooth mountain ranges in Nowhere, Montana, coyotes yipping. Catch and his girlfriend cozied on a couch, the Pacific Northwest rainy season underway. Angel somewhere down here in South America. Maybe. But likely to have found stability, happiness.

Then there was ol' Case, plopped in an obscure bar wrapped in the smell of wood polish and revolution—errand boy for the gnomes of Zurich. I refused settlement of too much of the blues and twisted my head around the reality of here and now. A man can take a certain amount of succor knowing the immediate future played to his strengths. I was good at this stuff and took pleasure working the puzzle. Alone, insular—which ratcheted the alert factor up a notch or two, and helped nudge the blues offstage.

The click of high heels alerted me to her entrance. She'd made a solid attempt at "been awake the whole time," but telltale puffiness under her eyes told of a hurried preparation after the hotel staff woke her during my check-in. I clocked in at work, game on.

Chapter 11

Heels, long slit skirt, with a taut leg exposed at each step. A silk blouse with two too many buttons undone. Tawny hair cascaded and framed a Slavic high-cheekbone face. A looker, big-time. But not a prostitute. The countenance, the well-practiced smile, the shaded eyes—all pointed to another type of pro.

A pleasant nod my way, and she eased onto a seat, left an empty barstool between us. "Hi," she said. "I'm glad someone else is up late."

Her voice held no accent, Indiana flat. Her movements and demeanor confirmed the professional status. A Russian. They trained their people to sound like a newscaster, with no inflections. I saluted with a raised glass, remained silent, and returned a tight-lipped smile. She addressed the bartender, ordered a Scotch and soda, and swiveled toward me with a smile that offered vast promise.

"You must have just arrived. Quite a pleasant surprise, I must say," she said.

"How so?"

"You're a cut above the usual mining engineer that visits Paramaribo." Her eyes crinkled with good-natured humor and a light challenge.

I was to approach her, cross the empty barstool divide, show male intent and interest. Then reveal anything she wanted. At least, that was her plan. Classic tradecraft. And I damn near complied. Elegant and charming, well versed in male ego massage, her appeal grew by the second, but I remained planted. She'd have to come to me.

Delta had trained us well in the tradecraft of spies. Crank up the senses, spot nuance and subtlety—the mark of a pro. They'd also trained us not to screw around and play their game. Under the professional spy's rules of engagement, they had the upper hand. Every time. We'd been trained to eliminate their advantage and recalibrate the relationship.

"Wouldn't you prefer vodka?" I asked.

The hesitation in her movement as she lifted the Scotch and soda lasted milliseconds, long enough for confirmation. She knew it, too, and as her facade tumbled, she delivered a sardonic smile toward the polished bar top. With a slight shake of her head, still smiling, she returned the glass and pulled a cigarette from her purse. She waited, poised. I stayed still, and the bartender lit it for her.

"I'll have what he's having," she told the bartender and pushed the Scotch away. Her liquid slide over to the empty stool between us allowed ample viewing pleasure.

"Sorry to get you up," I said.

"Why, my gracious," she said with an exaggerated syrupy Southern accent. She leaned over, exposed more décolletage. "Arising for a fine-looking gentleman such as yourself is hardly a burden."

We both laughed, pro to pro. She straightened back up, took a sip of her just-arrived vodka, and said, "Nika."

"John. John Bolen."

We tapped glasses. A formal recognition and shot fired at the starting line for the ensuing conversation. After a tight sip, I placed my glass well beyond Nika's reach. The bartender donned earbuds, hummed along with an unknown song.

She'd know of Hines, the Suriname CIA station chief, and would eliminate me as another spook, recently arrived. Had I been CIA, the embassy would house me, provide cover. It left several options for her consideration—arms dealer, corporate spy, hit man.

"You have a keen eye, John. Now allow me to suggest you're not here on commercial or diplomatic business."

The unspoken acknowledgement of her as Russian intelligence licensed her to dig around John Bolen. Tit for tat and fair enough. I'd present a half-truth picture, watch my *p*'s and *q*'s, and gather what I could. Focus on my mission. She'd misdirect, twist, and seek advantage. The clandestine game. And she would be dangerous. Jules's warning at the Clubhouse flared.

I laid a truth card. "Checking things out. Simple gig. Independent contractor for an NGO."

Global Resolutions *was* a nongovernmental organization. And I was an independent contractor.

"How about you?" I asked. "SVR? GRU?"

A stomp on my side of the teeter-totter. Keep things off-balance, in the operational realm. My turf.

Russia didn't have a Suriname consulate, much less a full-fledged embassy. Her appearance here wasn't happenstance. Either SVR—the Russian Foreign Intelligence Service—or GRU—the Foreign Military Intelligence branch of the Russian armed forces.

She ignored my question and took a sip of her drink. Long, polished fingernails tapped the side of the glass when she set it down.

"Independent contractor. I see. Somewhat vulturelike, isn't it?" she asked.

"How's that?"

"Lurking while this unfortunate place is in the throes of a civil war."

"Civil war, coup of the month, or something else?"

"I wish I knew."

She throttled up her tradecraft. A long-nailed hand scratched my upper-arm shirt material, catlike. The sound of nails on pressed cotton accompanied her visual assessment of me, feet to face. Her eyes crinkled again, nostrils flaring. Man, she was good. The allure and sensuality of Nika's every move lapped at my personal barriers. The two of us, alone in a strange, small South American country, offered ample opportunity to toss aside purpose and indulge in brief, dangerous pleasure.

I took her hand off my arm, squeezed with appreciation, and placed it back on the bar top.

"My client wants information on the situation here. Any personal insights?"

Not my best moment, but at least our interaction returned to terra firma.

"We're merely curious," she said. "The little incident with the Suriname president's son. Allowing a terrorist group sanctuary—well, none of us want that, do we?"

"Lots of *we*'s, Nika."

"Let's just say we—you and I—may have common cause."

Misdirection and fog. She'd move through the clandestine mist, and I'd fulfill my contract. Two different animals. There were overlaps, sure, but I'd move on after this assignment, without a scorecard. She played a different game. Zero-sum. A winner and a loser. Whatever her assignment here, the intent was to win. It made her a dangerous player.

A brief weariness descended over me. My jaundiced view of this, and all the geopolitical chess games, originated from not giving a damn anymore. These global endeavors ended, always, with uncertainty and trauma and death.

"From a strictly personal perspective, the whole regime-change strategy has given us some damn poor outcomes around the world," I said, marker placed. I took a sip and watched the seated bartender nod in time to unheard music. "Your bosses may want to consider that."

"An observer of affairs," she said. "That's my role. A precaution and little more. Regime change and all that would entail is, to use an American expression, above my pay grade."

She chuckled, low and sultry. It didn't cover her lie. The possibilities loomed large and sure. The Monroe Doctrine—US foreign policy since 1823—made it clear that any outside efforts to colonize land or interfere with states in North or South America would be viewed as acts of aggression, requiring US intervention. Cuba had been the key example, and damn near triggered a nuclear war during the sixties. When the USSR collapsed, so did Cuba, and the United States' rapprochement with that Caribbean island brought the Western Hemisphere back under some semblance of US control. Other power players, using the guise of commercial interests, encroached—China and its commercial control of the Panama Canal, the most glaring example. But nothing on a military level—a major no-no for the DC crowd.

The appearance of Nika might have been a simple fact-finding mission, similar to mine. Or she could be supporting the insurgency right under the nose of the current Suriname power brokers. If the latter proved correct, then Russia would establish a new Western Hemisphere foothold. Shit would hit the fan, big-time. Saber rattles from the DC crowd, emergency meetings called, hands-on-hips posturing. Harrumph, harrumph.

I just didn't give a damn. The power-player games had screwed up more people, killed more innocents, and resolved jack shit more times than I could count. This was a bit-player third-world country filled with former Africans, Javanese, and Hindi Indians—all brought by their former colonial masters, the Dutch. It defined messed-up. But they went about their days, lived life as best they knew how, and deserved better than the role of pawns on a chessboard. So screw it. I'd find answers, do my job, file a report with Global Resolutions in Switzerland, and return to the *Ace of Spades*.

I downed the last of my drink and stood. "Above my pay grade, too. I'll be here a few days, talk with folks, report back, and head home. Nice chatting with you." Her arena, her game, and hanging around raised the odds of a slip, a mistake on my part.

She let me take a few steps toward the bar's exit before replying.

"There's another option, John."

I turned and captured a view that would make any strong man weak. The Nika train roared through the tunnel, and once again I stopped, stood, and considered. She perched on the barstool, legs crossed. The slit of her skirt exposed a high-jumper's leg. Long hair fell across perfect shoulders. Her high, defined cheekbones accompanied a torrid-possibilities smile.

"While we may not be working together," Nika said, pausing to stub out her smoke, "our situation doesn't preclude recreating together."

"What'd you have in mind? Golf?"

She laughed, deep, low. "I was thinking of a more horizontal activity."

I stared at a black-widow spider, albeit a beautiful one. "Let me sleep on it. Have a good evening."

The polished wood floor echoed my footsteps toward the hotel elevator.

Chapter 12

Automatic gunfire woke me. A semiregular third-world occurrence, and the appropriate response mechanism kicked in. Slide out of bed, crawl to the wall beneath the room window, safe from stray bullets. Bring a pillow. Stretch on the floor, wait it out. Stare at the ceiling. Ponder whether revolution was under way or a trigger-happy soldier had gotten drunk or the national soccer team had just won a major game, eliciting gunshots of celebration.

I contemplated my means of escape, preplanned. Standard operating procedure upon any arrival. I always kept it simple. Here, head to the docks, steal a boat, and get salty. French Guiana was a short distance to the east. The firing tapered off, and sleep returned, the hardwood floor cool.

Dawn and street silence greeted me outside the hotel. Paramaribo had the feel of a town on edge, awaiting an outcome. Murmurs of collected soldiers at street corners, sharing smokes. A nod in their direction as I passed brought no response other than cold stares.

The contact Jules had given me for acquisition of a weapon owned a ship chandlery—a store for anything marine. Rope, welding supplies, paint, fishing nets, turnbuckles, maps, pipe, electrical conduit—you name it. De Groot Marine occupied a spot at the end of Keizerstraat, on the dilapidated wharf above the roiled-coffee Suriname River. Wooden creosote piers jutted, occupied by fishing vessels and tramp steamers. Life on the docks began early, and several people were out and about on their vessels or meandered along the wharf. Smatterings of languages—Sranan, Dutch, English, Spanish—floated over the water. It had the look of a movie set, unorganized, the director not yet ready to film. It had the feel of a place where you'd best keep your back against the wall.

The bell over the door of De Groot Marine announced my entry. The sound prompted hurried activity far down one of the material-laden aisles. A wiry man wrestled with a chain-and-tarp-wrapped lump near an open trapdoor, far back in the bowels of the chandlery. With a final grunt, he shoved the substantial package through the opening. A muted splash returned from the deep river. The place smelled of weathered wood, mold, and cigarette smoke.

The man dropped the trapdoor with a bang, hitched his pants, and turned. He acknowledged me with a hooded focus. I returned the universal "I didn't see anything" motion—a lift of my chin and tight smile. He nodded back, moved toward me, and wiped his hands on the seat of his pants. I'd come to the right place.

He was of indeterminate old age, bald except for random stubbles of white hair. His dark leathery skin indicated years of sun and salt. A plain white cotton T-shirt in need of a wash tucked into pants belted far too high. The cuffs, rolled up, exposed thin ankles above rubber tire sandals. His hands were large, powerful, and his eyes focused with intensity, returning no emotion.

"I need a special tool."

My statement could have meant anything in the world of boats and ships, but the rubber-banded roll of Benjamins I laid on the counter specified, unspoken, the type of tool.

The door rang behind me, and a seaman of Javanese extraction wandered in holding a broken shackle. The proprietor of De Groot Marine scooped the roll of bills and pocketed them. He would provision my request; another tight nod my way. I studied marine charts pinned on the walls while the shackle transaction took place.

The Suriname River was over a mile wide at this location. Five miles from the Atlantic. It would make a fine naval base for any interested parties, protected from storms and deep enough to accommodate warships.

New shackle in hand, the seaman left. The proprietor followed him and locked the door. He didn't bother glancing in my direction and disappeared into the long warehouse-like shop, accompanied by the shuffling of treaded sandals. A few minutes later, he returned and dropped a cheap plastic grocery bag on the counter with a clunk.

I removed the semiautomatic pistol—a small high-end Kimber .45—and checked the action, dry-fired it several times, confirmed functionality. All good. The bag also held twenty loose rounds of ammunition, and I inspected each one. Again, all good. The magazine held eight of the rounds. I pocketed the remaining bullets and chambered a round so it was ready for action. I tucked the weapon into the back of my jeans, hidden under the lightweight rain jacket. I was good to go.

I gave a final nod, he nodded back, and I left. Other than my initial request for a special tool, we had not exchanged a word.

Government functionaries require a waiting period before accepting an appointment. So I strode several blocks toward the Ministry of Economic Development, low clouds overhead. Dutch colonial architecture displayed across this section of Paramaribo. Clapboard two- and three-story buildings, painted bright white and topped with steep-pitched roofs of green or red. Each with rows of perfectly spaced small windows. Several had a series of ascending large porches across the front facade, the upper-story balconies supported with precise round columns. Tight, wooden, well architected. Very Dutch.

It began to sprinkle. I turned a corner and stepped back to the protection of a building when gunfire rang out. One or several of the soldiers stationed at a road intersection had clearly seen something they didn't like. A perceived rebel soldier or wandering dog or old family enemy—it didn't matter. Revolution was under way, and soldiers were on edge. An occasional potshot was to be expected. Chalk it up to nerves or the settling of old feuds.

I retreated to the front porch of the building, out of the rain, and waited for the weather and street corner soldiers to calm down. A nice lady opened the front door to ask me if I'd like coffee. She chose to speak English. Americans have a look, a countenance, an attitude identifiable for most folks around the world. The way we wear our jeans, our physical stance, the quick smile. My current cover showed a tourist or businessman or wayfarer, benign, with none of the macho Ray-Bans or strut. A nice guy, albeit a nice guy armed with special skills.

"Thanks. That would be great."

"Cream and sugar?"

"Just black, please."

Minutes later, she joined me on the porch with two cups of coffee. She was middle-aged and of Asian Indian lineage, her ancestors likely brought by one of the Dutch East India Company outposts. She commented on the current situation.

"Bad times."

"Seems like it. Thanks again for the coffee. And the roof." The drizzle had turned into a tropical downpour and hammered the tin roof of the front porch.

"American?"

"Yes, ma'am. Here on business." The flooding rain brought a thick, junglelike smell.

"I believe business may be poor for a while." She sipped coffee and used her other hand to indicate the streets of Paramaribo. "We have troubles at the moment."

"I may leave tomorrow and come back at a later date. How long do you think this will go on?"

Collecting information. A nice lady, a resident, would provide another perspective. Information shoved into the data bank and distilled.

"His Excellency, the president," she said, smiling, "seldom allows such things to continue longer than a few weeks." The tired mirth in her eyes indicated the lack of respect she had for the current president for life.

"What's the deal with this Joseph Hoff?" Hoff, the rebel leader, controlled areas west of the Coppename River, sixty miles from Paramaribo. Little was known of the man other than a short stint in the Suriname army.

"Who can say? We all wonder who is supporting him and his efforts. Your country is on the top of the list." She smiled again, offering no critique of the possibility that the United States backed the rebel insurgency.

Her statement came as no surprise. Large swaths of the world attributed any calamitous event, including inclement weather, to US efforts. Specifically, the CIA. It made for a good catchall boogeyman and fed conspiracies.

"I hope not. This stuff never ends well."

Maybe we *were* behind Suriname's troubles. His Excellency's son, with his Hezbollah antics, had kicked the clandestine anthill. The current rebel insurgency brought out the big dogs. Enter the Russian connection. Nika. Maybe a fishing mission, similar to mine. It was hard to say. My job was to find answers. Global Resolutions of Switzerland expected no less.

"I would agree. Do you have family?" she asked.

One of the great divides between developed countries and the third world was personal interest. In the States or Europe, conversation swirled around jobs, economies, current events. In poorer portions of the world, family status was inquired of early. It always struck me as a nice touch, grounded.

"I do. Back in California. They're doing well." I lied about the location out of habit. "And you? Your family?"

She informed me of a son recently married to a girl that may not have lived up to her expectations. And two daughters who consumed a great deal of her time searching for acceptable spouses. And a husband who lacked the appropriate verve in this husband-finding endeavor, a major bone of contention. I loved it—real, personal, here and now.

The rain abated, became a drizzle, and no other shots had sounded during the coffee interlude. I thanked her again, we wished each other well, and I started again toward the Ministry of Economic Development to arrange a meeting with the minister, His Excellency Ravindu Tjon. Jules had identified him as a conduit of information. A conduit with a serious cocaine habit.

The small ministry building—three stories of white clapboard— was quiet. A young lady at the entrance counter greeted me with a smile.

"John Bolen. American businessman. I was wondering if it would be possible to set an appointment with His Excellency the minister for this afternoon."

She asked me to wait while she "checked his calendar," which consisted of gliding upstairs and presenting my request to Tjon. Several minutes later, she returned and said the minister would not be available.

"Tomorrow?"

"I'm afraid not."

All righty, then. The minister of economic development, His Excellency Ravindu Tjon, wasn't prepared for any dialogue with an American businessman. Easy to interpret the larger picture: Tjon hiding, aligned with somebody, told to keep his mouth shut. The details—who, what, how, where, when—I'd have to dig for.

I thanked the young lady and moved through the light rain, halting at each street corner. Pressed against the nearest wall, I glanced down the intersections to confirm no new gunfights. At several corners, members of the Suriname army watched my precautions, pointed, and laughed. All the better. A frightened American making his way somewhere. Not a threat and damn good cover. I smiled wanly at the clusters of soldiers after checking both streets, played the church mouse role to the hilt, and took solace knowing they wouldn't be laughing if I meant them harm.

The US embassy stood a few blocks away, on Dr. Sophie Redmond Straat—one of Paramaribo's main drags. The building was large and impressive, the ubiquitous high walls surrounding well-maintained grounds. Construction was under way for a new embassy several miles away. Why the hell we needed a new embassy here would remain one of life's mysteries. The current one appeared functional, safe, and well situated. Odds were the State Department had excess funds a year or two ago. To protect their budget, they allocated money for a Suriname boondoggle.

A young man, local, occupied the entrance lobby. A marine guard stood nearby. I tossed a quiet "Oorah" his way. He cracked a return smile and nodded. I had come through the army before Delta Force but admired the tenacity and in-your-face attitude of our Marine Corps.

"May I leave a note for the agricultural liaison? Mr. Fletcher Hines?" I asked the local.

"Certainly, sir."

The written request was short and sweet. *Meet across the street. Café. Noon. Case Lee, Esq.*

The *Esquire* bit signaled clandestine operations when used between American operators. Hines would search his CIA database and ascertain my background and current world role. Then he'd shove aside any meetings he had scheduled and accommodate me. I asked the young man for an envelope, dropped the note inside, and sealed it. For the eyes of the agricultural liaison only.

Hines would be pissed. When someone of my ilk showed, unannounced, in his backyard, it wouldn't foster a warm relationship. So be it.

The tropical drizzle continued as I made my way north for the next meeting with a prominent Dutch businessman. After handshakes and niceties, the two of us would lie to each other, glean information, two-step the dance floor. There was one large difference. He would seek an advantage, based on economic leverage. Money. I wasn't burdened with that perspective.

Chapter 13

Luuk Hoebeek, owner and president of the Eerlijk Trading Company. *Eerlijk*—Dutch for honest, fair, aboveboard. We would see.

Jules had sold me his name and contact information. The best-connected Dutch businessman in Suriname. Owner of a trading company. You can't get away from trading companies. Sprinkled around the world, the name is used as a catchall for activities too varied for a specific category of business. The Dutch, Chinese, and Lebanese tended to dominate the trade. The Dutch from the days of the Dutch East India Company. The Chinese from the days of the Silk Road. The Lebanese—spread everywhere—had been at it since the days of the Phoenicians. Hell, I wanted a trading company. Case Lee, Esq. President. Home office: the *Ace of Spades*.

Lush landscape surrounded Hoebeek's understated office building. Bougainvillea, tropical foliage, manicured lawns. A large water feature—boulders and more tropical foliage—marked the entrance. The light rain had stopped, replaced with low clouds and a steam bath. I tugged at the rain jacket, avoided outlining the pistol. The thick air carried the scent of tropical blooms, bright and sweet.

The glass doors opened and hit me with cool AC, a welcome relief. A circular reception desk dominated the entrance rotunda, manned by a large and dour Creole receptionist-slash-guard. He registered zero emotion as I approached and asked to see Mr. Hoebeek.

"You have an appointment?"

"Nope."

We shared stares. The water feature gurgled outside the front doors. I tugged again at my light jacket and continued. "I'm an American businessman. I'm here to discuss business opportunities with Mr. Hoebeek."

He returned a cold stare and stone-statue silence.

"Mr. Hoebeek will be *very* upset if he misses this opportunity. Upset with *you*, my friend. Not a good thing."

The large man picked up the phone, pushed a quick-dial button, and glared at me while he spoke Dutch. His short conversation with Hoebeek provided access.

"Elevator. Third floor."

We wouldn't become bosom buddies anytime soon.

"Thanks, bud. Been a hoot chatting with you."

Hoebeek occupied a corner office with floor-to-ceiling windows, decorated with hand-carved furniture of local wood that would land you a jail sentence stateside. Jungle ebony, exotic mahogany—dark, rich, impressive. Native throw rugs adorned the polished wood floor. The largest rug had several golf balls scattered on it. A putter leaned against a chair.

The man himself stood and extended a hand. Tall, thin, with well-coifed sandy hair. The reading glasses perched on his nose lent an air of affability. And why not? He owned a trading company.

"John Bolen, Mr. Hoebeek. I appreciate you taking the time to see me without an appointment."

Polished, suave, he gestured toward a large chair across from his desk. "I'm certain it's my pleasure, Mr. Bolen. What may I do for you?"

His English was impeccable, the Dutch accent guttural. I'd bet good money he spoke a half dozen languages. That's what trading companies do.

"Well, again, thanks. You must travel a lot, so I'm lucky to catch you in." I didn't have a clue whether he traveled a lot, but time to collect information.

"A part of my job, I'm afraid. All the travel."

"I'm sure."

I waited for elaboration. None came.

"I represent interests in Switzerland, Mr. Hoebeek."

True enough, and a potent declaration. Whatever Hoebeek thought of the Swiss, he damn sure respected their handling of money.

"Yet it would appear you are American."

Fair enough. He would do some collecting of his own.

"California. However, like you, our organization has interests worldwide."

"I see." His smile was pleasant, noncommittal.

"I don't want to give any false impressions. Nor deal in hyperbole."

"I appreciate that." He adjusted some perceived flaw in the crease of his pants.

"My job is to investigate opportunities. Rather mundane, I'm afraid."

"Due diligence is never mundane, Mr. Bolen."

We nodded together—two businesspeople with respect for both opportunities and risk. Global citizens. Comrades in commerce. He asked if I'd like to remove my jacket. I declined.

"It's a matter of stability, sir."

Bona fides semi-established, we now entered the opaque world of feeling each other out. Hoebeek offered me something to drink. I politely declined and continued.

"We tend to focus on stability."

"Your Swiss client."

"Yes, sir. Clearly, we prefer engagement with a local partner of integrity and standing within Suriname's business community. But prior to that, the issue—the due diligence—regards political stability."

Trading company negotiations. Open-ended, cautionary, carrot-dangling.

"We've been through many changes, and regardless of the regime, business continues unaffected. I can assure you." He removed his reading glasses for effect. "As for a trading partner, your client should know our experience in Suriname goes back fifty years, beginning with my father."

Here sat a man as apolitical as they came. He'd play one side against the other, or play both sides concurrently with allegiances spread among the current power brokers and potential power brokers to come. I didn't begrudge him this approach. It took strategic thinking and a set of balls. It also pitted him against anyone who might disrupt his personal apple cart.

Hoebeek sat back, crossed a leg above Italian shoes, and emanated benign confidence and stability. Calm, cool, collected.

"I'm sure the Eerlijk Trading Company has navigated rough waters in its time, sir. Which is why I'm here. Can you tell me anything about the current, um, troubles?"

"Ah, yes. The current troubles." Spoken and presented as an afterthought. He'd salve my client's Swiss angst. Troubles. Nothing he couldn't handle.

"I have an obligation to my client."

"Of course. Due diligence."

"And you're the best source in town, from what I understand. Certainly, the most respected."

A massaged ego never hurt.

"Who can point to the reason for such actions? Disgruntlement over a perceived failure of the current regime? A grab for power, perhaps? The reasons and rationales are endless."

"And this Joseph Hoff? The rebel leader. Can you tell me about him?"

"Very little, I'm afraid. Former military. As you Americans would say, a small fish."

Luuk Hoebeek profited from stable times, but the big money came during change. It was the same the world over for those tapped into a fluid power structure. Not always a wholesale government change, but change in the culture, the business community. Change fostered opportunity. This guy would avoid and resist geopolitical change that led to total chaos. But he'd embrace a shift toward acquiring more power and money. A challenge, balanced on a razor's edge, but Hoebeek clearly had the ability.

"Is someone pulling his strings?" I asked. "Sorry for the colloquialism. Is someone, or some foreign power, directing him? Funding him?"

Hoebeek chuckled and shifted his chair, viewed the panorama of Paramaribo through glass walls. "This is Suriname, Mr. Bolen. One seriously doubts this is a location for international intrigue."

He'd had enough probing of local current events and began an inquiry regarding my business focus. A conversational quid pro quo. I lied about "infrastructure investments" and "natural resource extraction." Hoebeek nodded and probed. We did the dance, polite and professional.

Then I spotted it. Of the several golf balls splayed near the man's putter, one insignia was plainly visible. The other golf balls' positions showed partial insignias, but one faced me, clear as day. It didn't say *Titleist* or *Nike* or *Calloway*. *IDEX* was stamped on it, black, with a small red flag underneath. I could make out a larger gold star and four smaller stars alongside. The flag of the People's Republic of China.

IDEX. The International Defence Exposition and Conference, held annually in Abu Dhabi. State-sponsored and private arms dealers from around the world descend on that Gulf State each year to ply their wares. Everything from fighter jets to troop carriers to field cannons were splayed across the cavernous exhibit hall. I'd been there twice—once as a member of Delta Force and once as a private contractor. IDEX offered the opportunity to see and inspect what I might face in the field. Solid research, needed more often than I'd like.

Mr. Luuk Hoebeek had gone shopping. The golf balls indicated he'd, at a minimum, chatted with a Chinese government arms dealer and collected swag in the form of golf balls. Interesting. The question was whether he'd popped over to IDEX for the current regime or for the "small fish" occupying the western part of Suriname.

"I've always found the Swiss excellent business partners, Mr. Bolen. If you have any questions—any at all—please don't hesitate to communicate with me. Do you have a business card?"

"I'm afraid my client prohibits contact information during these preliminary stages. That said, I appreciate your openness to engage any of their concerns."

A semi-legitimate response. Swiss investment firms seldom opened a channel of communication until lay of the land had been established. We chatted on. Hoebeek assured me that whatever the outcome of the current strife, Eerlijk Trading Company would be around to facilitate business.

I stood and wandered over to his wall of windows, complimented the view, and passed by the scattered golf balls. From this new position, two more IDEX/China insignias became visible.

A cordial goodbye as he walked me out, his handshake firm, sincere. The front desk guard glared as I exited and made my way toward the café across from the US embassy. Hoebeek had held his cards close, but conversation intimated a willingness to play either side of the current situation.

I stopped at a tiny coffee shop and loitered at the entrance for thirty minutes, sipping from a heavy porcelain cup and killing time until the lunch meeting with the CIA. The coffee was fresh and strong and just right.

Luuk Hoebeek. A player in all this mess, although how deep and for whom was a big TBD. But a player, no doubt, and of a type well versed in calculating tide changes. And a potential danger. He'd play for keeps.

The profile and walk and turned heads among a cluster of soldiers alerted me to Nika's presence. She was headed in the direction of Hoebeek's building, confident and tight. The overcast clouds remained, and the lightest of drizzles started again. Oppressive weather; hot and wet and filled with uncertainty.

I followed, a full block behind. She crossed a street and made her way into the entrance of Eerlijk Trading Company. Hoebeek had a relationship with the Russians. No uncertainty there. Enough time had passed since my meeting with Hoebeek for him to have contacted her and to suggest she drop by for a chat about John Bolen.

A failure on my part. Hoebeek hadn't bought the Swiss investor story. I had left enough doubt, made an errant move, and set off Hoebeek's personal alarms. It happens. Part and parcel when you moved fast, assessed, probed.

I'd gathered good intel from the meeting. IDEX. China. His style and demeanor. A better than decent trade-off for him questioning my cover. And now a checked box in the Russian relationship column. I'd watch my back with Mr. Trading Company.

Chapter 14

A smattering of locals occupied the roti shop across from the US embassy. A handful of cats wandered beneath the tables, the aroma of curried meats permeated the place, and cheap posters of happy people from around the world plastered the walls. The eatery was open-air, the patrons displaying a sheen of sweat. The rain jacket came off. In a practiced move, I removed the .45 from my back waist and hid it during the process. Two folds of the jacket, then laid on my lap, the pistol accessible.

I'd been exposed to roti shops in the Caribbean and had passed half a dozen during my morning walk in Paramaribo. Roti was a curry stew of chicken or goat or shrimp served with Indian flatbread. I waited for my lunch guest.

Fletcher Hines—the CIA station chief—exited the embassy compound and crossed the street. Average height, fit, coiled, with an athletic walk. Khakis, white button-down shirt, close-cropped black hair, and the ubiquitous Ray-Bans screamed "Company." An easy man to spot.

A lifted chin drew him over. He sat without shaking hands or introductions.

"Let's start with the basics," he said. "What the hell are you doing here?" Hines removed his sunglasses and hung them from his front pocket—Company-style.

"Pleasure to meet you, too, Hines."

We exchanged stares.

"And it's John Bolen. Feel free to call me John."

I smiled. He didn't.

"Global Resolutions," Hines said. "Tell me."

He'd done his homework.

"I'm not discussing my client engagements. Just know it's plain vanilla. Information only. No action."

I owed him my operational framework. He'd weigh my assertion of simple information collection as a potential lie. He sat and stared, waited.

"What I'd like to discuss is the current mess in your backyard," I said.

No response.

"Share with me, Hines. Let's bond."

Hail fellow, well met failed to appear. I didn't expect it. I'd worked with the CIA—the Company—numerous times as an active member of Delta Force. Committed professionals, they held a skeptical view of the world, considered it nuanced, angled. I considered them wrapped too tight around the intrigue and analysis axle. Occam's razor, baby. The answer with the fewest assumptions—the simplest possibility—was usually the right one.

Plus, the Company viewed Delta as muscle. A hammer. They categorized our less violent abilities as encroachment on their special skill sets. Rivalry wasn't an appropriate description—wariness and not-of-my-tribe more apt.

A young man approached and took our order. We each ordered a Parbo beer, and Hines ordered the chicken roti.

"Why don't you try the special, Mr. John Bolen?" He delivered the suggestion with a smirk.

"It is most excellent," the waiter added.

A cat rubbed against my leg. I glanced at the cat, then Hines, and settled on the waiter.

"Chicken for me as well," I said. Hines chuckled.

I understood and empathized with Hines's attitude. This was his show. I'd arrived uninvited. But we would play our private version of the Clubhouse, trading information, cautious.

When the waiter left, I said, "I was thinking of a western tour. Past the Coppename River. Any recommendations regarding sights and areas of interest?"

The Coppename River separated Paramaribo and government-held territory from rebel turf.

"From an agricultural perspective?" Hines asked, poking me over his ostensible role as agricultural liaison.

"From a tourist perspective."

The beers arrived, bottles sweating.

"I'd advise against it." He took a deep swig of beer, eyes hard. Chatter volume increased as more patrons meandered in and took seats. The rain continued. Road traffic was minimal.

"Yeah. Understood. But I have a strong curiosity regarding Mr. Joseph Hoff." The rebel leader was an enigma and required clarity. The street corner collections of soldiers and random gunshots confirmed urban rebel guerrilla activity. Hoff's capital-city influence indicated strength, commitment. "And why does his reach extend to the streets of Paramaribo?"

"Hoff is run-of-the-mill," Hines said. "Former Suriname army. Popular with a segment of the population. The Paramaribo activity is a nuisance. Small scale. A few sympathizers. Not a danger for the current regime."

"Current?"

Hines had made a simple designation or a slip, indicating regime change in the works. Or it was purposeful misdirection. Hard to say. Dealing with spooks—Hines, Nika, or any of the others—was a pain in the ass.

"His Excellency is aligned with us now," Hines said. "A bumpy past, admittedly."

Well, yeah. His Excellency's son offering the Lebanese terrorist outfit Hezbollah a foothold would qualify as "bumpy." The food arrived, steam rising from the plates. Curry filled the air. The chicken was excellent.

"Hoff's ideology?" I asked.

Hines took a bite of roti and reset the conversation. "We should talk about Case Lee, Esquire, and his current activities."

"I'm happy to oblige, Hines. Really. And I have information— good, salient information—that would interest you. I'm only asking for background."

My playing card was laid, facedown. Hines eased open the kimono and showed a bit of skin.

"Hoff's ideology is collectivist."

It made sense. A catalyst—the strong-arm tactics of the current president—would provide a coalescing of angry citizens, but an ideology glued a rebel force together. Collectivism had a strong pull in this part of the world.

But there were three revolutionary components—catalyst, ideology, and funding. The last one held the most interest. At the moment, I would place the bankers as the United States, Russia, or China. The CIA agent across from me wouldn't share intimate knowledge, but he'd dance around the edges for a look at my facedown card.

"Who's bankrolling the effort?" I asked.

"We have our suspicions."

"So do I. And one of them is you."

He shook his head and squinted. "No. Not this time."

I bought it, to a 70 percent confidence level. His admission of "not this time" was a truth pill, and acknowledgment the United States wouldn't hesitate to back regime change.

"Middle East?" The Hezbollah connection.

Hines gave a tight shake of his head, rejected the possibility. Dismissive, he didn't verbalize his statement. Okay, then.

"Leaving the Russians or Chinese," I said.

Hines declined to respond, so I turned over my table card.

"There's a Russian in town. Either GRU or SVR."

Hines stopped midbite. He lowered his fork, took a swig of beer, and stared, unblinking.

"She's at my hotel."

"I haven't received word of any such individual," Hines said. "And the hotel staff is amenable."

He meant on the payroll.

"Yeah, well, she's here. You've had your 'amenable' staff outbid." Informants flipped, flopped, and double-dipped. Old story.

A potent card had been delivered. Now I'd test the waters for a bit of quid pro quo. "What can you tell me about Luuk Hoebeek?"

Hines stared at the street and digested the Nika information, formulating plans and activities. I let him digest. Eventually, he responded.

"Hoebeek. Respected businessman. Maybe *the* most respected businessman in Suriname. He has a cut of the new embassy contract. Organizes the building materials."

Damn, I needed a trading company. Meanwhile, I kept Nika's Hoebeek visit under wraps.

"What about equipment? Small arms, personnel carriers?" I asked. If this whole revolution thing was going to work, it required men, firearms, and armored vehicles. Hoebeek's little Abu Dhabi shopping trip was off the table as a discussion point. For all I knew, Hines may have sent him there.

Hines ignored me.

"I'll drop a dime on our Russian friend. Tell me about military equipment."

The Nika-Hoebeek relationship would have high value. Overlay a 30 percent probability the United States was funding the revolution, and you had a big, murky mess. Welcome to the world of global spy craft and political chess games.

Hines weighed the options and decided to reveal equipment intel.

"Satellite images show the unloading of military vehicles in Niew Nickerie. At night. Tarp covered. By daylight, they're jungle covered. Source of the material, unknown."

The small town of Niew Nickerie sat on the banks of the Courantyne River. The large rain-forest-fed river formed the border with Guyana. Niew Nickerie had a small set of docks, barely large enough for a tramp freighter, but it would do for discreet unloading of military equipment. Military equipment purchased from anyone. Golf balls pointed toward China.

But the supplier and the sponsor might be two different players. A different supplier would help the sponsor cover its tracks. What a freaking mess. The gnomes of Zurich expected answers—correct answers. Hines would seek the same, unless the United States had funded this little soirée. If so, what the hell was a Russian spy doing in the mix? I'd have to head west, into rebel turf, and seek answers. Son of a bitch.

"Okay," I said. "Here's the dime. The Russian—a stunning woman—paid Hoebeek a visit after I left him. It wasn't an accident. He called her about my arrival at his office."

"You visited Hoebeek?" he asked.

"Courtesy call. Sniffing."

"Then the Russian visited him?"

"Eyeball confirmed."

Hines would simmer that stew for a while. You could damn near see the wheels turn as he contemplated the ramifications. Another cat rubbed against my leg, the dishes were removed from the table, and I ordered two more beers. The drizzle had stopped, and shafts of blistering tropical sunlight broke through the clouds. The steam bath cranked up.

So far, this had gone about as expected. Little of a definitive nature, all fog and avoidance. Still, thin and opaque ties formed among the players—each nebulous. Welcome to Spookville.

The rebel force sponsor, military equipment, and trading company conversation had run its course. Hines itched to get back across the street, unleash assets, and find answers. I wanted a few more insights.

"Tell me about the minister of economic development, His Excellency Ravindu Tjon," I said.

Hines still chewed on the Nika-Hoebeek connection and stared into the big empty. He addressed me as an afterthought. "Attends embassy functions," Hines said, uninterested. "Eats a lot. Drinks a lot."

Neither a ringing endorsement nor an indication Tjon held much sway over events. A bit player, in his eyes. Now, one other individual required addressing.

"Chopper jock. Bishop?" I asked. The mercenary helicopter pilot, as per Jules, in country.

"The three Indian-manufactured helicopters His Excellency purchased have fallen into disrepair. He requires aerial transportation other than fixed-wing," Hines said. "Why ask, Lee? Other than birds of a feather and all that."

The statement grated, big-time. Hines's assertion lumped me with the likes of Bishop. Whatever you said about my current employment, I didn't take gigs that fostered mayhem and death. Or trade in chaos and suffering. Hines may have mentally acknowledged such a distinction, but the "birds of a feather" comment bit deep.

"I play in a different class."

"Yeah. Right."

No point presenting my case for a higher life, so I didn't dwell on the subject and asked how to find Bishop. And worked on lowering my blood pressure.

"Whorehouse," Hines replied. "Every night. He lives there. Thanks for lunch."

He stood and left me with the bill as a small dig. "Next time, try the special." He chuckled.

"I'm crossing the Coppename River."

That stopped him.

"Again, I'd strongly advise against it. But I know you. Your kind. Delta Force. Cowboys. Shoot-'em-up. If you make it back, fill me in. You owe me that."

"I don't owe you shit, Mr. Agricultural Liaison."

"Maybe not. But for God and country." He leaned from the waist, curry thick on his breath. "You're still an American, aren't you?"

"Don't wave the flag at me, asshole. Don't even try. I've been the hammer for the likes of you for years. Delta took out your garbage."

He straightened up. I let it rip.

"And unless you've held a fellow soldier while he bled out in some godforsaken shithole while doing our country's bidding, don't try and play the patriot card, you son of a bitch. Ever."

The CIA station chief exited the roti shop without another word.

Chapter 15

Hines performed his pissed-off CIA operator walk back across the street and entered the embassy compound. I drained my beer. Pissed or not, he wouldn't screw with me. He'd categorize me as a soft asset, unreliable perhaps, but of potential use. He was enough of a pro to accept the opportunity I presented.

I calmed down and strolled to a rent-a-car establishment. Hines had gotten under my skin. The initial pricks and jabs, expected, hadn't busted my cool. But he'd lumped my endeavors with those of a common mercenary and violated a personal demarcation—a division Hines had been aware of and casually ignored.

I had a legit Swiss client. Gigs with them had an element of danger, but no fireworks, no hits. I didn't hang in whorehouses. The heavy-handed lean on patriotism broke the dam. Hines could shove it.

Time to check the countryside, cool off. A beat-up Toyota Land Cruiser fit the bill. The rental-car clerk tried an upsell, but the job required off-road capabilities. I wouldn't cross the Coppename River until tomorrow or the next day, but a drive to the river crossing would provide a feel, a sense of the other side. A view of rebel-held territory. And an opportunity to pull it back together.

A quick stop at the hotel provisioned the afternoon trip. A lanyard with a laminated *John Bolen, Reporter, Rolling Press International* hung around my neck. Rolling Press International didn't exist, but it looked official. A version of the official press pass, also laminated, was tossed on the dashboard. An old camera as added cover. The rain jacket would remain folded on the car seat, the .45 handy.

Before leaving, I went online and rescheduled my flight out for tomorrow. A variety of clandestine services—American, Russian, Chinese—would have backdoor access to the passenger lists. I wouldn't make the flight, but it added a layer of misdirection and safety. Nika, Hines, Hoebeek—I occupied a large blip on their radar.

The drive to the bridge over the Coppename River showed more violence than I'd been led to believe. Burned-out troop carriers and cars, some still smoldering. Evidence of firefights, violent, at night. The burned husks littered the fifty-mile coastal stretch of two-lane potholed road—the country's sole highway. The Atlantic Ocean was on the right as I traveled west, thick, uninhabited jungle on the left. Jungle extending a thousand miles, deep into the Amazon drainage.

I slowed for three checkpoints manned by His Excellency's soldiers. The press pass, camera, and a brief explanation sufficed for semi-safe passage. The soldiers were armed with Uzis—Israeli submachine guns. Marksmanship wasn't the order of the day. Just pull the trigger and spray lead in the general direction of the enemy. They kept their helmets on in the heat—a bad sign. Few developing country soldiers tolerated the added weight and heat of a head bucket. Unless they thought it would save them from an imminent headshot. The wall of jungle, dark and deep, began fifty yards from the highway.

The final checkpoint stood at the tiny village of Jenny on the Coppename River. The soldiers had established a battle line at the edge of the river bridge. Sandbags and machine-gun placements marked the end of government-held turf. I waved the press pass, parked under a tree off the road, and took photos. Acquiring "news." I suppose I was. The soldiers wore newish uniforms, tan. The officers strutted with maroon berets. They weren't about to give up the cool factor of the berets for a little added safety. But they'd damn sure be the first to dive behind the sandbags when bullets flew.

The captain in charge of the bridge crossing asked pointed questions. "Why are you here?" His English, tinged with an amalgamation of accents, came across as chopped, accusatory.

"I'm a reporter. Rolling Press International." I lifted the lanyard press pass and waved it in his direction.

"Why?"

"To report. The world is interested in your excellent efforts."

He glanced down the bridge, chewed on his options. It was time to grease the ego.

"Can I interview you? Take your picture?" I lifted the camera, waggled it, and continued to smile.

The opportunity for his fifteen minutes of fame won out. He gestured to a nearby shack. I conducted a bogus interview, scribbled in a notebook, and clicked the camera a few times. He admitted to nighttime attacks—at the bridge and along the road to Paramaribo. We walked back to the sandbagged machine-gun position. To his credit, the guy was a decent soldier.

I opted to tell him I'd return the next day and cross the bridge. Visit rebel-held territory. He lowered his sunglasses, stared, and shook his head with a "you're crazy" expression. He had that half right.

My intentions revealed, Hines or a government functionary could hear about it and attempt to stop me. Ugliness of the serious kind would ensue. And my ruse of a departure on the morning flight was now compromised.

The upside—a big upside—it would trigger word of my travel to filter across the river. Alert the rebels. A lot of these guys standing around with submachine guns would play both sides and wait for a winner. Passing word of my trip would curry favoritism with the rebels if that side won. A reporter, crossing the Coppename tomorrow. Only a reporter. With Rolling Press International. No surprises. Everyone stay calm.

I took a few more photos, flipped open the small spiral notebook, and pretended to take more notes while I asked a few questions, smiling and nodding. The muddy Coppename pushed past; the occasional tree and other jungle detritus bobbed by. A fisherman cast his net from a dugout canoe, upriver. He drifted by and ignored the battle-ready environment on the bridge.

The *whomp-whomp* of an approaching helicopter sent me back to the tin-roofed shack. I ducked inside. Beer, soda, and sundries. The ubiquitous river-crossing depot. Shelves filled with rice, beans, and tins of fish. An old lift-lid refrigerator held Parbo beer and Pepsi. Several machetes were for sale, as well as three hoe blades. Folks in undeveloped countries don't pay money for a handle they can make from jungle wood. Two tubes of antibiotic cream and one ACE bandage rounded out the pharmacy portion of the establishment.

I bought a bottled water and fried plantain chips at the small counter and wandered onto the covered porch. A Hughes 500 light chopper dropped, twisted, and pulled a sports-car landing on the highway, near the bridge. The whine of the engine shut down. The infamous Bishop, helicopter mercenary, had made an appearance. As the noise died and the five-blade rotor slowed, Fletcher Hines climbed out. Bishop, wearing a baseball cap and large aeronautical headphones, stayed put.

The CIA station chief met with the captain, listened, and nodded as the military man spoke. Toward the end of the conversation, the captain pointed at my Toyota. Hines scanned the area, dark Ray-Bans on full display, and observed me taking a sip of water. I smiled his way. He shot me the finger; I returned the gesture. Bosom buddies. Hines turned and delivered instructions to the captain. Five minutes later, the helicopter fired up, and Hines departed.

Well. Hines shouldn't object to my crossing into rebel-held turf if I brought back valid intel and shared with him. A big if, but he was professional enough—emotions and feelings aside—to appreciate my reconnaissance skills and take advantage of them. But if the military at this bridge stopped me tomorrow, it sent a clear signal Hines had been less than honest about whom the United States backed.

I wandered back on the bridge, snapped more photos, and addressed the captain again. Time to find out what Hines had told him.

"Thank you, Captain. I'll be back tomorrow or the day after. To cross the river. You okay with that?"

"I agree with the other American." He meant Hines.

"Agree to what, Captain?"

"That you are foolish. Reporters will not be greeted well by the traitors across the river."

"You're probably right, Captain. But it's news. That's my job." I lifted the laminated fake press pass again and smiled. The captain shook his head and turned away, barking orders at his men.

I started the Land Cruiser. An hour or so until dusk, and—given the fire-gutted military vehicles littering the side of the road—it was clear things tended to get lively at night.

Friendly waves and "I'll see you folks soon" preceded my departure from the bridge over the Coppename. I kept an eye to the right during the hour-long drive. Toward the ever-present wall of tall tropical jungle lining the road. There be dragons in there.

The hotel café stood empty. Sufficient time for a meal prior to nighttime calls on Tjon and Bishop. A personal break to collect my thoughts on the Suriname puzzle. I caught a glimpse of the chef, Javanese, so I ordered a *rijsttafel*—a Dutch-influenced Indonesian array of small bowls and plates, tidbits of food, with a variety of textures and spices. When in Rome. Or Suriname.

A Niew Nickerie trip loomed. Rebel turf. Damn, Sam. But at this point, collected information painted a hazy picture, nothing clear. Shadows and fog. Players moving, lies, hidden secrets. The possibility of definitive answers lay a hundred miles away through revolution-torn property. But this was why Global Resolutions continued to hire me. To find answers. Go the extra mile. Cross the damn Coppename River.

The finger bowls and plates began to arrive. Pork belly with soy sauce. Spring rolls. Several flavors of fried rice. Banana fritters. Shrimp crackers. Stewed duck. Skewers of satay. And a wide variety of dipping sauces—peanut, chili, and coconut. Pick and choose, mix and match. It was delicious.

Start with the knowns, consider broad assumptions, identify the unknowns. Hezbollah had attempted the establishment of a South American beachhead. A known.

The United States had reacted and reinforced its Suriname presence. Odds were a verbal bitch slap of His Excellency ensued, with threats of economic disaster and worse. An assumption. Whether the United States saw a more stable partner in Joseph Hoff, the rebel leader, was an unknown.

The rebel army had funding. A known. By whom—an unknown.

Russia sent a pro here. A known. Whether to buttress the current regime or oversee an investment in the rebel cause—an unknown. The Russian—hotter than a firecracker. Definitely a known.

Luuk Hoebeek, Mr. Trading Company, had a Russian connection, evidenced by Nika's visit after our meeting. Known. And he'd been to IDEX. A known.

The minister of economic development, Mr. Ravindu Tjon, had refused a meeting with John Bolen, a nice American businessman. He was dirty. Known, but murky.

I ordered espresso and mused over the possibilities while the dishes were taken away. Drizzling rain had started, the night dark and dank. Time for an unannounced call on Ravindu Tjon. And ample time lay ahead to also visit Bishop at the whorehouse. Part of the job, sure. But still . . . and the blues crept in. I needed a trading company.

Chapter 16

A tall wrought-iron fence surrounded Ravindu Tjon's two-acre estate. Landscaped grounds—unlit islands of tall plants and wandering paths—offered excellent approach cover. The three stories of wraparound verandas shone as welcome mats for silent entry and search. I waited to ascertain if a dog or two roamed the premises. No dogs. I dropped into Tjon's backyard. The ground yielded, soaked. The tropical drizzle had stopped, the air thick and still. I left the rain jacket, folded, at the fence. The .45 was tucked into a front pocket, the grip exposed. Insects sounded from the pockets of bamboo, bougainvillea, bromeliads, and ferns.

Tjon was hosting a party. Screened windows allowed sounds of gaiety to float across the backyard. My movements were swift but not rushed, using my friends—night, darkness, shadow. I paused at one of the back corners of the house at the edge of the ground-floor veranda. A heavy chain, in lieu of a gutter downspout, hung two feet away from the series of veranda-supporting columns. It was anchored at the roofline. More welcome mat.

Through the large ground-floor windows, servants scuttled about setting out plates of hors d'oeuvres and delivering drinks to a crowd of several dozen guests. Men in suits and women dressed to the nines moved about, chatted. One of the young women stopped at a low table, squatted, and inhaled a line of white powder from a mirror placed for that purpose. Neat rows of the drug, prearranged, offered guests immediate gratification. A large corner bar, manned by another busy servant with a dark suit and bow tie, stood nearby.

I performed a hand-over-hand ascent of the thick chain, aiming for the top floor. The stout wooden columns supporting the tier of verandas offered more shadow, more darkness, and protection from the light cast by the large windows. Standard Delta stuff; I operated in confidence. A recognizable voice moved across the first-floor veranda and stopped my ascent at the second floor.

"Positioning, Ravindu. Never forget that. Remain neutral by all appearances. I have a great deal of experience in such things."

Luuk Hoebeek. I rested a foot on the second-floor railing and pushed out to view the conversational participants below. Hoebeek addressed an impeccably dressed Creole. Ravindu Tjon, minister of economic development—rotund, imperious, and more than a little dismissive of Hoebeek.

Ravindu waved an irritated hand. "I do not need to be reminded, Luuk. Enough. By the way, an American businessman came by my office today."

"His name?" Hoebeek asked, leaning in.

"Bolen. A Mr. John Bolen, according to my receptionist. American."

"And?"

"I declined to see him. Simply too much going on to see people now."

"A wise decision, my friend. A wise decision. He is to be avoided."

"You know him?" Tjon asked.

"We've met. Avoid him."

Nika's influence shone through Hoebeek's statement. She'd presented me as a danger. Fine. I'd still sleep at night having failed the friend test with Mr. Trading Company.

Tjon nodded, looked into the night, and collected his thoughts. The ice cubes in Hoebeek's glass clinked as he drained his drink. Tjon glanced through the windows at the gaiety inside, then back to Hoebeek. I checked for any upstairs veranda guests. None appeared.

"I can administer to this American if you think it proper. Dispose of him," Tjon said.

"No."

"I can ask one of my people to handle it tonight."

"No, Ravindu."

"This is a critical time. We cannot have disruptions," Tjon said.

"No. The matter is being taken care of." Hoebeek started to move away, and added, "I cannot emphasize enough the importance of secrecy. You did well regarding this man."

Tjon smiled at the compliment, adding, "What is not secret are the beautiful girls and cocaine available at this moment."

Tjon laughed. Hoebeek scowled.

"So come inside, my friend," Tjon said. "This is a party. I have a few girls I'd like you to meet."

The French doors swung open to the floor-level veranda, and several guests spilled out, stopping their conversation. An issue was made of the host and his good friend not joining the festivities, laughter echoed across the lawn, and the entire veranda crowd moved inside. Except for Hoebeek. I plastered myself against the chain, nestled ten feet above him against the support column. He remained contemplative, face grim. Then he turned and joined the party inside.

Another conversation about Case Lee, Esq., getting whacked. Great. I shoved the conversation aside and focused on the mission. The chain proved stout and quiet as I approached the third-floor veranda. The rooms visible through windows stood empty, the door leading off the veranda to the hallway unlocked.

The inside wooden floor squeaked at my first step, so I moved against the wall where subfloor supports were strongest. Laughter and chatter drifted up from the party. The first room's door was wide open, and luck provided my objective. Ravindu Tjon's office.

Large framed photos of Tjon and His Excellency the president hung alongside photos of Tjon on a golf course, Tjon at a grand-opening ceremony, and Tjon bundled in ski wear. The enlarged ski photo's backdrop displayed a French après-ski restaurant. The minister enjoyed the French Alps. A large desk, a four-drawer wooden filing cabinet, and a substantial safe filled the room.

His desktop and desk drawers revealed little. I was rifling through the top filing-cabinet drawer when steady squeaky footfalls approached. Not good. The space behind the open door offered a hiding place. In marched the minister.

He squatted on large haunches, worked the combination of the safe, and pulled open the heavy door. My vantage point allowed view of his activities but not the safe combination. Tjon removed a cigar-box-size container, wooden, and lifted the lid. The interior was filled with white powder. Tjon dipped a fingertip into the substance, raised it to a flared nostril, and inhaled with gusto. A shake of his head and a positive "Yes, yes," followed.

The safe held other items—papers, a leather sack, and a roll of what looked like blueprints. Pay dirt. Tjon stood and leaned over, the wooden container in one hand, and prepared to close and lock the safe, spinning the safe door's combination. That wouldn't do.

The sleeper hold, well practiced by Delta Forces, blocks both the left and right carotid arteries, causing a cessation of oxygenated blood to the brain and loss of consciousness within seconds. Improperly applied, it kills. Two long silent strides, and seconds later, Tjon took a short nap.

He'd come to in a minute, more or less, leaving little time. I started with the rolled-up blueprints within the safe. Spread on his desktop, a heavy stapler and desk lamp holding the edges. A detailed diagram of extensive docks, piers, and support structures lay before me. A quick turn of the pages showed more granular detail. A massive project. A navy facility, complete with dry docks. Bingo.

The lower right corner of each page displayed the same statement. *Prepared and Presented by The Eerlijk Trading Company.* Double bingo.

A global power saw Suriname as a vassal state, a pliable country. One that would support the big dog's military operations. A naval base, home for aircraft carriers, destroyers, amphibious assault ships. The diplomatic shit would hit the fan, condemnations and economic sanctions threatened. The remaining question was the identity of the big dog. The blueprints gave no indication.

Down the hall, stairs creaked. Someone climbed, approached the third floor. Tjon moaned, regaining consciousness, his box of cocaine spilled alongside him. Time for Case Lee, Esq., to skedaddle.

Out the door—a quick glance ensured the arriving guest hadn't reached the top of the stairs yet—and onto the veranda. I started down the drain chain, stopping below the third floor. If I continued my descent, I risked the new person noticing the heavy chain's movement. Best to hunker down, be quiet, be still. The ground-floor party remained in full swing, the laughter raucous. I hung suspended, plastered again between the chain and support column, hidden by the shadows.

The footfalls moved toward Tjon's office. Above me, a muffled admonition, unclear and frustrated and angry. Then movement. One body stumbled, unsteady. The other moved with sure intent. Both came closer, together, exited the veranda door, and approached the railing above my head.

A brief "Whaa?" and the minister of economic development flew several feet past me, headfirst, toward the ground three floors below. Two sounds—a muffled impact similar to a sack of rice hitting the kitchen floor, and the discernible crack of neck vertebrae. Ravindu Tjon sprawled on the dark stone pathway below, dead.

A face peeked over the railing, focused on the fallen man. Luuk Hoebeek. He pulled back, and his footsteps retreated. The party remained inside. No screams or horror-filled recognition as a body whipped past the ground-floor windows and made a lethal stop. The laughter and good times continued.

Mr. Trading Company played for keeps. Just ask the *former* minister of economic development. And, in a heartbeat, he'd turn the same attitude toward Case Lee, Esq. Fine. Him, Nika, whatever. But I wasn't just another shmuck, another victim. Delta Force, baby. And if you had any intentions of tossing my butt off a balcony, you'd better bring several dozen large men.

I eased down the chain and jogged into darkness, through elephant ears, canna lilies, and banana plants. Rain jacket retrieved, wrought-iron fence hurdled, I continued to jog until, several backyards later, I hit a street. The noise of the party behind me carried through the dank air.

Chapter 17

Paramaribo's finest whorehouse—a two-story wooden building with low outdoor lighting—stood four blocks from my hotel, tucked into a large tree- and vine-covered three-acre lot. A few vehicles were parked on the gravel drive out front. Music—a bass-driven American pop song—filtered through open windows. Two prostitutes smoked and chatted, occupying the front porch. They dropped their smokes, ground them out, and struck a pose as I approached. I nodded and smiled, passed them, and entered a world of sadness and despair. Another day at the office. Witness a murder, drop by the local cathouse, and chat with the resident mercenary. Mom would be so proud.

Christmas lights, a permanent fixture, were strewn across the ceiling and wrapped around any vertical room support. A small bar, arrays of liquor, and more Christmas lights. Cheap wooden tables and a small dance floor. Painted velvet art festooned the walls. A sci-fi goddess astride a dragon, gravity-defying boobs and six-pack a sign of her power. Another painting held her counterpart, some dude with a minimalist loincloth. He gripped an ax, scowled, long hair streaming. And another of Elvis. On velvet, crooning. The poor bastard.

A dozen women milled about. A variety of sizes, shapes, and colors—both the women and their attire. It smelled of cigarettes, liquor, sweat, and sex.

I took off the rain jacket, the pistol protruding from my back waistband. No worries as no one would blink an eye at its display.

My guy sat at a corner table, a young woman perched on a knee. Two others occupied adjoining chairs. Mr. Air Jockey, stud of the universe, filled a one-piece flight suit covered with aviation patches. A long, thin cigar smoldered in a stamped-metal ashtray. Bishop. Have chopper will travel.

I approached, and the girls scattered, leaving the two of us alone. My demeanor, look, or walk indicated "other business." Working girls had a keen eye for the inherent dangers of the here and now. An American approached the helicopter pilot, and their internal radar sent a signal—step aside. Leave. Leave and not overhear anything they could later be associated with. Pure survival instinct. A core skill set among prostitutes in a gritty country.

A merc is a merc, and Bishop would focus on business. I sat near him, back against the wall, and signaled, smiling toward the nearest working girl. A beer. She returned a nod and left.

"I sense another operator," Bishop said. He grinned and plucked his cigar from the ashtray. He could have passed for a NASCAR driver with all the commercial patches on his one-piece. "A man smelling easy money," he added.

Great. Another bosom buddy. A quick recon of the room confirmed no immediate danger.

"Something like that," I said.

My heart broke in these dens of cheap life. The girls, often teens, plied the world's oldest profession out of desperation. Parents had sold them, pocketing cash while their daughters immersed themselves in the deep pits of a miserable life. Some were kidnapped and held as slaves. Desperate poor countries with desperate people. Their next meal was a constant concern. Beaten, fed drugs, abused mentally—a shitty life, a downward spiral. I never contributed to their decline. Sad and depressing. Vile bastards like Bishop fed the beast. A user of others' pain and struggles.

A small lizard ran up a nearby wooden support pole and found a perch on a red bulb among the Christmas lights. The music changed, another pop tune. Tires crackled on gravel outside—another customer or two arrived. A sad damn place.

"John Bolen. Not an operator. Information only," I said. My head craved such a demarcation.

"Sure," Bishop said, smirking. He hadn't bought the separation. "Whatever you say, *John*. Clever name. You sure we haven't crossed paths? Sudan?"

Not Sudan. Neighboring Eritrea. We hadn't made physical contact in that war-torn African country, but Delta knew of his efforts. He flew for the highest bidder, carnage be damned.

"Never worked that part of the world," I lied. Misdirection, head him off any potential past trail. My beer arrived. "And no desire to. How's this gig treating you?"

His answer was dependent upon several factors, not the least of which was liquor consumption. Sufficiently lubricated, the macho mercenary bullshit might surface and legitimate answers be given.

"Lots of opportunity. Lots of money. Lots of girls. A man could do worse."

Well lubricated. All good.

"You're the Suriname Air Force at the moment, I understand."

He took a large swig of beer, puffed his cigar, and added, "Seems that way. As usual, flying for the HCIC. Head clown in charge."

Head clown. Suriname's president. Bishop's lack of class shined bright.

"Side gigs?" I asked.

"Poor boy has gotta eat. What did you have in mind?"

"Nothing at the moment. Just checking availability."

He'd already demonstrated willingness to take other clients. Hines's arrival at the Coppename bridge, for instance. What other players utilized his service?

"Give me a heads-up twenty-four hours in advance. I can bullshit the HCIC and get you where you want."

"Good."

"Two grand an hour."

"Reasonable."

"Including standby time. Minimum three hours. That's six large for those of you challenged by math." He laughed, drained the beer bottle, and waggled the empty toward the bar.

"Good to know. Just don't want to cut in on someone else's schedule."

His beer arrived, and he fished the cigar from the ashtray, relit it. As he puffed, the mercenary shields rose. Bishop had lived this long knowing when to shut up, regardless of booze consumption. Damn.

"Nope. Just the chief and his army commandant." A lie, and his hooded expression gave clear indication he wouldn't tolerate much more digging.

I plowed ahead, took another sip of beer, and remained sociable. I had to choke the beer down—the room held such a rank smell, the whole landscape tawdry.

"You know the minister of economic development? Ravindu Tjon?"

"Heard the name."

"Luuk Hoebeek?"

"Look, asshole. I have a good thing going here. Chill with the all the damn questions."

The music switched—a god-awful Dutch pop tune. Two girls wafted by the table, smiled, and trolled for business. Fatigue washed over me. A busy day. The establishment's vibe of desperation overlaid with cheap perfume and cigar smoke added weight, depression.

"What you need is to get laid," Bishop said. "Learn to relax."

I couldn't handle any more beer. One more question, then exit.

"Now, I'd suggest the one over there." Bishop pointed out a young woman in hot pants and halter across the room. "Will tear you a new one."

He laughed. I feigned a smile.

"Or the one with the sarong. Lie back and let her drive. A spinner."

Visions of a white-picket-fence future shimmered, unreachable. This current path skirted the possibility, led to muck and mire. Led to those that relished the filth and degradation. All right, the money was damn good. Mom and CC received most of it. But the thought of family and a past life with Rae, in this place at this time, had me circling the drain.

I cleared my mind of loved ones. This was work. I was good at it. Damn good. And in a couple of days, I'd be back on the *Ace* a million miles from this setting. I shivered, let it go, and did my job.

"How about a blonde hanging out at the hotel? Seen her?" A bit of a stretch, as Bishop lived at the whorehouse and worked at the airfield, keeping his bird mechanically fit for service. He wasn't the type to hang at decent hotels.

"Sweet piece of ass. Seen her. That's it."

"That's it?"

"That's it for this supersleuth bullshit you're playing." He turned surly.

"Dude, I'm not an operator. An errand boy, nothing more." I held up both hands, palms facing him.

He didn't buy it.

"It's a good gig I've got here, Bolen. Too many questions makes me uneasy."

"Not my intent."

"Harshes my mellow."

"Understood."

"So before you ask the next one, let me preempt the effort."

"Okay."

"Shove it up your ass."

Several of the girls had started dancing—desultory moves, prompted by an unseen command from management. Bishop, agitated, raised a hand toward the bar and signaled a "come here" to someone.

Someone was the large bartender, muscle for the owner. Backup followed. Classic other-world bar scenario. The lead big guy, muscle number one, would inquire if Bishop—his best customer—was all right. He'd also want information about this strange man that kept Bishop from buying the girls drinks and spending money in the usual manner. I was bad for business. The guy behind him, tall and wiry with more than a few face and neck scars, stood a discreet two steps back.

"Everything okay, Mr. Bishop?" muscle one asked, his voice an amalgam of accents.

Bishop leaned back, swilled beer, and cast a smile my way. "Everything okay, Bolen? Why don't you tell my friend everything is okay?" He chuckled, back in control.

I assessed the large muscle. Tall, broad, and a face long bereft of a good-natured grin.

"Everything's fine," I said. I'd had enough of Bishop. Exit time. Graceful or humble or violent—it didn't matter.

A young girl came around muscle two and stood, her look nervous, fingers fidgeting. Drugs—meth, coke, or a god-awful combination that might include laundry powder, snorted or injected. She was lit, high voltage, and scratched her forearm. "I'll sit with Bishop if you'd like, Bello."

She tried to placate big muscle, start the party again with Bishop, and do her bit to alleviate any unnecessary activities. A legitimate attempt, and she deserved a hell of a lot better than she received.

Bello glanced over his shoulder and backhanded the young girl. She yelped, grabbed her cheek with one hand, and fled to a corner of the large room. Another prostitute comforted her, rubbed her arm, and whispered in her ear. Someone turned off the music.

There's not a caped-crusader trait built into my character. I wanted out of the place, to walk away. But this hellhole of an establishment deserved a lesson in manners.

"Best of luck, Bishop," I said, standing. "I'm fairly certain the Stingers I smuggled in a couple of days ago haven't been deployed yet."

Chopper pilots weren't fond of small-arms fire from the ground, aimed skyward, but they were shit-scared of the shoulder-mounted Stinger missiles. It was total bullshit I'd smuggled any of them, but Bishop wouldn't know that. And the possibility of a Stinger in the wrong hands induced ulcers for chopper pilots of Bishop's ilk.

Bishop's eyes went wide, any semblance of curled-lip mirth long gone. I turned and addressed the large muscle, Bello. "Stop hitting the girls. They don't like it. I don't like it. Any questions?"

He telegraphed his next move. His torso turned toward the backup muscle as he prepared for a backhanded head blow. It came as expected. I caught his wrist, stepped close, locked eyes. He struggled against the pain in his now-bent wrist, his body a shield between me and muscle number two. A short vicious kidney punch put the large man on the floor. The wrist grip remained, and his kneeled position revealed the backup muscle with a flicked knife, flashing under the low lighting. He moved laterally, kept the knife low—a legitimate knife fighter.

Pulling the .45 remained an option, unneeded. A quick hand signal toward Bishop—*stay put*. I stepped past the large man on the floor, used the momentum to snap the wrist he'd used on the girl. He screamed. The white-hot cry of pain echoed off the low ceiling, and the working girls huddled, grouped against the walls.

I advanced toward the knife-wielding muscle, forced him to make a move. A move on my terms. The knife came low, deadly. I caught his forearm, punched his throat, and as he fell, broke his knife arm at the elbow. He rasped a bellow of pain, tried to breathe, no longer a threat. A quick glance confirmed Bishop had heeded my signal and declined participation in the festivities. It was over in under ten seconds.

A settled intermission filled Paramaribo's best whorehouse. Case Lee, center stage. Bello's scream lowered to a guttural moan. Muscle two joined the chorus, short violent gasps for air, emphatic exhales, attempting to control the pain.

"Behave, Bishop."

He nodded, relit his cigar, and leaned back. Saved some face.

"That's sound advice," I added. "Behave."

I checked the room for any additional assailants, grabbed my jacket, and made a calm exit. A light rain had started. I jogged away. The rain washed, cleansed. The whorehouse event faded, shoved deep, racked up, and discarded. Another sad vignette, played out on life's garbage-ridden stage. Sad, tawdry, lonely.

Fatigue flooded me—a full day. A quiet, clean drink at the hotel bar called. I jogged in that direction. The movement provided more physical release, tuned both body and mind. It also saved my life.

The angry bee-buzz of a bullet whipped past my neck. The echoed crack of a pistol followed. Someone had missed his or her running target, me, by an inch. The bullet's movement past my head and the sound of the retort identified the general location of the source. A parked car provided me cover. The drawn .45 presented a deadly fact— I'd deliver the next shot.

This could have been related to the whorehouse incident, but mental alarms screamed otherwise. I scuttled near the front bumper of the vehicle, stayed low, surveyed the direction of the shot. The glint of a metallic firearm revealed my adversary's position—across the street, a dark shape also crouched behind another vehicle. The .45 took aim.

Automatic gunfire blasted down the road. Tracer rounds, mixed with regular bullets, left brief red lines in the night air. A cadre of scared soldiers, posted at the nearest street intersection, didn't bother ascertaining what the hell was going on. Instead, they had opened fire with their Uzi submachine guns toward the general direction of my assailant's shot. Bullets pinged off parked cars and struck the street with a wet whine. The cacophony continued for fifteen seconds, then stopped. Hushed commands and back-and-forth arguments among the group of soldiers floated through the light rain. Dogs barked, and heavy wooden house shutters slammed.

A quick glance across and down the street revealed a retreating shadow, quickly covered by the night.

Chapter 18

The front desk staff lacked the usual smiles, eyes toward the floor when I informed them of my scheduled departure on tomorrow morning's flight. They were cautious, wary, and less prone to engage. Someone had delivered them a first-class ass-chewing. Fletcher Hines, CIA. A man upset over their lack of prepaid loyalty. And upset with himself for having been outbid by a Russian spy. I settled the bill with cash.

"Pleasant evening?" Nika asked.

Alone, she worked a hotel bar drink. Tight jeans, black running shoes, and a dark maroon hoodie. She oozed sexuality from such a casual outfit.

I sat two stools away and ordered a Grey Goose on the rocks. Her presence prompted a new review of the possibilities. The bullet with my name on it, close. Too damn close. A pro must have fired it. I had presented a nighttime running figure, and the shooter had missed by an inch.

Hines, maybe. The CIA would consider me a loose end that required tying. A well-trained hit man hired by Luuk Hoebeek, another possibility. Ravindu Tjon had tasted, for the final time, Hoebeek's displeasure.

Or Nika, now sipping her drink, cool as a cucumber.

If she was the shooter, then brass balls led her to inquire about my evening. Perhaps she considered the hotel bar neutral ground. There wasn't a damn thing neutral about the black widow perched several feet from me, smiling. Her hoodie's large front pocket showed signs of something small and heavy nestled within. A pistol. Of course, she *would* carry, part of her motif. Whether she'd used the weapon this night was the $64 question. The metallic coolness of the .45 pressed against my lower back, tucked inside my jeans, provided comfort. If gunplay ensued, I could draw faster than her. Maybe.

"It's been a hoot so far. How about you?" I asked.

Long red fingernails performed a light bar-top staccato, similar to a piano player, bored. She smiled, ignored my question, and asked, "Such a peculiar life we live. Do you tire of it?"

"I'm tired of being shot at."

The light clack of her manicured nails stopped, and a look of concern—real or fake—appeared. "Someone shot at you today?"

"I didn't say today."

"I assumed."

"You assumed right."

At least the tawdry atmosphere of the whorehouse had been replaced with a civilized, albeit lethal, venue. Another office setting for Case Lee, Esq.

She sent her right hand into the hoodie's front pocket. I reciprocated, slid my hand over the pistol grip at my back. We both froze, locked eyes. Then she smiled again and shook her head.

"Really?" she asked.

"As real as it gets."

Still smiling, she slowly extracted her hand, showed a pack of smokes and a lighter. The heavy bulge remained in her hoodie pocket. I returned my right hand to the bar top, took a drink with my left.

She lit a smoke and addressed the bar-length mirror. Bottles of booze blended with her reflection. A little finger corrected a perceived issue with her hair.

"I've discovered something interesting, Case. And I do like your name. It fits."

John Bolen hadn't lasted long with her. I did a quick replay of the last twenty-four hours. I'd been careful. Discreet. Unless Hines had shared information with her. You never knew. Then it hit me. My Grey Goose glass from last night. Fingerprints. The glass taken, the prints lifted, digitized. Then combined with photos she'd taken of me with a hidden camera. Zip it up, hit "Enter," Moscow bound. Voila—the profile of a Mr. Case Lee emerged. Damn. I should have taken the glass with me. Her physical allure had worked—caused a slip. A stupid misstep on my part.

"It will come as no surprise that inquiries were made," she said. "I've received background information. And I must say, you do have an interesting past." She continued an inspection of herself in the mirror and took a drag of her smoke.

"And that's all it is. The past. I'm boring now."

"Boring?"

"And tedious. Client-based sleuthing. Run-of-the-mill stuff."

She turned, faced me. "The bounty on your head is hardly run-of-the-mill."

"Remnant of the past."

"Even so. My, my. Quite a sum of money."

I downed the Grey Goose and held the glass suspended, toward the bartender. He nodded back and prepared another. He showed no interest in the conversation. Too cryptic, perhaps. Or too dangerous to have any claims of overhearing. Nonplayers go deaf with regularity.

"You looking to collect, Nika?"

She laughed and took another drag of her smoke, exhaling toward the ceiling. "Oh, Case. I'm long past such endeavors. Like you, I focus on the mission."

"The mission."

"Yes. And the suggestion I'd be motivated by mere money actually hurts."

She stuck out a lower lip as an exaggerated affront at my question. Then she broke a wry grin, shook her head, and added, "Still, it must keep you on your toes."

"Yeah. I'm a regular Gene Kelly. Dancing in the rain while dodging bullets."

She gave a "Hmm" and moved on. "Well, be assured this is friendly turf."

"The bar."

"Yes. I want you comfortable, relaxed. The night is young." She winked and took a sip of her drink.

A hotel front desk employee stuck her head in the bar and called the bartender. He left, and the low-ceiling room now held just the two of us. The damp rain spots on her hoodie and jeans hadn't dried. She laid her smoke in the ashtray, undid her ponytail, and shook her head, releasing a cascade of blonde tresses.

"Think about it," she continued. "Ships passing in the night, pleasure taken, no strings."

Quiet footfalls on hardwood outside the bar, murmurs from the front desk, and the aroma of expensive perfume a few feet away. Chanel No. 5.

"Just so I'm crystal clear on this moment, you're intimating we have a drink, conduct a little belly rubbing, and forget our daily woes? Am I hearing that right?"

Lunacy, plain and simple. Neutral ground and a roll in the hay. Sheer lunacy, but an attribute common among clandestine professionals. They weren't my tribe, but I'd worked with them and understood where she came from.

She took a drag, locked eyes. "You should go home, Case. Report to your client the rumor and speculation you've uncovered."

"And that's about all I've got."

"Sufficient for a job well done. Leave the international gamesmanship to the professionals."

"Like you."

"Like me."

Odds were stacked high she was malevolent, hollow, a stone-cold killer. A possible attempt on my life twenty minutes ago, not quite acknowledged, now shunted aside. An alluring new proposition made. The thought of passion spent with her brought shivers, most of them the wrong kind. Most, but not all.

"Let's talk about your day, Nika. Idle chitchat. Get to know each other better."

"If that's what it takes."

"Takes to do what?"

"To salve your 'get to know her' prerequisite."

"Just being friendly. And professional. Not a prelude for other activities."

I drove that stake in the ground for two reasons—to set boundaries for this little interaction and to ensure I didn't slip. I'm a straight man. And she looked like a Victoria's Secret model. Break out the resolve tools, nail certain doors shut.

She chuckled—low, sexy, lethal. "My day was certainly more mundane than yours. Not a single bullet passed me by. I feel left out. What's a girl to do?" She played a bit more fingernail piano, smiled, pleasant.

I shifted on my seat, the cold steel at the small of my back reassuring. "So if you were betting, who's ramrodding the rebel effort?"

"Back to work subjects?" She cast a false pout.

"This is no small shakes. The taking over of a sovereign country by insurgents," I said. "Plugging in a new leader."

"Plugging in a new leader. How Soviet."

"A leader very amenable to the desires of the funding power player."

She took a sip, swayed to unheard music, bored.

"You think it's my team?" I asked.

Throwing out the possibility of a United States–led effort provided a starting point. No accusations, no denials, and acceptance of the possibilities. Her turf, and I wouldn't linger long.

"It could be. Don't look at me for answers. I'm trying to find out. Like you. Except this is my job. You're a freelancer."

"I'm pretty good at it."

"I imagine you're better than good at other things."

"Let's stay on topic."

"Again, why don't you call it over and done? Report what you've found, and head for the hills or wherever it is you live."

Absent the bartender, she stood on the bar's foot rail and leaned far over, retrieving the bottle of Grey Goose. I watched the whole show and avoided staring at her ass. Her hoodie pocket thumped on the bar top and caused a casual freeze of movement. She looked over her shoulder, gave a friendly raise of her eyebrows.

"Oh, my," she said, then continued on her mission and poured us both another drink.

In for a penny, in for a pound. This was liable to be the last time I ever saw her, so I opened my kimono a bit, starting with a half lie. "I'm heeding your advice, Nika. Leaving this place tomorrow. First flight."

She'd buy it, after checking with the front desk and going online to backdoor the airline's passenger list. A layer of cover while I mucked about on the other side of the Coppename River.

"All the more reason for a bit of relaxation," she said, cocking her head and raising the corners of her lips.

"Couldn't afford it."

"Afford what?"

"The emergency-room bill at Paramaribo's finest hospital."

She laughed. It was getting late. Tomorrow, another busy day. This was her turf, her game. Time to shake and stir, tilt the seesaw, then leave.

"Ravindu Tjon is dead."

An ice-cold expression fell across her face.

"And you know this how?"

"Eyeballs."

"Who did it?"

"Your dear friend, Luuk Hoebeek."

She lit another smoke and pursed her lips, thinking. A single polished fingernail tapped the bar top. She stared into the mirror. "You've certainly been a busy little beaver today." The statement was directed at her reflection. The next one locked eyes with me. "Busy, busy. That can be very unhealthy."

"I take vitamins. Whose payroll was Tjon on? Yours?"

"I hate to say this, Case. I really do. But you're out of your league."

"And I just met with a merc. Name of Bishop. Chopper pilot. You know him?"

A broadside effort, firing definitive statements and blunt questions. No subterfuge, no spy craft. My rules.

"Everyone knows Bishop."

"If Bishop is double-dipping with you, he won't last long."

"They come and they go," she said.

"I'm discounting the Chinese."

"Unwise."

"They have too many commercial interests in this neck of the woods to risk screwing it up. So it's either your side or my side."

"You've left out commercial interests. The world runs on money. Big money."

A Nika feint. The blueprints from Tjon's office showed massive docks, piers, and repair yards. A naval base, not commercial.

"I'll give it a toss-up. United States or Russia. That's going in my report."

"Highly speculative. Bordering on unprofessional."

She had ceased any warmth toward me, thrown the off switch.

"Goodnight, Nika. And goodbye." I slid off the barstool and backed toward the door. "It's been, well, different."

I no longer existed for her except as another chess piece. Another pawn. She glanced my way, turned, and contemplated her reflection while she mused, planned. The next move, who to influence, who to kill. She soaked in her world, alone, deadly.

Back in the room, I locked the door and slid a chair under the door handle. Gathered bedding and two pillows, closed and locked the bathroom door. The bathtub made for a secure bed. I slept with the .45 and dreamed of darkness and purple streets and death.

Chapter 19

The lobby's glass front doors revealed predawn blackness. My travel rucksack slung over one shoulder and the displayed .45 pistol sent a simple message. I'm leaving. Don't mess with me.

A wave and smile at the two front desk receptionists returned neither movement nor emotion. The "strange" factor cranks up in developing countries when revolution is under way. The front desk folks accepted the necessary behavioral changes, chose to navigate through this unsettled period with temporary blindness the mantra of the day.

The press badge dangled from a lanyard around my neck, the larger version placed on the dashboard. Both helped when I was stopped at a checkpoint at the edge of town. Tired soldiers shook their heads and sent me on my way. The sixty-mile drive to the Coppename River took over an hour. No new burned-out military vehicles littered the lone coastal two-lane.

I kept an eye to my left, toward the wall of jungle. Wild turf. Muzzle blasts from military types tucked into the foliage would have shown, pinpoints of fire from the black sanctuary. Had someone taken a few potshots, a duck-down-and-stomp-the-accelerator strategy would ensue. But the ride, tense and grim, proved uneventful.

Dawn lowered the anxiety a notch or two. The same group of soldiers that had met me yesterday shuffled around the safe side of the long bridge. They stretched, yawned, the night shift over, uneventful, relieved. The same captain approached my vehicle. I reviewed my news-reporter task again, and—as so often happens—a new day had dawned, so he'd check with headquarters, confirm my passage. With Tjon's death last night, complications were liable to arise at my departing government-controlled territory. When the captain strode toward his command post, I eased off the clutch and rolled across the bridge. They wouldn't pursue me into enemy territory, and no one fired, either out of confusion or disregard. It didn't matter. The view in the rearview mirror was the last I'd have of them.

Rebel-held territory. Eighty miles to Niew Nickerie, the town on the Courantyne River that separated Suriname from Guyana. A nowhere town and odds-on favorite for the rebel leader's stronghold. Past experiences had shown that rebel leaders—and this Joseph Hoff fellow would be no exception—held firm exit strategies. Hoff might pull off a strong assault on Paramaribo and ensconce himself as the new president for life. Or the current guy in power could launch a major military assault on his position and destroy the rebel army. If the latter, Hoff would want a quick exit available. Cross the Courantyne River and find himself on the safe turf of Guyana. Live to fight another day.

Overcast, the gray day met the strip of asphalt on the horizon. Ocean on the right, jungle to the left, screwed-up revolution ahead. I had no edict from Global Resolutions for this jaunt, no macho desire to mingle with the other side. This was my job. If pressed, I might admit an adrenaline-driven desire to hang it on the edge. But at the end of the day, it was my job.

Behind, questions and obfuscation and at least one murder. The blueprints in Tjon's office portrayed no backer, no banker. Just Hoebeek's trading-company stamp, leaving the door wide open for several possibilities. One thing for certain: Hoebeek played for keeps. Just ask Ravindu Tjon, who'd failed to sprout wings when he'd departed the third floor of his house.

Nothing cut and dried about any of it at the moment, and clarity wouldn't come in Paramaribo. Another bullet aimed my way, perhaps, but no clearing of muddy waters. So I'd take my chances in a new venue. Niew Nickerie. The rebel army and Joseph Hoff. At least they hadn't shot at me. Yet.

I focused on my job—satisfying the gnomes in Zurich. Overarching games of global intrigue meant nothing. As a member of Delta, I'd done my part. Hammered the requested nails, killed and wounded and gathered information. The past. Today would be about finding a semblance of truth, report out, and let the chips fall where they may. And while subsequent global chess moves were made, I'd motor down the Ditch on the *Ace*.

I stopped at two armed checkpoints on the Niew Nickerie run. At each one, the rebel soldiers—dressed in a variety of ragtag uniforms and hand-me-downs—looked at my press pass, shook their heads, and signaled me to pass. One reporter, one old Toyota Land Cruiser—no threat. They carried a variety of arms: Chinese Kalashnikovs, Belgian

FNCs, Israeli Uzis, and a sprinkling of US M16s. Several donned black berets. Most wore Chinese Ray-Bans, a badass look.

It took two hours—the road potholed and rough—before I arrived at the third checkpoint on the outskirts of Niew Nickerie. Another ragged collection of soldiers allowed passage after they performed their soldier strut, circling the vehicle. I rolled along the main drag and pulled up to a small hotel, clapboard and clean. The town had the eerie feel of a place that might not have been fond of the current His Excellency, but wasn't enthused with Mr. Replacement now occupying the town. Looks over shoulders, tight nods of greeting. Let us do our business, live our lives, and don't shoot us. A reasonable outlook.

I booked a room and asked the owner how I might go about meeting Joseph Hoff. A reporter, looking for a story. He shook his head no. The three Benjamins slipped across the desk counter changed his outlook. I was assured, in broken English, he'd at least make an effort.

Now that I'd arrived, the first order of business was how to get the hell out. I scouted escape routes. The Nickerie River, small, ran alongside town. Three miles to the west, the larger Courantyne River— the primary objective for a shit-hit-the-fan scenario. Crossing it put me in Guyana, semi-safe turf. Joseph Hoff and I already had common interests—the same exit plan. I strolled west, rucksack over one shoulder, stretched my legs. The pistol remained hidden under the untucked tail of my T-shirt. Rain threatened but didn't fall, the sky gray, low.

Jules had been wrong—I knew how to exit gracefully. True enough, running wasn't in my nature. Because running left you exposed. I preferred to cover my tracks with a planned exit and avoid violence directed my way.

At the edge of town, I stopped for something to eat. The small, neat café held a few locals who returned tight nods at my smile and hand wave. The owner attended me. He tried Dutch, Sranan, and then Hindi. I tried Spanish and Portuguese—little point in trying Arabic. The other diners chuckled and smiled at the linguistic impasse. The owner raised a hand, disappeared into the kitchen, and returned with a teenager, his daughter. She spoke English, laughed, and informed me a typical Niew Nickerie breakfast was just what I needed. I let her know that as long as it came with coffee, I'd be good.

The java, excellent. The meal, different—rice, a slab of dense bread with local goat cheese, and dried fish reconstituted with curry sauce. The owner's daughter asked if she could sit with me while I ate. She was a delight.

After explaining my job as a reporter for Rolling Press International and my desire to interview Joseph Hoff, I asked questions.

"Are you safe here? I mean, while the conflict is going on?"

"We are not affected. Unless we wish to travel to Paramaribo. That is dangerous now. But, yes, we are safe."

"Have you met Joseph Hoff?"

"No. I have seen him. Often."

"Do you go to school?"

"Yes. Senior school. Not quite a university, but good."

"How'd you learn English?"

She giggled. "You have heard of the Internet? It is mostly English. Do you have a Facebook page?"

"Afraid not." She wasn't surprised. I occupied the ancient side of the age scale.

"Where do you live?" she asked.

"California."

"Ah." It brought a wide smile. "Hollywood." A statement rife with possibilities and wonder.

"Has there been fighting here? In Niew Nickerie?"

"No. Do you know any movie stars?"

"I'm afraid not. But I've seen a few. Do you know how many men Joseph Hoff has?"

"A lot. I suppose. What stars?"

"Arnold Schwarzenegger. Jennifer Aniston. Are there any large military vehicles here?"

"Some. In the jungle. What were they like?"

"Very nice. They smiled. What do you think is the best way to find Commander Hoff? I have to write the news story."

"He will find you, I'm sure. Any others?"

She meant movie stars. I'd never laid eyes on Schwarzenegger or Aniston, and I'd wearied of lying to this wonderful young lady. "No.

That's it. I want you to be careful while all this is going on. Will you do that for me?"

She laughed again. "I'm careful. There is no worry."

I finished breakfast, washed down the dry bread and goat cheese with black coffee. Then off again, strolling toward the Courantyne River. The road changed from asphalt to dirt, potholes filled with rainwater. The few occupants of ramshackle shacks scooted inside when I meandered by. A couple of mangy dogs barked, and tall, thick weeds lined the road.

Larger vessels, including one tramp freighter, were tied up along the dilapidated docks. The Courantyne River, here at its Atlantic Ocean mouth, was two miles wide, the current swift. A ferry capable of carrying six vehicles ran a twice-daily service across the river and provided connectivity between Suriname and Guyana. The normal route for a traveling tourist. Upriver of my riverbank position, tied to high-water poles driven into the ground, were dozens of small fishing vessels. Mixed with them were a handful of viable exit craft—dugout canoes. Exit strategy of Case Lee, Esq.

On my way back, an old motorcycle approached from the rear. I turned and stepped aside, waved. The slow-moving bike held the driver, his wife and child, and a pile of baskets roped together. The man ignored me, the woman stared, the child pointed and giggled. The dirt road returned to silent and empty.

A quarter mile later, a small Datsun pickup truck rambled my way. Four armed soldiers occupied the truck bed, two more in the front seat. The truck stopped fifty yards away. I continued walking toward it, waved and smiled. One of the clowns in the truck bed cut loose with his Uzi, the bullets zipping down the other side of the road. Two others joined the game. So damn typical.

Bored and exhibiting their badass control of all things before them, rebel soldiers the world over delighted in scaring the hell out of innocents. I presented a prime target for their testosterone exhibit.

Diving into the head-high brush along my side of the road provided two options. I could wait, the scared reporter, until they finished their firearms display. Or lose the rucksack and pull the pistol. Circle behind them through the thick brush, and—six shots later—end their day. I chose the former, although the latter option held strong appeal. Being shot at does that to me.

The firing stopped, the laughter continued, and the Datsun ground into gear, approached.

"Reporter?" the soldier in the passenger seat called as they stopped near me. "Reporter?" They exchanged more laughter.

"I'm a reporter!" I yelled back, hidden.

"Yes! Yes, reporter. I know." A lighthearted exchange in Sranan among the pickup occupants was cut short by someone's command.

"You are not in danger, reporter. Come, come."

I stood and became visible. The good news was nobody pointed his weapon my way. The lanyard with the fake press ID still dangled from my neck.

"Yes," I said. I affected a look of fear, eyes moving from one rebel soldier to the next, body hunched, apprehensive. If these guys knew the real deal, they wouldn't have smiled. Hell, a couple more shots my way, and they wouldn't have been breathing.

"Yes, please don't shoot anymore. Please. I'd really like an interview with your commander. Joseph Hoff. For our international newspaper." I held up the lanyard; the laminated press badge twisted with the breeze. "More of a website these days, but we do still publish the old hard copy. Someone needs to use that paper we bought." A shy smile for my insider joke. All good humor. All in earnest. Mr. Passenger Seat lowered his fake Ray-Bans, his eyes bloodshot.

"Go to the hotel. We get you later." He signaled the driver to turn around. A five-point turn in the middle of the road; then they headed back toward Niew Nickerie. One of the truck-bed occupants waved his Uzi in my direction and flashed white teeth. Asshole.

Alone again. An occasional large droplet of rain splatted on the hard-packed dirt road. By the time I made it the half mile back to the hotel, the sun had broken through and fierce tropical heat brought rivulets of sweat. At least the discovery of the dugout canoes offered relief. Past experience dictated I wouldn't be taking the ferry.

Chapter 20

The small hotel front porch offered a comfortable rocker, a place to read a paperback, and watch life flow. Niew Nickerie displayed more normalcy than Paramaribo. Joseph Hoff had taken the fight to the capitol city.

The town's traffic flow, both vehicular and pedestrian, appeared typical. No soldiers guarded intersections. The hotel owner kept me supplied with coffee. I hadn't unpacked, and the afternoon rolled on.

An old Nissan pickup arrived, brakes squeaking. The lone occupant, elbow out the driver window, showed a camouflage shirt and black beret. He lowered his fake Ray-Bans, and we locked eyes. The engine idled.

Several seconds later, he asked in broken English, "You have car?"

I nodded back.

"Follow."

I retrieved the Land Cruiser from around the corner and pulled behind him. He stared at me in the rearview mirror for a good thirty seconds before pulling away. I followed.

We drove south, parallel with the Courantyne River, and left asphalt after five miles. The track became enclosed; tight jungle pressed against our passage. The smell of decayed vegetation, the detritus of the jungle floor, mixed with the dank humidity. At irregular intervals, we slowed for checkpoints, manned by rebel soldiers armed with automatic weapons. The assortment matched what I'd seen earlier—Chinese, Belgian, Israeli, US.

The checkpoints coincided with undergrowth-cleared areas where men had pitched tents and now lounged in hammocks. Sprinkled among them, hidden from aerial view by the large canopied jungle trees, were military vehicles. Chinese. Type 92 armored personnel carriers. Wheeled, amphibious, with a 25 mm canon and 7.62 mm machine gun. They could each carry nine fighting men plus a crew of three. Perfect for Suriname. They could cross rivers if bridges were blown. Small enough for tight turns and urban warfare.

We passed through five checkpoints over the next five miles. Each contained several Type 92s as well as assorted pickups and four-wheel drives, several with mounted heavy machine guns. Smart money would be on the rebels—under appropriate leadership, at night, and spearheaded by the Type 92s—taking over Paramaribo. My professional opinion, and dependent upon the leadership component.

We continued, bounced over ruts and holes, traveled down deep-shit avenue. I estimated the river a mile off the right. Potential exit strategy.

The path ended at a large clearing. I took the time for a two-point turn and parked with my vehicle pointed back down the trail. Nearby, trees had been felled, opening a small pocket of cleared space. There was only one reason for such a clearing. A helicopter landing zone.

This was the main camp. A hundred men milled about, along with more Type 92s and a mixture of civilian vehicles. Campfires burned, tents and tarps strewn about the area. An extra-large camouflage tarp hung suspended between trees. Underneath, a few chairs, wooden boxes, several men. And Joseph Hoff.

He perched at the edge of the tarp-covered area, sideways in a hammock. Booted feet planted on the ground, he swung the hammock with leisure, waved at my approach. A powerfully built man, jet black, shirtless with camouflage pants and a bright red beret. A Maroon—descendent of slaves brought by the Dutch who had escaped into the jungle and formed their own society. He smiled wide at my approach. I reciprocated.

"My reporter!" he said, slapping his muscled belly. "Come! Come!" He gestured toward a couple of wooden boxes. I took a seat.

His English was excellent. I suspected a connection of some sort with neighboring Guyana, a former British colony. Men milled, and he offered me a warm Pepsi. I accepted, the goat cheese and curry-laden fish still not settled. A young man grabbed two soda cans from another crate and, as he passed by Hoff, received an ass pat. Hoff's lover.

I carried a small spiral notebook and pen. We chatted—rebel leader to professional reporter. I asked if he minded my taking photos. He agreed as long as the camera focused on him. No pictures of the military vehicles allowed. I snapped random shots with the beat-up camera. He posed.

A nearby soldier laughed a comment, and Hoff snapped back. "What? Tell me what is so funny!"

The soldier moved away, beyond the wrath of the commander.

"Can you tell me about your cause?" I started.

"It is a movement," Hoff said. He started the hammock swinging again. "A movement of free people. A movement to return power to the hands of the people."

The usual. At least this guy didn't come off as a psychotic thug, often the case. The people of Niew Nickerie hadn't been killed or harassed. They went about their lives, and Hoff left them alone. At least for now.

"And what drove this rebellion? What specific things did His Excellency do to cause your actions?"

Hoff took a hard turn down a personal alley and heaped a long litany of deprivations on the head of the current president of Suriname. I nodded, scribbled.

"If victorious, will you hold elections?" I asked. Background information for the gnomes of Zurich. I didn't care if Hoff's government drew straws at election time.

"Of course." His boyfriend plopped on the hammock and rubbed his back. "I have no interest in a dictatorship, unlike the current president. Your newspaper must tell this."

I assured him his story would get out. But things change. Hoff, if successful, might find he liked the trappings of office. And he'd have intimate dealings with his unknown sponsor, who would want more than a little input on a governing arrangement.

"Are other interests, other countries, helping your efforts?"

His defenses flared. "Those who support the oppressed. Those who wish liberation from iron fists. Those who support positive change. There are many in the world who wish this."

Well, yeah, bud—but not too many willing to bankroll it. Joseph Hoff had been instructed, in no uncertain terms, to keep a lid on his army's sponsor. The last piece, the missing ingredient.

Then the magic key appeared. A radio, sitting on another crate, crackled. A quick glance confirmed its origin. Russian, military grade. Everything came together.

The fighting military hardware—Chinese in this case—could be purchased on the open market by anyone. Luuk Hoebeek had done a little shopping and would have turned a profit during the process. But communications for these little global surprise parties were tightly controlled by the bankroller. Every time, without exception. As sure as the sun would set, that radio had locked frequencies, Moscow-bound. All communications monitored by satellite, sifted, acted upon. Russia intended to establish a Suriname naval base, move into the neighborhood. Move into what the United States considered its own backyard. Hot times at the global geopolitical dance.

A sense of relief at finding the answer—a job well done, but no alarm. No real concern. Case Lee, Esq., no longer played that game. I continued to nod and scratch on the spiral pad. Mission accomplished, a well-written and informative report soon sent to my Zurich client, contract completed. Not all the loose ends tied up, neat as a bow, but loose ends were the warp and woof of life. The big stuff, the overarching strategy, had enough evidence for a proclamation, an answer. The gnomes would be pleased. Now to get the hell out of there.

The radio crackled again, this time with a voice and the *whomp-whomp* of chopper blades as background. Bishop. No surprise, and he announced his intended arrival. ETA ten minutes. Fine. I'd be gone.

We chatted further about Hoff's military efforts, he bragged about holding half of Suriname's territory, and I snapped a few fake closing photographs. We shook hands. I half liked this guy. Sincere, candid—except for his funding source—and a leader of men.

The sound of the approaching helicopter signaled one last comment for Commander Hoff.

"I appreciate your time, Commander. Gotta go. I really don't want to get too involved." I head signaled toward the radio. "That helicopter means more involvement."

He stood, hand in hand with his lover, and nodded, grave and understanding.

"But I do want to leave you with one thing," I said.

"Yes?"

"Take it for what it's worth, Joseph Hoff. Vladimir's Christmas list changes regularly. And his friends tend to disappear."

Hoff smiled, laughed. Unexpected, but he understood the message and was willing to take his chances. A massive Russian naval port would seem far-fetched, far outside his current interests. Vladimir Putin wouldn't have the same perspective, guaranteed. Russia had invested time and money. There would be a return on their investment. They played for keeps.

I fired the Land Cruiser and paused, twisted my body, and viewed the clearing where the helicopter was landing. Bishop would be transporting supplies, contraband, defectors eager to join Hoff's army. He worked both sides, double-dipped, and surely had his own private exit strategy. Ballsy, stupid, worth the risk. Take your pick. The life of a hard-bitten mercenary. Jungle debris—decayed matter, leaves, twigs, and bark—filled the area as the chopper settled and the blades wound down.

Nika climbed from the passenger side, dressed in a ball cap, khaki shirt, jeans, and jungle boots. Hell's bells. Should have seen it coming, screwed up, had to make a last comment. Great, Case. Just freakin' great. I punched it, and the Land Cruiser leaped forward.

She'd meet with Hoff, he'd tell her about the reporter, and she'd connect the dots. And go ballistic—ordering a quick and violent termination of my assignment. He'd radio the checkpoints that lay ahead. Shitfire and pedal to the metal.

Five checkpoints before exiting the camp areas. The old Land Cruiser's engine howled, protested. I made it through three, barreled past men with their hands held high, ordering me to stop. Sorry, fellas. Gotta go.

I flew along, bounced off pressed-in trees, lost a side mirror. Exit time. Get to Niew Nickerie, steal a dugout canoe, paddle to Guyana. Cover my tracks, watch my back.

A tight skid around a sharp turn, and the fourth checkpoint appeared, ruining the exit plan. A Type 92 armored personnel carrier squatted in the middle of the path, its 25 mm cannon pointed my way. Double shit.

Adios, Land Cruiser. I slammed the brakes, grabbed my rucksack, flung open the door, and took off into the bush. Almost made it. The cannon roared, the Toyota exploded, and the blast caught me in the back. Lifted from the ground, I tumbled forward, rolled, and got up running. The adrenaline masked any injuries as the dense jungle swallowed my progress.

I angled back toward the checkpoint—a ploy the enemy seldom expected—and hunkered among deep foliage, reconnoitering. My breathing calmed, the .45 pulled. The pistol reach caused a twinge of pain that shouldn't have been there, and my gun hand returned bloody. Triple shit.

Loud calls and the breaking of jungle limbs surrounded me. Armed movement hunted, scrambled, searched. I reached back with my free hand, assessed, and found a small piece of Toyota Land Cruiser, a shard, embedded in my ass. Great.

My private Suriname offered even thicker vegetation nearby, so I crawled into the dense mass of ferns, brush, vines, small trees. The rucksack contained a first aid kit, Delta-style, and I tore off a piece of bandaging. An ass is a hard thing to wrap, so out with the three-inch piece of metal and in with the wadded-up bandage, shoved deep into the hole. It would have to do.

The first wave of soldiers had passed, and several of them doubled back, rechecking the turf they'd already gone over. One passed within three feet, his boots visible as I lay on my side. He paused. Distant calls continued while he remained, still. The possibility of a rifle barrel aimed my way prompted a minute repositioning of my pistol. He wouldn't have the opportunity to fire more than one shot. More yells, calls. He moved on. Then quiet.

Nika and Hoff wouldn't be far behind. A camp vehicle to load them and drive the same distance meant I had a couple of minutes, at best. Critical minutes, because they'd direct the men in a less random search. Right now, the soldiers ran around, helter-skelter.

Rucksack on my back, I made my way toward the river, moved fast, thirty yards at a time. At each stop I dropped to the ground, listened. Visibility was poor in the thick growth, but sound still carried. Another thirty yards, another drop. The key—depart the immediate area, the search zone, and make a silent dash for a watery escape. Dusk descended, a positive factor.

Yelps and calls surrounded me. Then the booming voice of Hoff, commanding. Chaotic running stopped, orders passed, and a methodical search begun. No more yelling, no more crashing of brush. Just the near-silent stalking of men closing on their prey. Commander Joseph Hoff had been trained. Not by Nika—battle operations wouldn't be her thing—but trained nonetheless. And given the movement of the men around me, trained by an expert. Hoff's success at armed revolution became clearer. He'd had help, guidance from a player other than Nika.

Two options loomed. Hunker down again inside the thickest jungle available and hope the now-disciplined waves of rebel soldiers passed, or take the elevator. Surrender meant death. Not an option. So I climbed.

A nearby tree pointed straight toward sunlight through the dense canopy, tall, fast-growing. A thick competing vine wrapped around the trunk, also climbing toward light. It provided a solid grip, and I moved upward. Now the danger zone. Movement. Anything moving at eye level to thirty feet up might draw attention through the thick foliage. With rapid, quiet, rhythmic movements, the ground fell away. The danger zone passed, and I continued climbing. At fifty feet, I stopped and wedged inside several branches, hidden from view. My butt wound howled with pain. A quick check ensured the emergency plug of bandage remained.

Several hundred rebel soldiers, reacting to Hoff's passed-on hand signals, canvassed this stretch of jungle in waves. Along with one Russian. Nika had drawn her pistol and moved with surety—low, steady. A jaguar, hunting. Glued to the trunk among branches, I watched her work and aimed the .45. If she sighted me, she'd kill me. Unless I killed her first.

Squads of soldiers cut focused swaths through the surrounding area, then moved farther away. Their presence receded, and I lost sight of Nika. Deep dusk brought birds flying to roost—parrots, toucans, kingbirds. The air cooled, and the jungle breathed night-blooming flowers as it morphed into nocturnal life. I waited as time and light clocked by.

Near full darkness, the turbine whine of Bishop's helicopter carried through the jungle. Nika had called it quits. Hoff's men would soon follow suit, drift back to their camps, start fires, cook supper. I adjusted position, accommodated the wound, still waited.

Thirty minutes passed. I climbed down, silent, and made my way to the river. Away from its mouth, it remained a mile wide, muddy, roiling. Google Earth had shown no roads on the Guyana side until close across from Niew Nickerie, several miles downstream. Cutting through jungle at the riverbank's edge, I walked north. Men's laughter drifted from one of the soldier camps, hundreds of yards inland. The quarter moon provided sufficient light to make out a dugout canoe, tied at the river's edge.

I slipped into the dark waters of the Courantyne River, paddled from a kneeling position, alert for deadly obstacles. The powerful current fought me, pushed, ocean-bound. Rain-forest debris, including massive fallen trees, washed toward the nearby Atlantic. I paddled hard across the current, intent on making the Guyana side. A glow, city lights, more than a mile downriver on the Suriname side announced Niew Nickerie. I flinched when a river dolphin surfaced and blew an exhale. I bit the paddle deeper, pulled, breathing hard.

The canoe met resistance, and I edged through aquatic vegetation announcing the west bank. A silent thanks for the dugout owner, the craft now secured by the thin bowline to a tree. I slid through the Guyana jungle. A gravel road appeared after several hundred yards. A quarter mile later, the faint electric glow of a small village shone through the night.

A few dogs barked as I entered the outskirts. A cow lowed alongside the road, tied with a long rope to a sign, which read *Crabwood Creek*. Guyana.

Chapter 21

Relief. Relief, lowered adrenaline, and full recognition of an aching ass wound. Out of immediate danger. Out of Suriname. They ought to make a movie.

Crabwood Creek, Guyana. An official greeting cow tied to the town's sign. Welcome, Case Lee, Esq. A well-built house, one of the first in town, looked to be my best bet. I approached with caution, and several people on the front porch stopped talking.

"Hi." There wasn't much more I could add, other than I was damn glad to see them.

"Hello," the matron of the group responded.

"I'm looking for a place to stay the night. I'll pay. One hundred US dollars."

The gathering, apparently a family, looked at each other and exchanged expressions of "Why not?" The matron spoke.

"That should be fine." She turned to a young man—her son, it turned out—and ordered him to prepare his room for the stranger. It helped that I stood at the dark edge of the light cast by their porch. I would have looked a mess in the full light.

"And I need a ride to Georgetown in the morning. I'll pay another one hundred US dollars for that."

"That should be fine as well." Whether the old British Land Rover parked nearby provided transportation or another village vehicle mattered little. The matron would arrange things and take her cut. Good for her.

I'd taken off the reporter lanyard and used another false name during introductions, in case any Surinamese crossed the river looking for a reporter. A simple lost tourist, and no further elaboration provided or asked for. Just another crazy American.

I was shown to the son's room, and the shower was pointed out down the hall. The bloody gob of bandage protruding from the seat of my pants was pointed out as well.

"Fell. Cut myself. It's nothing."

The matron rolled her eyes, turned, and headed for the combination large kitchen and dining room. The first order of business—sew up the wound and get clean. Dinner would be served in an hour, and it was made clear my presence was expected.

The rucksack joined me in the bathroom. A large mirror hung above the sink. Standing on a short stool of the type kids used to brush their teeth, a decent view of the issue reflected back. Twisting to look over my shoulder in the mirror, orienting to the reverse view, I maneuvered my upper body sufficient for use of both hands. The medical kit held sutures, forceps, tweezers. The operating room was open.

Standing naked on a child's stool in the boonies of Guyana, I smelled the barn. I'd use the satellite cell phone and reserve a seat on the first flight north tomorrow. Norfolk by dark. It took more tugging than I'd hoped to pull the cloth plug from the wound. Fresh blood oozed down the back of my leg. A small vial of hydrogen peroxide provided antiseptic, and a clean bandage pressed hard stanched the bleeding.

Georgetown, one hundred miles away. I held high hopes the road would become asphalt close to Crabwood Creek. The less jostling of my rear end, the better. I grabbed the suture needle with forceps and braced. Seven stitches would suffice, spaced wide. Using the mirror helped—the physical concentration required to sew the wound shut in a reflection took my mind off the pain. The first one always hurt the most. Subsequent stitches had a known level of ouch factor to expect, and that helped.

Mom and CC. And Tinker Juarez. I wondered how they were doing. I'd been gone three days. Tomorrow, the fourth. A short, high-octane trip.

The first stitch was key. Drive the suture deep, all the way through, before coming up through the other side of the skin tear. That was important. A person's butt, unless you intended to spend the day on a couch, was an active element during movement. The stitches needed to hold. The first one rang the pain bell, loud. Son of a bitch. Blood oozed, dripped. I tied the stitch off and snipped the nylon thread.

Tomato plants. Bo would have watered them and looked after the *Ace of Spades*. Fall season on the Ditch. Snowbirds cruised south, headed for Florida, their large expensive cruisers loaded with winter supplies.

Now two more centered between the first stitch and the edges of the skin tear. The suture needle drove deep, a muted groan as metal pierced flesh. Sweat poured down my face.

Russians. A brassy move on their part. And a massive amount of investment money. Small wonder Mr. Trading Company had been willing to kill to ensure the plan stayed under wraps. He stood to become a very, very wealthy man if Joseph Hoff's troops took over the country. I wondered how long before the Russians started construction of their naval base. Not long. President Hoff would receive a call from old Vladimir shortly after trying out the sheets at the presidential palace.

Simple surgeon knots tied the stitches shut. Nothing fancy, and they'd hold. I'd been through this more than once before. The whole wound screamed, on fire, as the curved suture needle drove down for the third time.

Blowback. The lion's share of gigs ended clean. Information gathered, delivered, and I'd fade back into the shadows. This had been one of the rare ones. The hornet's nest kicked, my name attached. There was likelihood of an aftermath. Blowback of the Russian variety. Russians don't forget. Or forgive. The Sicilians might take top spot in the revenge category, but Russians were a strong second.

Now two more stitches spaced between the center one and the last two. I squirted more hydrogen peroxide, and it bubbled, drooled down my leg, mingled with the blood.

Nika. If the Russians decided to exact revenge, she'd spearhead the effort. Her mission had been exposed and would soon be delivered for consumption by my client. Being away from the Ditch, away from the *Ace of Spades* and home turf, exposed me to Russian tenacity, vengeance. Her catching a short flight to Georgetown—where she'd figure I'd head—wouldn't be a stretch for such a mind-set.

A gentle knock on the bathroom door inquired if I was all right. Too much time had passed, and the shower hadn't started.

"Fine," I replied, an attempt at casual, teeth clenched. "Fine. Just about to jump in the shower. Thanks."

I fought the urge to vomit and finished off the fifth stitch, hands quivering with the last square knot. Keep it up, Delta. Stay tough. Two more near either edge of the skin tear. My side began cramping, protesting the twisted position. Blood oozed at the nonstitched edges. Dr. Lee, on the home stretch.

I'd file my report ASAP. Global Resolutions, pleased with my findings, would drop it in the geopolitical hopper for either a prepaid client or for high-bidder dissemination. I'd stop by the Clubhouse after I landed. Chat with Jules. Exchange information. And watch my back. The Russians could be rash and enact swift retribution. Still, home turf. My terms.

One more, Mr. Man of Intrigue. Get it done. The wet squeak as needle pierced flesh, down one side of the tear, up through the skin on the other. Flop sweat pooled on the stool and the floor. I wondered if these kind folks had anything resembling Grey Goose. Or anything resembling liquor. Beggars—or naked, sweating fools perched on a stool in nowhere, Guyana—couldn't be choosers.

Tie it off. Whew. Whew and son of a bitch and shit. Shit, enough of that. Final inspection of my handiwork—not bad, with the guarantee of a Frankenstein scar. Onto the tile floor before I did a header in that direction. Completion brought a flood of tremors, the job done. I should hang out a shingle. Dr. Lee, ass-repair specialist. Son of a bitch.

The tile floor, drain in the center, helped the cleanup process. The shower, warm and gentle, was fine. A clean towel and then some antibiotic cream, gauze, and tape applied. Clean clothes from the rucksack. Good to go.

Most of the family remained on the porch while the matron supervised two teenagers in the kitchen. I thanked her for the shower. She introduced herself as Molly and announced supper would soon be served. I wandered onto the front porch and joined the others. Not a peep regarding my arrival, not a single question about how I had gotten lost. They required no elaboration. Just another American, peculiar, reasons and motivations unfathomable.

The oldest gentleman, perhaps the grandfather of the bunch, gestured toward a wooden chair and offered me a smoke. When I declined after a gentle landing, he pulled a bottle of local rum from under his chair and offered it. I grabbed someone's empty glass from the porch railing.

"No, no," he said. "A clean glass, my friend. Wait. Wait."

"Not necessary, sir. Not at all. Pour away. I insist."

Crazy Americans. Harmless, but crazy. He poured two fingers of the amber liquid, rested the neck of the bottle on my glass, and lifted his eyebrows.

"A bit more. Please."

Another finger's worth flowed, and I nodded, "Enough." Ambrosia and nectar of the gods—a fine distilled product from Guyana's sugarcane fields. I'd taken three ibuprofen, and the rum added to the drug's efficacy. Relaxation took a foothold, although the .45 stayed hidden under the tail of my shirt. You never could tell with the likes of Nika. I called Air Guyana and booked my flight. Ten thirty in the morning. The *Ace of Spades* called, waited.

Supper was excellent, the chatter filled with love and good-natured kidding. Fine and good folks. I was lucky to have stumbled across them. Assurances were made that the midmorning flight time wouldn't be an issue. After one more porch trip for an after-dinner rum, I hit the bunk bed and slept fitfully, a chair propped under the door handle and the .45 at my side. Dreams of jungle, red and vivid, while I huddled, hid from massive crunching footsteps, the enemy unseen.

Chapter 22

A CIA greeting committee of one met me in DC. Not a complete surprise, and the midnight hour added to the clandestine theme. Bone-tired, big-time ass ache, lousy flight—Guyana to Trinidad to Jamaica to New York City to DC—put a heavy thumb on the *so what* side of the scale.

The ancient Land Rover had covered the one hundred miles to Georgetown in three hours. We'd left well before dawn, and Molly had provided a small, clean tin bucket with cold rice and beans for the trip. My driver had ended up being the young man whose room I'd occupied. We'd talked of weather, food, sports, and girls. A nice kid.

The Georgetown airport immigration agent pointed to the lack of an entry visa stamp for Guyana. Under the guise of trying to find it, I retrieved the passport and inserted a Benjamin. Both edges peeked as it slid back across his desk, and it was discreetly pocketed. An entry and exit visa were thwacked on an empty space in the passport. The .45 pistol was lowered into a bathroom garbage can, the fingerprints wiped clean.

The long flight offered ample time for writing on the laptop, producing the Global Resolutions report. Sent from New York, dark web. No names. Players were identified as *US interest, Russian interest, Rebel leader*, etc. A report framework had been established years before. I would supply answers, not identify people. Global Resolutions, satisfied, accepted valid information over detailed operations. The report did outline Russian intent, with backup information and qualifiers. I'd never know if the Suriname information had been requested by a single entity, or if my client would auction it on the underground market. Not my concern.

I changed the wound bandage during the long New York layover and tried contacting Bo. No response, but no worries as he answered to whatever whims circled his head at any one moment. I also went deep web and sent Jules a message, requesting a Clubhouse rendezvous the next morning. A quick check-in, feed the Clubhouse, and gain currency for future transactions.

Her reply—short and surprisingly prompt—read *1100*. Eleven a.m. tomorrow I'd play intelligence poker in Chesapeake. I called Mom and chatted for a while. I was reminded again of the available young lady in Charleston she'd vetted, and then spent time with CC, laughing and teasing.

Boarded the last leg to DC and counted on Uber for a Chesapeake, Virginia, ride. I wouldn't crash at a hotel until three a.m. Or so I thought. The CIA had a different schedule planned.

A far cry from statuesque, she carried an air of surety, confidence, and intellect. An expressive face and a quick, genuine smile. Somewhere near thirty. She flashed the Company ID as I exited the Jetway.

"Mr. Lee. Agent Abbie Rice."

She extended a hand; we shook. A pixie haircut, the tips of her ears pointed. Large horn-rimmed glasses. I never knew if such eyewear was worn out of necessity or as an affectation implying seriousness, professionalism. She also had a small crease scar along her neck.

"Can I have a word with you?" she asked.

"Sure. A word. Maybe two."

"Great!" Her smile flashed, she turned on her heel, and set a brisk pace toward the airport exit. I followed.

Outside, she continued apace, turned at regular intervals, and checked my tag-along, smiling. She moved with a hidden strength, small, wound. Martial arts. She compensated for her size with practice, muscle memory, and knowledge. Standard CIA protocol. And another layer underneath—athlete. A jock. At the short-term parking, she opened the door of a plain black sedan and signaled me to join her in the front seat.

"Agent Rice."

She'd climbed behind the wheel, reversed actions, and now smiled over the top of the sedan.

"Yes?"

"A word. Not a drive."

Her face fell. "Oh. My apologies. I meant at Langley."

The CIA headquarters. Twenty miles away. I remained still, silent.

"Given your background," she said, "I just assumed."

I'd visited Langley twice before, both times as an active member of Delta Force. Operational meetings and debriefs. As a civilian, I had no obligation to go there now.

"Nope. We can talk here."

"Here?"

"Standing up, in your car, over coffee. But not Langley."

Her wheels turned and weighed. Her instructions were no doubt specific. Bring the guy to headquarters. I'd put her in a tough spot.

"Sorry if it causes problems. But there's not a lot to say," I added.

She chose the car. I added coffee.

An all-night diner greeted us five minutes from the airport. On the way, she discussed my background and hers.

"First, I want you to know how much I, and the CIA, appreciate all you've done for our country. Amazing operations," she said.

A pleasant change from Mr. Agricultural Liaison's perspective. "Delta was unique. And I was honored to be a part of it."

"Unique? To say the least. I mean, holy cow."

There was a bit of a starstruck-groupie thing going, and the little ego massage was appreciated. But the possibility she was playing me like a Stradivarius remained lodged in my thought process. "I'm the first Delta you've met?"

"Yes. At least one-on-one."

"So what's your background, Agent Rice?" I asked. "And if we're going to have a chat over coffee, how about Abbie and Case?"

"That works." She swerved around slower traffic. "Colorado born and raised. Master's degree. Harvard Kennedy School, International and Global Affairs."

A live wire, she drove fast, aggressive.

"Tae kwon do?" I asked.

"What?"

"Your training."

"Oh." A quick glance my way, another bright smile. Cute. Cute and intense and lacking the aloof Company demeanor. "Judo. Judo and krav maga."

The Israeli fighting discipline. Short violent exchange, brutal, eliminate the opponent's threat.

"Potent stuff."

"It works," she said. "I was also good at tennis but lacked the size. Couldn't take it to the top level."

"Well, I'm sure the Company is glad you're on board."

"Then biking. Road races. Turned out I'm a good climber."

"Good for you." I had no clue where the hell she was heading.

"Kicked ass when we raced the hills."

"Got it."

"Good runner. Distance. And swimmer. So combined the three. Triathlons."

"I'm sensing a competitive streak." Boy, howdy. It rang loud and clear.

"That's swimming, biking, running."

"Got it."

"I still compete," she said, stirring her coffee.

"Do tell."

She paused and reloaded. I took the opportunity and tried a different direction.

"Family?" The drain of arduous travel, relief at home-turf proximity, a desire for real connectivity? Hard to say what prompted my inquiry. A roundabout approach to ascertain her relationship status? She didn't wear a ring. The Rae guilt pang came, went, wafted back, lingered. But so did my interest in Abbie.

Identifying the allure of her specific attributes challenged me. Each time the attraction pull came, it baffled me. Sometimes it was a nose crinkle when a woman smiled, a raucous laugh, an attitude. Movement, assuredness mixed with vulnerability, the way a woman walked or addressed me. Never could figure it out. But it existed, and Abbie had it. The indefinable combination of attitude, inflections, looks—put together as a whole, she had a strong appeal. Maybe I'd been isolated too long, or maybe she struck a chord because the attraction was right, natural. And maybe she came across as the opposite of the black widow, Nika.

"I'm not allowed to talk about that," she said. A wry smile, another quick glance. Damn, she was cute.

"You hurt?" she asked.

"Why?"

"You're shifting in your seat."

"Butt wound."

"Suriname?"

"I'm not allowed to talk about that."

We both laughed. A diner back booth offered seclusion. The seat—hallelujah!—well padded. We both ordered coffee, black. I added bacon and eggs. The diner night shift had mopped the floor, and disinfectant hung in the air.

The pull of old obligations, real, coupled with male interest, also real. If asked by my government, I'd supply. To a point. As with Global Resolutions, no names, only solid information. I didn't mind sharing with the CIA. They kept information close to the vest. I still considered us the good guys, albeit with a hell of a lot of gray areas. My Swiss clients never asked if I'd revealed found information to the US government. Perhaps they assumed I did when the stakes rose this high.

The great exception for the whole business relationship was slaughter, terror. When encountering those facets of global chaos, crafted and pushed by evil individuals and organizations, I'd damn sure name names. Including the ones I'd personally taken out. As ugly as Suriname had gotten, it didn't near reach the level of abject horror. Where did I draw the line? Gut feeling, shaky moral compass, pain and suffering. A Case Lee line, and no apologies.

"So, we received word," she said. "From Suriname."

"I bet you did."

"You covered your tracks well."

"Not that well. Here I am."

A half smile returned. "Well, we do have certain tools."

Face-recognition software at major airports, for one.

"I gave Hines hard intel. Actionable."

"I know. And we appreciate it."

The waiter brought more coffee. We waited for his departure.

"Can you tell me about Joseph Hoff?"

"Didn't chat long. Things got dicey."

"Hot-fire situation?"

"You'd know about those."

She reacted and touched the scar on her neck, a light flush rising. "Cyprus."

"It's hardly noticeable."

True enough and immediate regret on my part. She clearly considered it a big deal. Abbie shifted to a more professional footing. A stupid statement to highlight a minor flaw in her appearance. I considered a mention of the jagged stitches in my posterior to offset the faux pas.

"Tell me about Hoff's military equipment."

"Chinese. Type 92 armored personnel carriers."

"And?"

She'd gone full CIA debriefing mode. Damn. "Mishmash of small arms. Chinese, US, Belgian, Israeli."

"Other heavy equipment?"

"Just pickups."

"Odds of success?"

She requested my assessment of Hoff's army taking over the country. "Fifty-fifty." The other facet of rebel help, the outside training, was left unmentioned. I didn't have a feel, a grip, on the military trainer. Most likely Russian.

The bacon and eggs arrived; I dug in and waited for the big question. It came right away.

"Funding source?"

I had torn allegiances revealing the global player behind it all. If identified, the CIA was liable to pour on the juice, reinforce the current regime with military advisors and hardware. Or the Company might wait, assess, and validate my assertion. Then apply political and economic pressure.

And nothing against Hoff, who appeared a decent enough guy. He'd come across as legit. As legit as most rebel leaders. Then again, he *had* tried to kill me.

"Russia."

There was no point beating around the bush. The naval port issue they'd discover for themselves. It wouldn't take long. A land base for military elements was self-limiting. A large airfield possible, but still static. Immobile. A naval base, including aircraft carriers, made more sense. The analysts at CIA headquarters would suss it out within days.

She'd acquired the big fish. The answer. The wheels turned as she stared into the coffee, unblinking. Abbie would arrive bright and early at headquarters and file the report. She'd caveat the hell out of it with "he contended," and "reasonable degree of assuredness." But a career-enhancing enchilada nonetheless, and Agent Abbie Rice would receive kudos and documented accolades. Good for her.

I ate, she cogitated, and the waiter did another flyby, refilling our coffee mugs.

"Can you validate?" she asked.

A mention of the Russian military-grade communications used by Hoff and the rebels would trigger the NSA to search and find the appropriate frequencies. Then eavesdrop, monitor. But they'd figure it out without my help.

"Short answer, yes. There won't be a longer answer."

We locked eyes. "It would help a great deal if you did a full debriefing," she said. Their original intent. Haul my butt to Langley. A well-lit room, conference table, video recording. It wasn't going to happen.

"I'm a civilian, Abbie. Tourist. Wandering investigator."

The CIA had no jurisdiction inside the United States. They'd have to engage Homeland Security and the FBI for any arm-twisting of Case Lee. My reply had established a boundary and emphasized the bureaucratic turf.

"And that's that?" she asked. Signs of a smile returned. It was good to see.

"Actually, no. Could use your help."

"Is this the part where I swoon and say 'Why, anything for Mr. Lee?'" Delivered with a big smile. We both laughed.

A fine line, mixing business with pleasure. But the upcoming request addressed a big issue—removal of the target painted on my back.

"Consider it quid pro quo. I need a reliable source inside."

The idea was so outlandish—asking for a private mole in the Company—that she continued smiling, stared through the diner's window at the dark Virginia night, and shook her head.

"Bit of a reach, isn't it?" she asked.

"For information regarding me," I said. "Some upstream swimming. Identify a paymaster." A limited request, personal.

"I'm all ears." She used a hand to flip a pointed ear toward me, eyes bright behind her horn rims.

"I have a bounty on my head."

She sat back. I'd provided a twist and new information. Others in the Company might know of this, but odds were stacked high, it wasn't on anyone's priority list. Buried, page thirty-seven of a filed report, long forgotten. The Russians, on the other hand, were very aware of the price on my head. Just ask Nika.

"A bounty."

"Me and some friends. Million bucks a head."

No elaboration was required. Abbie would figure out the Delta Force connection.

"Chunk of change," she said.

"Yes, it is."

"But since you're a civilian, we really can't operationalize any effort. Unless it affects our mission."

A jab in my direction, delivered with good humor, and accepted the same.

"Name and location of the bounty's sponsor. I'll take it from there."

"I bet you would."

"Can you blame me?"

"No. No, I wouldn't blame you. And I'm very aware of what you've contributed during your Delta Force stint."

"So you'll do it?"

A glance back inside her coffee mug and an oversize eyewear adjustment.

"I'll sniff around. That's all I can do."

"If you find a trail, will you follow it?"

"No promises."

"I'll take it. Thanks. The intel has to be accurate. Deadly accurate."

A hard stare her way, a returned nod. There was no mystery regarding the action I'd take.

Between Abbie Rice and Jules, an answer—an individual—might crop up. The importance of accuracy couldn't be overstated. Because once identified, I'd find and kill the sponsor. Without remorse or hesitation. A brief flash of Rae sprawled on the floor of our Savannah bungalow filled my head.

"Again, no promises," she said.

"Got it. Again, thanks."

"Consider it a double quid pro quo."

It came unexpected, and I went on high alert. The past had seen too damn many games played out, and I'd walked away from the gaming table. She'd invited me back.

"I can't say I'm all ears."

She edged over the table and entered my personal space.

"Since this," she said, rubbing the neck crease, a remnant of a grazing bullet wound, "I've been pulled from field ops. Turned into a bureaucrat. Desk jockey."

"Okay."

"Can't stand it."

"All right."

"I want to get into what you do. Private contractor."

It came from left field, a zinger, ridiculous. I sipped coffee to cover my surprise. She stayed in my space, eyes drilled through owl glasses.

"I've thought this through," she said.

"Got my doubts about that."

"Look, Case. If we're going to work together, you'll have to understand my commitment. My sincerity."

"We're not going to work together."

"You need to listen." Delivered like a schoolteacher.

"You need to understand. Not going to happen."

Statement ignored. "I have the talent, a range of field ops you don't possess. Tradecraft."

"La, la, la." I plugged my ears, attempted humor.

"Stop. I'm serious."

"I was going to ask you out. A date."

She sat back, sipped coffee, and reloaded. Then back across the table, invading my space again.

"You're good enough looking, I suppose."

"Good enough? Glad I hit the high bar."

"Great character. No question."

"And?"

"And not my type."

"What's your type?"

She ignored me and moved on. "And it would disrupt our partnership."

"There's no partnership."

My statement was ignored, again.

"So I'll root around. Maybe find the source of the bounty. Prove myself."

"I'm revoking my request. I'd rather go on a date."

"Too late. Now think of it. Your connections with a paying client. The two of us in the field. A potent pair."

This had slipped off the rails at an amazing speed. The waiter poured more coffee, and I laid a twenty on the table. Exit strategy. Abbie held strong appeal, but it was time to fold my cards and walk. Man, I was tired, and the toothache in my butt pounded.

"Let's mull it over. My way of saying no. No, Abbie."

"Tell me the downside."

"Getting killed."

"I'm not afraid."

"I am. And looking to retire from my current vocation."

"All the more reason for a partner. Continue the tradition."

"There is no tradition."

"And we'll be unstoppable. Think of the skills I bring to the table. Skills you don't have."

My hackles rose. Beyond the absurdity of her career plan, I still sat on top of my game. A few skills lacking here and there, but damn few.

Agent Abbie Rice and I were through, for the moment. As we exchanged contact information and a nebulous agreement to keep in touch, she tossed a final pitch.

"I'm very, very serious about this," she said.

"I can tell."

We stood outside, and she pressed in, smelling of lavender. A half step back opened personal space again.

"I could play the femme fatale. Gather intel in ways you can't. Have you ever seen how effective a female approach can be?"

"Once or twice."

"And electronics. Computers. A strong suit of mine."

"Gotta go, Abbie."

Her lips pursed, joining a hard stare.

"You'll consider it?"

A pit bull on a fresh bone, and I'd lost the energy to pull the treat away. An Abbie Rice wear-them-out strategy. It worked.

"I'll consider it."

She smiled large and extended her hand to seal the deal. We shook.

"I'll consider it, Abbie. No promises."

"All I'm asking. You need a ride?"

"No, thanks."

"Going home?"

"Yeah."

"Where's that?"

"Not far."

She smiled, conceded my obfuscation, and waved as she drove away. Fatigue settled, heavy. The Uber driver cruised the three hours to Norfolk, happy about the lucrative pickup. I traded between nodding off and snapping awake—tired, wounded, finished. Contract fulfilled, it was time to slip back into the rhythms of the Ditch.

Chapter 23

I retrieved Bo's old pickup from the Norfolk airport parking lot and confirmed the .40-caliber Glock remained stuffed deep into the seat cushion. Armed and on home turf. The Clubhouse meeting seven hours distant, I checked into a decent hotel and crashed for five hours.

It's an otherworldly experience waking in a safe environment after a mission. Four days afield. Shorter than usual for a Global Resolutions gig. But a busy four days. Added points for meeting Abbie Rice, on a personal and professional basis, with one big asterisk. The "let's join forces" bit remained beyond the pale. So I wallowed in the Abbie Rice situation to find an out, a letting go of a possible personal relationship.

I'd asked Abbie to poke around the Company and look for tips or trails identifying the bounty sponsor. She'd do it to prove herself, and expect our next steps toward a partnership. It would be sweet information to identify the paymaster of the bounty, but I'm not a user. And Abbie would be used, without any intention of forming a team. Not a good thing.

I waded in the "let's find some negatives" pool, ammo to salve a guilty conscience. She'd invaded personal space. Went into too much detail about everything. Thought ol' Case had more than a few rough edges. Well, she had a point about the last one. But it would still be wrong, using her with no intention of fulfilling her expectations.

And her mild negatives aside, she appealed to me. Funny, bright, cute. But she'd drop me like a hot rock when the partnership thing didn't develop. I offered Ditch life and a lack of stability—broad brushstroke warning signs for a woman you liked. The possibilities of a relationship became opaque, distant.

The head games started, mental ping-pong on occupational selection. Suriname had been a success. I was good at this stuff. Damn good. But the business had serious downsides, including violent death. Mine and others. And continuation of my career ensured another shot at the white picket fence remained distant. Odds of a solid, long-term relationship were slim to none as long as I plied my current trade.

After I showered, the view from the bathroom mirror reflected the less-than-ideal stitch work on my rear end. I dressed the wound again and made a mental note for stitch removal in eight or nine days. Another round of bacon and eggs called, fuel for the fire.

I parked near a drugstore and café and bought a small bag of Australian black licorice—a weakness of Jules's. Over breakfast I tried Bo again. No luck. I texted him and sent an email as well. Shards of worry etched fine lines of bother and concern. But time and schedules failed to resonate with him, knowledge that helped with the concern. When the waitress poured more coffee, I ordered an extra round of bacon to celebrate home turf.

Familiar blank, hooded stares greeted me at the Filipino dry cleaners, the pistol again placed and covered. The stairs still squeaked. Two knocks, the clang of the electronic deadbolt, and the usual pirouette for Jules. Pockets emptied while she verbally poked and prodded, shotgun aimed at my torso. I held a money clip and the licorice.

"Word has it, Horatio, things became a tad active down there." Inspection over, she lowered the shotgun and retrieved the cigar that was balanced on the edge of the desk. How Jules could have known about Suriname would remain a mystery. And there was a chance she didn't know but surmised so from my past missions; stating a good-odds proposition added to her mystique.

"Walk in the park."

"You're favoring that right leg."

"Right butt cheek."

"Tough park."

I shifted in the hard chair, dispensed with hiding my discomfort.

"Piece of a Toyota."

"At least you were facing the appropriate direction when you received it, dear." She cackled, her eye squinting with pleasure, then held in a sneeze. Her body jerked. The shotgun was grabbed, then lowered.

"So how you doing, Jules?"

"Mesmerized, as always, by the abject stupidity of our fellow travelers on this earth," she said. "End games. Planned, modeled, gamed, and triggered even when the unintended consequences loom heavy on the table."

"Anyone in particular?"

"Our world leaders. Dumb as a sack of rocks. Would that be for me?" She pointed to the licorice.

I tossed it on her desk with a smile. She took the lit end of her cigar and burned a hole in the wrapper. Inserting two thin latex-covered fingers, she plucked a piece of the candy and popped it into her mouth. The chair squeaked as she settled back, closed her eye, and chewed.

"Yeah, well, I've quit worrying about it. World leaders, sacks of rocks."

She swallowed, grunted, and reengaged. "Their ineptitude is a blessing. Business is good. As is this licorice. You are a dear boy."

"I try."

"Speaking of business, a ficus tree informed me of an endeavor by three gentlemen of Central Asian persuasion looking to fatten their bank accounts several months ago."

"Do tell."

"Mucking about south of here." She blew cigar smoke at the ceiling, her hawk eye focused on my expression. "You failed to mention that little fandango when last we met."

"They're taken care of."

Jules always amazed. Tendrils—some thick, some minute—spread across her world. Conduits, rivers, trickles of information. Even from the depths of the Dismal Swamp.

"With a degree of finality, I would hope." Her expression remained hard, stonelike.

A tight nod from me ended that train of conversation.

"Let us discuss another item in the same vein," she continued. "And it distresses me to view you in such obvious discomfort. Are you taking medication?"

"Bacon."

"Splendid. Never doubt the efficacy of that product." She leaned back, her old wooden office chair protesting again, and flicked ashes on the floor. "A wandering child may have returned. A previous affiliate of yours. So word has it."

Few possibilities fit the descriptive. William Tecumseh Picket topped the list. Angel.

"If it's Angel, I'd love to see him again. Last I'd heard he was in South America. Bolivia, maybe."

Jules turned and stared at the old *Casablanca* movie poster on her steel wall. Bogart and Bergman, love unfulfilled. The Clubhouse AC hummed; I shifted again.

"People change, Case. Hardly a revelation on my part, but one you might move to the forefront of your ruminations."

I didn't have a clue where Jules was heading with this. Silence offered her the opportunity for elaboration. She declined.

The chair squealed a different tune as she turned. "Provide me an overview of your little Suriname tryst. It shall put me in arrears for our next transaction, but such is the cross I bear."

"No trysting. Although one of the players made a strong case in that direction."

She laughed. "The Russian?"

I gave her an overview, culminating with confirmation of Russia's move for a naval base. I halted halfway through the debriefing, eyebrows raised toward her abacus.

"Ye of little faith," she said, and then sighed as she shifted several black abacus balls.

I finished my delivery. She peered at her abacus. "The blueprints for the naval base were in Tjon's safe, you say?"

"Yes."

"Although no guarantee they remain there now, given the proprietor of the trading company's intolerance for shoddy discretion. Correct?" she asked.

"Correct. I didn't hang around to see what Hoebeek did with them."

I'd spilled the beans three times over the course of twenty-four hours, each with varying degrees of detail. My client received the most in-depth report, Abbie the least. Jules held the high points, furthered her cause, and provided me credit. A murky world; feints and maneuvers. But at the end of the day, Executive Decisions would be more than satisfied, the CIA—still on my side of the fence—alerted, and the Clubhouse bucket tilted in my direction. I'd tilt it more and cover my back in case the Company took a dim view of my activities. You could never tell with Spookville.

Meanwhile, Jules inspected the end of the cigar, tried a few puffs, and relit it.

"I was met at the DC airport last night. CIA."

"Perhaps they missed you, dear. A simple open-arms gesture."

"Agent Abbie Rice."

I delivered it with a tinge of guilt. Jules, if she didn't already know of Abbie, soon would. And the Clubhouse would relay any pertinent information about her, for a price.

"And?" Jules asked.

"I gave her Russia."

A scowl, grunt, and an irritated motion on the abacus. Two balls slid up a rail.

"You've lowered the value of my information." Blunt, businesslike, her eye hard.

"She'll sniff for the bounty sponsor."

Her countenance softened. "Then I shall partially forgive you. Admittedly, this poor creature has failed you in those endeavors."

"No knock on you. At all. It's important you know that."

She plucked more licorice from the bag, eye closed as she chewed. The AC hummed.

In due course, she peered at the abacus. "You've racked up a substantial credit. Even after accounting for spoilage."

"How much?"

"Substantial. Would you care for information on Angola? Tasty items, fresh."

I had no interest in West Africa. "No, thanks."

"Ukraine? You do seem to have a Russian motif working."

"I'm headed for my old boat. Semiretired, for the umpteenth time. A little more information about the wandering child would be worth a lot."

She shook the abacus; the black balls slid down their rails, the math erased. "I'm suspicious by nature, dear. And perhaps you should be more so."

"Not following, Jules."

"Timing. Merging activities. Drivers of human emotions."

"Let's focus on the activities." Alarms tingled. She knew something.

"Let's focus on the drivers. Power, money, sex."

"Sure wish you'd be a little less cryptic."

"My nature, Monsieur Lee. My nature. Now pay attention."

"Always do."

"My personal joss rattles on the shelf. And so I offer a rare gem out of amity and the discomfort of carrying a debt."

The sage of the Clubhouse. An offer, attached strings to follow.

"Describe this crown jewel, and I'll decide if it has immediate value," I said. "Not knocking your offer, but I'm off the clock at the moment."

"We have no rest, you and I. Merely pauses. I'm offering a conduit. Communication with the Clubhouse, deep web only. No voice communications, of course."

She plucked another licorice, chewed, stared with an eagle eye and continued.

"Not to be overly Conan Doyle about events and activities, but something is indeed afoot, dear boy. I don't like it."

Jules had always refused communication via telephone, and deep-web messages were for face-to-face appointments at the Clubhouse. This was a major departure, and my gut knotted. If she offered this unheard-of present, events were still active. Very active. Son of a bitch.

"Thanks, Jules. I'll accept. Sincerely, thanks. I assume you'll keep tabs on my balance if I resort to using your offer?"

She flicked an abacus black ball up its rail, then back down, smiled as she chewed, the attached strings identified.

"Allow me to express what has promulgated such an offer," she said.

"All right. Can I have a licorice?"

"Just one. It is possible your association with Suriname began prior to your departure. Certain facts, hazy at inception, have presented themselves with more clarity since your departure."

"Okay." The candy was okay. I didn't get the big appeal.

"Your belief that our Mr. Hoebeek purchased military items for the rebels would buttress the rumor he also hired a trainer. A military trainer, for the rebel forces."

I remained silent and reflected.

"Any sign of that, dear boy?"

"Yes. Signs. No identification."

"Ah." She gave a tilt of the head and benign focus toward me.

"So what does this have to do with me prior to my Suriname departure?"

Jules leaned forward and plucked another piece of licorice from the bag. She convulsed with a held-in sneeze, hand reaching for the shotgun. There was a suspension of activities, then quick recovery, and candy popped in her mouth. She spoke with her eye closed, worked the licorice, relishing the experience.

"Lovely tidbits, these. Lovely. And now we loop back. The wandering child. It would appear the military trainer working for Hoebeek, and by association your Russian amour, is an American."

I didn't see that coming and refused to accept it. Angel might have done a lot of things, but setting up rebel armies in the employment of Russia wasn't one of them.

"Not Angel," I murmured.

"Hmm."

"Blood brother."

"Of course."

Quiet shared stares and unspoken communication. Her hand disappeared underneath the desk, and the metallic click of the door unlocking followed. The meeting was over.

"Yes, well, as I have stated, the lines of communication will be open in the near term twixt you and I. Now depart," she said. "Attend to your posterior."

A mild groan, standing. It ached, and the *Ace* called.

"Flee to your haven," she continued, an arm wafting. "An ostensible wandering existence on a well-defined watery path. You do see the incongruity, don't you?"

I did.

Chapter 24

No returned messages from Bo. Fine—I was going home regardless. A large sporting goods and outdoor supply store across the bridge in Newport News had a selection of canoes.

"I'll take the ten footer, green, out front," I said, pointing toward the front doors of the store. "And a paddle."

The man behind the counter had the earmarks of retired navy—a forearm tattoo of an elaborate anchor with a US shield, and an attitude.

"Flotation device?" he asked.

"No, thanks."

"Extra paddle?"

"Nope."

"You'll have to register it as a watercraft. The morons in Richmond say so. State law."

"Fine."

He pulled below-counter forms, shook his head, snorted, and found a pen.

"All right. Name?" he asked.

"Kofi Annan."

He looked up, chuckled, and asked, "Spell that with a *K*, right?"

"Indeed."

"What address you want me to put down, Kofi?"

"Make one up."

"Can do easy. This going to be a cash transaction?"

"Indeed, again."

He helped me load the canoe into the bed of the pickup and tie it down. I'd be at Bo's old barn to park the truck in a little over an hour. Concern for my friend grew, tempered with the knowledge he was liable to be sitting in a tree, contemplating, and had decided to remain there for a day or two. It was quite possible. And now the news of Angel. Not confirmed and hard to wrap my head around. If—and it was a very big if—he'd trained the rebel forces in Suriname, maybe he worked directly for Hoebeek. It was false hope, grasping at straws. He would have figured out the backer, the power player. It made no sense. He didn't need to take that kind of gig. Ex-Delta members had plenty of other opportunities. Opportunities on this side of the fence.

A tinge of fall weather hinted, suggested, as I hid the truck in the barn. A short trip to carry the canoe across the small two-lane highway and down the trail to the Ditch. Across from the canal, the Dismal Swamp waited, primal, separate, and ancient. A living, breathing thing. There was no boat traffic. Dead silence interrupted only by nature's scurries, calls, splashes.

The muted sound of the paddle brought a sense of calm and separation. I shifted on the small hard canoe seat and eased the butt throb. Going home, each paddle stroke propelled toward a place where safety and love reigned. The world would move on, babies born, people dying. Laughter, love, tragedy—baked in the cake. Archimedes had been wrong. No lever of any size or power was sufficient to move the basics.

I reversed the paddle stroke. Something was wrong. Where a fine trip wire—fishing line—should have been stretched between two cypress trees, the line dangled. A near invisible filament, cut. The Glock, pulled from the rucksack, rested on my lap. A quarter mile later, another cut trip wire. Shields raised, all senses alert. Movement of small animals brought focus; silence offered no surety.

The canoe drew only two inches of water, so I took a different route to Bo's houseboat and the *Ace of Spades*. I approached from the opposite side of the island where they were parked and stopped a hundred yards from the island. I left the canoe wedged between two cypress knees, water waist-high. Submerged to nose level, I moved away from the canoe, waited, senses cranked high. Insects buzzed, ducks splashed in the distance. A rich, biting smell from the tannic water. Nothing. No human sounds or sights.

The last thirty yards of water were covered at a Delta Force pace— submerged, no wake, no noise. I paused before crawling onto the island, eyes, ears, and nose exposed. Waited, watched, listened, smelled. The last sense brought my heart to a jackhammer cadence. The smell— burned wood, thick. And death. Blood. And the millennia-old buzzing of fat flies. I snaked into the underbrush and waited again, then worked my way to the other side of the tiny island, silent.

A pool of coagulated blood, too much to have dried completely, maggots working it. Signs of battle, struggle. The remains of Bo's burned-to-the-waterline houseboat. The *Ace*, parked behind it, showed evidence of flame licks on the bow but appeared otherwise undamaged.

I didn't move a muscle, observed, breathed deep and slow for thirty minutes. It could be a trap, a setup. The half hour allowed time for horror, grief, betrayal, hatred, and revenge to run their course. Then I stood.

No sign of Bo Dickerson. Blood brother, dearest friend. Gone. No one could have done this except another Special Forces member. No one. British, Israeli, Russian. Or American. No run-of-the-mill bounty hunter could have taken out Bo. A specialized pro, either rogue or sent by an order from some government. My gut tightened as Jules's words echoed. People change. Wayward son. Angel.

I refused to accept his death and held on to fragile hope. I moved with caution, performed battle forensics. Pieces of Bo's boat, blown onto dry land. It hadn't been simply set on fire. Empty shell casings, dozens. They matched Bo's weapon. Firing had come at him from the swamp, the attackers' shell casings either underwater or on outlying islands.

I waded to nearby islands, cautious. Birds chortled overhead, undisturbed. The Dismal, dead quiet otherwise. More shell casings—Kalashnikov. AK-47 assault rifle. The most ubiquitous assault rifle on the planet.

Tossed in the brush near a pile of shell casings was the shoulder-mounted firing tube of an RPG. Rocket-propelled grenade. That explained the remnants of Bo's houseboat. The bastards had blown it up, and it had caught fire.

And blood. Splatters dried, rusty reddish-black. Then puddles, viscous and thick. Collected and pooled within the thick brush. Familiarity struck—bodies bleed out, blood collects in buckets. Universal and terrible and final. In this humid environment, it would take another day or two for it to dry or soak in. And it pointed back to a timeline—the attack had taken place in the last forty-eight hours. I moved on hands and knees, paused, checked. Swam the channels between bits of land, submerged. Crawled out, pistol ready. More blood. Three separate areas on two different islands. Bo had taken three of them out.

On a tiny hummock of land, another pile of shell casings. The caliber and ejection markings of an H&K. A Special Forces weapon. A Delta weapon. And no blood on that bit of dry land. Four of them had attacked. One lived.

Commitment comes in weighted degrees. The commitment to make the surviving attacker pay for this filled with the assuredness of the sun rising in the east. I'd find that son of a bitch. He'd pay.

A tour of the *Ace* to check for trip wires and booby traps, methodical and slow, revealed the surviving attacker had left well enough alone. Papers rifled through, opened cubbyholes, but nothing missing. I checked for explosives that could be triggered by the start of the *Ace*'s diesel engine. Nothing.

The *Ace of Spades* now functioned as potential honey, a lure. The assassin knew I'd return to my home sooner or later and had left it for me. Or had Bo been the prime target? Or was it only me they were after, and Bo was killed by association? Either way, time to get the hell out of Dodge. Remove the bait. Get on the offense. Hunt the bastard down. Or bastards. Didn't matter.

Bo was indestructible. As tough a fighter as ever lived. The killer may have come at night. Maybe a night-vision scoped rifle, striking Bo as he slept in his hammock. Bo's body wasn't around to confirm any theories. Fed to the alligators, or crawled and swam away to die. Too damn much firepower directed his way. Son of a bitch. I'd find the killer. Dead man walking.

I swam back to the canoe and rucksack, and called Mom on my satellite cell phone. Relief flooded when she answered.

"Mom, you need to take a break. Today. Now. Right now."

Our private code. Pack up, grab CC and Tinker Juarez. Leave town for her still-spry mom's place nestled in the forested rolling hills of Spartanburg County, three hours away. They'd be safe with Grandma Wilson, who kept a pack of loud, alert dogs around and knew how to use a firearm. It was a long shot thinking they were in danger, but no chances, no mistakes, until this matter was settled.

Mom didn't argue. This exit strategy had been used once before, and I had explained my rationale to her. She understood, accepted, and did nothing but warn me about taking care of myself. A world-class mom.

The canoe's bow grated up on the island. One more final act. I squatted near the largest dark wet spot close to the burned boat, flies buzzing, crawling. Bo's blood. A symbol, a totem.

I crumpled from my squat to a seated heap on the ground, shook my head, and cried. I already missed him, and the anguish twisted, tore. Pieces of possibilities, reenactments of the battle, clawing hope. But reality weighed, and dragged me down. Him residing in the Dismal, doing his unique thing, had always been an anchor, a set point in my life. Gone, gone.

I spoke, turned to address all around me, and said a prayer—talked to not only the higher power but to Bo, listening from another place, another celestial plane. Reviewed the tough times in mortal combat, the loss of other teammates. The laughter and relief, the absurdities we'd gone through together. And I told him how much I loved him and missed him already and asked for him to wait, hang out, because I'd be joining him. Maybe soon, maybe not, but I'd be there. The tears wouldn't stop.

The AR-15 assault rifle from the *Ace* joined me in the wheelhouse, loaded, safety off. I'd call Marcus Johnson. The former leader of my Delta Force team, now raising cattle in nowhere, Montana. But not yet, not now. Bo still loomed, swirled around me, as I maneuvered the *Ace* through the Dismal Swamp. He was part of the immediate—thick air, dark water, bird and animal noises, cypress trees, and brush. Life. I wasn't going to share this time with anyone. Just me and Bo. One last time.

Chapter 25

The *Ace* maneuvered out of the Dismal and into the canal, headed south. Windows and wheelhouse door closed, the glass bulletproof. Stuffy, sealed, it provided a capsule of safety and a hunting platform. It would be hours before I left the Ditch system and crossed larger bodies of water. During those hours, the slap of a bullet against the glass would indicate the general location of the shooter.

I'd then travel a short distance farther, tie off at the bank, and circle back on foot. Become the hunter. Find the bastard, or bastards. Kill them all.

Lethal thoughts fogged reason, pulled me away from a clinical approach, and allowed emotions steerage. My temples pounded with blood, and a sharp desire for steady talk—reasoned conversation—struck me hard. Marcus. Level-headed Marcus. In the middle of Montana. A friend, brother. I placed a call.

"Bo's been hit."

"He okay?"

"Dead."

"Tell me."

"No body. But his boat was blown up, burned. Blood nearby. Pooled. I just left the scene. Deep in the Dismal."

Silence as the analytical wheels of a Delta Force team leader turned.

"When?"

"The last forty-eight hours. Blood pools hadn't dried. Still smell the burned boat."

"The *Ace?*"

"Okay. Left alone."

Silence. A Ditch cruiser approached from the south at a sedate pace. A binocular scan highlighted an older couple, retired, headed north.

"Who?"

"Four attackers. He killed three. No bodies. Like Bo, fed to the gators."

"You don't know that."

"Yeah, I do."

Marcus chewed on my assessment; the *Ace* rumbled along. Trees and brush, close against the canal, flowed by. Shadows lengthened. The cruiser passed on my port, and the couple waved. I nodded back, grim, eyes working the tight tree lines.

"Tell me about the battle."

I reviewed my findings and clarified the scene. Blood, crushed foliage, the RPG tube tossed aside. We came to the H&K shell casings left by the fourth, still alive, attacker.

"A pro," Marcus said. "Special Ops. The other three could be anyone."

"Yeah."

"What are you not telling me?" he asked.

Classic Marcus. Something in my voice, my inflection, told him I withheld thoughts and perceptions.

"It was Angel."

Silence, as expected. Wind noise, a gust, came over the call. He stood outside on the Montana prairie.

"Tell me."

I detailed the feedback from Jules and the events in Suriname. Russians. Naval base. Everything. "The trainer for the rebel forces is an American. They've been trained. I saw it."

"So?"

"Plus a strong inference Angel is back on US turf."

"The Clubhouse again?"

"Yeah."

"That old witch doesn't know everything, Case. There's always been an element of self-promotion with her."

I wasn't surprised at his comment. Marcus viewed the whole Spookville world with derision. A battle leader, cut and dried. Solid intelligence was part of his action plans, but speculation led to waffling, indecision. If Marcus was anything, it was decisive.

"You shake the tree that hard down there?" he asked.

"Russians. You and I both know their tendencies. They don't forget. Or forgive."

"Fine. You pissed off the Russians. But the timeline is too tight. They'd have to have sent a hitter immediately."

"I know."

"A hitter," he said, "who knew of you. And Bo."

"Right back to Angel."

Silence. Another gust of wind on his cell phone.

"Or back to the Clubhouse."

A possibility only Marcus would have considered. But I couldn't buy Jules pulling the strings on this headhunting expedition. Then again, she offered to keep in touch. Or keep tabs on me. But why would she give me a heads-up on Angel?

"We live in a messed-up world, bud," I said.

"No shit, Sherlock."

A tiny town passed off the starboard side. Nothing moved but an old lab, who raised his head from a nap at the *Ace*'s passage, a single tail slap of "Hi," then back to sleep. The tight wall of trees on both sides of the canal continued.

"Okay. Back to the firefight," he said.

Again, classic Marcus. Digest the information, stay out of the speculative realm. Move to the immediate. "A pro and three mercs," he continued. "Bo cleaned the mercs. The pro is still out there."

"Yeah."

"Signs still point to bounty hunters. Collect a million bucks."

"My gut tells me otherwise."

"Your gut is full of shit."

I made a conscious effort and released the tight grip on the *Ace*'s wheel. Move. Hunt. They'd come for me. Movement afforded a level field of battle. Offered the opportunity for payback.

"I'm getting out of here. Head south. Draw the Special Ops bastard in. Finish it."

"Head west. Montana."

"You mean leave the operational area. Run. That's not happening."

"Reposition, dumbass. When the enemy knows your general whereabouts, reposition. Lie in wait. Take them by surprise," he said.

"Run."

A loud sigh. "Look, I'm not buying this as anything but collecting a million bucks for Bo's head. But if you're convinced you were the target, get your ass to Montana. The Special Ops hitter will have intel on me. I don't hide."

"So?"

"So he'll figure you've fled the scene, toward backup. Toward me."

"And put you in danger."

"Reposition. We'll attack if it comes to that."

"I've gotta draw him in. End it."

"Fine. End it. Head south, catch a flight. Reposition. Occupy different turf. Our turf."

"Bring my problems your way."

Another sigh, then silence. "Look, this is what we do, remember? Cover each other's backs."

Walls crumbled, and a strong desire hit hard. Marcus had offered sanctuary and relief from a solitary world. My friend, special and bright. I damn near cried again.

"I'll call Catch," Marcus said. "Tell him what's going on. Prescribe he lay low."

"You too, Marcus."

He remained silent. Marcus Johnson didn't hide or attempt anonymity. He lived an open life, albeit in lonely country. He wouldn't lay low. He'd lay prepared.

"Text me your flight," he said. "Pack warm. Fall comes early in the Rockies. I'll pick you up at the airport."

We signed off. The rumble of the old diesel, acute awareness I might be in a riflescope's crosshairs at this moment. Fine. Take your best shot, you son of a bitch. Take your shot. Then say your prayers.

Chapter 26

Resolution replaced anger. Cold, committed focus overtook the hooded mantle of revenge. Take care of the small things, clear the decks for what would come. I checked flights to Billings, Montana. Early departure from Raleigh, North Carolina, through Minneapolis, and land in Billings tomorrow afternoon. Norfolk would have been closer, more convenient. But I'd left a trail there and wasn't going to backtrack. Think, calculate, plan.

Over one hundred forty Ditch miles to New Bern, North Carolina. Twelve hours. I'd get there at dawn. Travel at night, using the light of the moon on the Intracoastal Waterway and GPS when I crossed Albemarle and Pamlico Sounds. Then up the Neuse River. Catch a ride to Raleigh's airport.

The satellite-enabled laptop beeped an incoming message. Global Resolutions. Business. Time to put a wrapper on Suriname, deny their expected request. The gnomes of Zurich would want me back in Suriname. A new gig, this time with more definitive outcomes.

Report accepted. Well done. Payment processed.

I wasn't in the mood, but appreciated the perk working for the gnomes—a personal Swiss bank account. The message went on. *We present another engagement. Same location. Engagement details: Stop—repeat—stop all destabilization activities by whatever means. Triple rate. Urgent response requested.*

There were two issues with the message. First, it wasn't sent deep web. Global Resolutions had violated protocol before, and I'd admonished them. They continued believing cryptic messages were sufficient cover. Wrong. After my chat with Agent Abbie Rice, she'd ensure the NSA focused on certain keywords within electronic communications flowing toward the United States. The Russians would already be working the same angle. Engagement. Destabilization. Catch words for the spy nets. I wouldn't be surprised if Nika got this shortly after I did. Good. It would keep her on her toes in Paramaribo.

And Global should have known I wouldn't accept this gig. Yes, I'd muck around most places around the world, probe, take chances, and find answers. It's why they kept hiring me. Several years before, they'd made a similar proposition. End things. Stop events. The quick and easy translation was, "Go kill the appropriate people." Their client—and it was clear they weren't auctioning my information—had made a request regarding Suriname. Fix it.

The client would remain unknown. Commercial interests, perhaps a multinational bank. Or a government, possibly my own. The perfect plausible deniability. Request action through Global Resolutions. Hands clean.

I was done with that world. Others—less skilled and more accepting of delivering death—were regularly deployed around the world for such duties. Case Lee, having left the US Army and Delta Force, wasn't one of them. There was a fine line between killing and murder. But a line nonetheless, and one I wasn't crossing. In a few cases, rare circumstances, one affected the other. Bo had been murdered. I would kill his murderer. We all live by a code, acknowledged or not. And the Global Resolution request resided outside my code, my boundaries.

I visualized the tight, soundproof, and elegant Zurich meeting room. A stainless-steel carafe filled with fresh coffee. Perhaps Swiss cookies or chocolates arranged on a Langenthal porcelain plate. Serious men, well-tailored suits. Suriname players discussed with hushed tones, a hit list compiled—orderly and neat. They knew they wouldn't have to spell it out for me. Luuk Hoebeek. Joseph Hoff. Nika. Cut off the head of the snake. Send Case Lee. Tight, tidy, problem solved.

Not going to happen. I responded with a message on the deep web.

Declined. Kindly use secure means for ALL communications.

They'd be disappointed but would get over it. They might even stop asking me to perform wet duties.

Fall brought early nightfall, and I made the lock ending the Dismal Swamp canal just as the single operator was calling it a day. He waved me in, lowered the *Ace* to sea level, and waved a goodbye. A Comanche moon showed close, full, bright. Tiny towns rolled by alongside the Ditch. Their lone bars sounded loud evening conversations and occasional laughter, audible in my wheelhouse enclosure. Then the trees and thick brush enveloped again until the *Ace* was spit into Albemarle

Sound. Open water, nighttime. I lowered the wheelhouse windows, relaxed, and gathered my thoughts. Set the GPS to track us along the dredged Intracoastal Waterway across Albemarle Sound. Considered pulling the Clubhouse fire alarm. I needed Jules's affirmation, an assurance. Marcus had tossed out a possibility, one that still gnawed. Decision made, I sent a message: *Bo Dickerson. Dead. Extreme malice.*

It was sufficient enough for Jules, a picture painted. I'd never communicated with her in such a manner. The reply cycle, unknown. If there was a reply cycle. One thing for sure, the spiderweb tendrils of Jules's world would vibrate, and word would move through the world's underbelly. Whether she'd reply, even with her offer of help, was another matter. Her silence would spell bad news. Conspiratorial news.

I plowed south toward New Bern, the mainland on my right and the Outer Banks to my left. Out on the Banks, Kitty Hawk, Kill Devil Hills, and Nags Head passed—their night lights dim across Albemarle Sound. Boat traffic was light, the occasional tug-and-barge combination my only companions. Autopilot allowed me to move about, fix a sandwich, prepare for the trip. Past images swept by: the team assembled, committed, and professional. Bo, Marcus, Catch, Angel, and I. We worked one challenging environment after the other. Marcus, several years older than the rest of us. Fair, tough as nails, and with an absolute commitment to the mission at hand. He displayed leadership attributes we operators looked for.

Bo, point man for high-fire situations. Marcus recognized in him some special juju, a reckless fearlessness coupled with a seeming immunity to bullets. A wild man, indomitable. Catch engaged the unexpected, the surprises. He never failed and ended threats with violent finality. Angel was the serious one, seldom joking or pulling pranks. Marcus kept Angel on our flanks, alert to rear actions and enemy subterfuge. My job—engage and accomplish after Bo's initial violent contact with the enemy. Bo had my back. They all had my back.

Yemen, Colombia, Indonesia—we were sent to hot spots around the world. A small tight band, and we sliced like a machete. Extreme prejudice. Then exit, mission accomplished. We'd never lost a man. Until now. The current situation cast a new urgency. They'd come before, the bounty hunters, and were eliminated. But now they'd gotten to one of us. Murdered one of us. And it could have been Angel. The ultimate betrayal. It wouldn't happen a second time. Not on my watch.

Chapter 27

The *Ace* soothed, rolled, chugged its deep rumble belowdecks. I'd started a slide toward deep-regret land when the laptop beeped an incoming message. Jules. *Target?*

She'd glommed on to my concern that Bo might have been collateral damage—I was the main target. And her response answered, at least for the moment, whose side she was on. If Jules guided the bounty-collecting exercise, she wouldn't have posed the question. Unless she was playing me like a Stradivarius. A possibility. I lived in one messed-up world.

I contemplated a response but voted it down. Her question of target was now stamped *food for thought*. The night salt air washed through the wheelhouse, and trusting the GPS autopilot, I moved to the foredeck, stared at the stars. Legs bent at the knees, riding the *Ace*'s roll, letting go, alone.

Agent Abbie Rice called. A quick glance at my cell-phone clock showed it was long after working hours. I answered after two rings.

"Hi, Case. Hope I'm not bothering you. But I've got a question."

"Not a bother." I focused on release and dissipated the killer mind-set, aware my voice carried it—tight, low.

"You okay?" she asked.

"Sure. Yeah. Glad you called. What's up?" I was glad she'd called. And I didn't want her experiencing this side of me.

"Our analysts have arrived at some interesting scenarios."

"I bet."

"And I was wondering if you might validate any of them."

"Such as?"

"Such as a naval port in Paramaribo," she said.

The CIA had hit the frantic switch, with scenarios and vignettes gamed out. This phone call attempted a semblance of confirmation.

"A possibility."

"Any thoughts on how possible?" she asked.

"Lots of factors to consider."

She sighed. "Do tell."

I couldn't help but crack a smile.

"I just got home," she continued. "Poured a glass of wine. Thought I'd give it a shot, calling you."

Another woman's voice sounded in Abbie's background, asking a question. A roommate, or a friend.

"Call any time. I like talking with you."

"Unless it's about naval ports," she said.

It was an easy picture to paint of her. Pixie haircut, feet up, tired after a long day. Maybe wearing sweats, a run contemplated, then discarded as wine won. And a roll of the eyes in response to my obscure answers.

"Let's just say you're barking up the right tree. End of that discussion."

"Fair enough," she said. "I appreciate it."

Silence dangled, so I jumped in. "I'll be in your neck of the woods before too long. How about sharing a bottle of wine?"

No subtlety, blurt it out. Whether circumstances drove the direct approach or it was a style I'd adopted over the years, I couldn't say. But I meant it, and perhaps she'd recognize my sincerity as having some value.

She hesitated. "Great offer. I may take you up on it. We can swap tales."

"Exactly."

"And discuss our business relationship."

"I was thinking we'd keep it social. As in, go out on a date."

The light sea chop slapped the bow of the *Ace*, the wind clean, a hint of fall, temperature dropping. Abbie mulled it over.

"So. Here's the deal," she said.

"We don't always need to speak in terms of deals."

She ignored me and continued. "This is a major, major decision on my part."

"It's a date. Maybe dinner."

"The decision regarding us teaming. I would appreciate it if you didn't approach it with such a cavalier attitude. Wait."

"Wait?"

"Wrong word. Not cavalier. Dismissive."

It was time to end the conversation, headed down the wrong path. So I copped out.

"I'm tired. On edge. Could we discuss this some other time?"

She spoke to her female friend. "A little more." Wine poured into a glass.

"Sure. Sure we can discuss this another time. As long as it's about our partnership."

The *Ace*'s deck rolled, sea legs rejoined my repertoire, and stars curtained the sky. The air fresh, salty, crisp. My spot in the world.

"Gotta go, Abbie."

"Back to that date thing."

"Thought we'd left that."

"I have a partner."

It was inevitable. Someone like her wouldn't be unattached.

"Got it. Sorry if I pushed."

"She's here with me."

I suppose she'd skirted it with the partnership talk and sent signals that flew right over my head.

"Got it. Sorry to push." Case Lee, man of intrigue and insight. Case Lee, Esq.—moron.

"No need. It's flattering to have you ask me out."

"Maybe you and your partner would share a bottle of wine with me sometime."

"I'd like that."

Romance dissolved, she still held appeal. A good person. And I was sincere about the three of us having a glass or two.

"Me too. And sorry again about, well . . ."

"Chill, Case. It's okay."

"All right. We'll talk later."

We signed off. A tug and barge passed to my port as the night dragged on. We moved into Pamlico Sound. The moderate breeze was welcomed as this body of water—fifteen miles wide and seventy miles long—could get rough with windy conditions. I followed the buoy markers along the Intracoastal Waterway. Salt air, the grumble of the diesel engine, and playing possibilities filled the space and time—as did acknowledgement of the defect that allowed me to mourn and seek female companionship at the same time. It was strange, peculiar behavior, recognized and chalked up to need. A need for positive human connectivity. A need for normalcy.

I checked the GPS, assured our position in the Pamlico, and reassumed lookout on the foredeck, nose to the wind. Moonlight, stars, and ancient connectivity with boats plying saltwater. Slow movement and peace. A headshake, musings of a messed-up world. Bo gone. Mom and CC in hiding. Thoughts of Rae, and thoughts of companionship. Female companionship. Taken as a whole, I'd screwed things up royally.

I looked skyward and sought connectivity. A tiny speck of humanity, rolling with the waves, insignificant beyond comprehension. If there was a plan, a path, laid out, I couldn't see it, feel it. Too much violence, too much hatred pierced my life. If the great master, the universal force, held a lifeline I could grasp, hold on to, it eluded me. But the twinge and nagging sense of something else pulled and tugged at me. A sure presence on the periphery of my being—one I failed to join, grasp. Yet I'd been blessed or lucky or fortuitous beyond my grief and hard knocks. Others—millions—fared less well.

It was three a.m. when I entered the mouth of the Neuse River and made for New Bern. Two hours later my preferred dock for the *Ace* showed empty in the moonlight. New Bern was a regular stop, and a favorite. I'd enjoyed it numerous times as an anchor, a resting spot. Now, at this moment, it would provide a launchpad.

I slid a note for the dock's proprietor—an old acquaintance—through the mail slot, letting him know I'd return a few days later. He'd look after the *Ace*. I added a line to please water the tomatoes. They were doing fine, and thoughts of Bo's ministrations brought back redheaded laughter and love and a painful grip on my chest.

A strange geographical angst struck hard as well. I was leaving the *Ace of Spades*, the Ditch, home. Tight canals and saltwater bays. Headed for big-sky country. Collecting, preparing, when maybe I should have been hunting here on my turf. I was angry, lost, and sick and damn tired of being sick and tired. But Marcus Johnson offered team and friendship and a united front.

An Uber driver waited for me, the pickup scheduled for a Raleigh airport delivery. I slept hard during the flights and landed in Billings early afternoon. Before nodding off, I ruminated on how much Marcus had changed. Visits to his lair were a semiregular affair, and each time I was struck by how well he fit into the local landscape. Physically and mentally, he'd become part of the Montana fabric. Live and let live, no ripples. A far cry from when we were operators.

***

A group of college kids on a marine research vessel had departed Kuala Lumpur, Malaysia, and sailed for Singapore. The five-day learning-at-sea excursion, with stops for marine-life sampling and research, should have been the highlight of their summer. Instead, it turned into a nightmare.

Malaysia borders one side of the Straits of Malacca; the large island of Sumatra, the other. It is still an important passageway between China and India for commercial ship traffic. And the thousands of tiny coves and islets along the five-hundred-mile coast of Sumatra had held pirates since time immemorial.

They struck at night, boarded the research vessel, and took twenty-one college kids as hostages. Europeans, Americans, Malaysians, Singaporeans. Tossed into fast pirate vessels, they'd disappeared into one of the hundreds of pirate enclaves that lined the Sumatran coast.

One of the kids had the great sense, as they motored toward the pirates' hideaway, to take multiple GPS coordinates on her cell phone. She'd texted them to her parents before everyone's cell phones were confiscated. Extrapolating from their direction of travel, authorities pinpointed a general location on the Sumatran coast where the kidnapped students might be found.

The pirates were well versed in kidnapping protocol. They contacted parents and government officials in Europe, America, Malaysia, and Singapore with ransom demands. Parents panicked, distraught beyond measure. Governments dithered. From past experiences, the pirates expected a large sum of money handed over and an exchange of the students consummated. What they didn't expect was a Delta nightmare unleashed.

Our Delta team deployed. An overnight Singapore flight, then we were helicptered to a navy support vessel. Six hours later, a Special Ops boat, the *Riverine*, was lowered into the water near the Sumatran coast. The five of us joined a crew of four boat operators. The *Riverine* fit the bill perfectly. Small, at thirty-three feet, it could maneuver through the bays and inlets of the coast. At fifty miles per hour, it could scoot.

The pilot manned the controls. The other three crewmembers locked and loaded an M2 .50-caliber machine gun and two M134 Miniguns, each capable of firing six thousand rounds a minute. A badass vessel, with a well-trained crew. And things would only get worse for the subject of our ire if the five of us exited the boat and hit the beach.

Marcus had mapped a string of villages in the suspected area, and we began paying visits. There may be honor among thieves, and clannish ties of protection, but impending devastation loosened lips. At each pirate village, under Marcus's orders, the *Riverine*'s crew fired a five-second burst of several thousand rounds over the pirates' heads. Opening negotiations. Then Marcus waded ashore and delivered the stone-cold assurance of nightmarish retribution unless they released enough information to point in the right direction of the kidnappers.

Three pirate enclaves later, we had a target, five miles away. Ten minutes later, the boat crew dropped us off a half mile down the beach from the suspected kidnappers. Angel skirted toward the back of the village and covered our flank. Catch followed us, crouched near the beach, and guarded against the unexpected. Bo, Marcus, and I approached through the jungle.

Sixteen college students were huddled inside bamboo cages, scared shitless. I couldn't blame them. Thirty-plus men wandered about or rested in hammocks, each armed with automatic firearms of all stripes. Evening sounds—insects, the clanging of cooking pots, low laughter—filtered through the foliage. I could smell fish cooked over a fire.

Marcus signaled for us to spread, away from the bamboo cages. Any return fire from the pirates would be aimed at us, the students out of harm's way. He hand-signaled Bo—wait two minutes while he and I repositioned. Then unleash hell.

It was over within ten seconds. Angel joined the melee, firing from the rear of the camp. Catch cut loose from behind us. Operators rarely miss, and the quick dispatch of a half dozen pirates facilitated immediate peace negotiations. Hands airborne, weapons tossed on the ground, the pirate band stared wide-eyed as Marcus, Bo, Angel, and I emerged from the jungle, Catch from the beach.

We released the sixteen students, and I asked the whereabouts of the other five. They pointed to a shack, offset from the main camp. Five pirates had dragged five of the students, young women, up the small rise to the privacy of the shack. Marcus drew his pistol, signaled Bo. The two approached it and entered. Five shots in rapid succession rang out. Then they exited with the five kids, all disheveled.

"Had they started raping them?" I later asked Bo.

"No. Close, but no."

Then Bo pointed at Marcus, made the sign of a finger pulling a trigger. "I never fired," Bo said.

No fuss, no muss, and no press covered the aftermath of the event. Delta slipped back into the shadows.

***

Marcus met me at the airport. The only black guy in the receiving area, tall, statuesque. More gray at the temples peeked from under his cowboy hat than the last time I'd seen him.

"Welcome to Montana." He smiled and delivered a big hug. It felt good and right, and for the first time since the Dismal Swamp, I didn't feel alone.

"You're not getting any prettier, Marcus."

"The hell you say. I'm becoming distinguished. You, on the other hand, look like refried turds."

We both laughed, and as we made our way to his Chevy Suburban, I said, "I'm feeling a few pangs of guilt. Involving you."

"I'm already involved."

Reiterating his point, the Chevy's back seat held two Colt 901 rifles and several semiautomatic pistols. Ex-operators don't scare. They fight.

Chapter 28

We rode forty interstate miles and turned onto a seldom-used hardtop toward the tiny town of Fishtail, thirty miles distant. Marcus's ranch was another ten miles of gravel road to the southwest of that tiny burg. High-country sagebrush, bunchgrass, and antelope casting a wary eye from the distance. Huge mountains loomed on the horizon. We didn't see another vehicle once we turned off the interstate. Both the Beartooth and Absaroka ranges, another twenty and fifty miles distant, had a dusting of fresh snow. We were thirty miles as the crow flies from the northern border of Yellowstone. Big, big country, and a long, long way from the saltwater estuaries and boundary islands on the Atlantic.

Geography imprints a heavy hand on culture. Tides, wind, and water marked events on the Ditch. Here, space and isolation dominated. North Carolina, where I'd parked the *Ace*, was one-third the size of Montana but held ten times the number of people. It requires a mental shift to accept taking a long drive and never seeing another vehicle. The theme song of tires on gravel provided a backdrop to life out West. With folks here, lonely wasn't a word. Alone was a more apt description. Privacy and leave me be.

"Cast and blast," Marcus stated as we drove. "Perfect timing, Case. Although any time is good, and I'm not sure what I've done to piss you off and keep you away."

He referenced a combination fishing/hunting trip while I was here. I explained other matters had greater import at the moment and changed the subject.

"How's Miriam?"

Miriam, Marcus's on-again, off-again lady friend lived in Livingston, ninety miles away.

"She's doing fine. We had dinner and saw a god-awful movie the other night. I fell asleep."

"I'm sure she appreciated that."

"Then maybe she shouldn't suggest a flick that lacked something called color. Set in London. During winter. Gray all the time."

"Probably wasn't important to the plot."

"They might as well have shot it in black and white. And constant rain."

"Listen to Mr. Cinematography."

"And the actors droned on about relationships. Constantly." He removed the Stetson, scratched his head.

"Stories. Relationships. What did you expect?"

"The whole thing was the film version of Ambien."

"Clearly, you didn't pick the movie."

"Was going to fake an upset stomach. But I've used that one before," he said.

"A memorable night for Miriam."

"A memorable night for me. I prayed for a theater fire."

Miles rolled by, sage and grasslands and rolling hills dominant. Antelope and mule deer grazed in the distance.

"You happy here?" I asked.

"You pose the same question every visit."

"Yeah. Just checking."

"Same answer. Who wouldn't be? This is my turf. Life is good."

Fishtail, less than a hundred hardy souls, had a bar named Dead Solid Perfect. The locals referred to it as The Solid. We both carried holstered sidearms into the near-empty establishment. An old habit, and legal in Montana. The interior hadn't changed since my last visit. Wooden-plank walls, a potbellied stove occupying a corner. The neon Jack Daniel's sign still had the *J* out of commission. Beer Nuts, pork rinds, and a two-gallon glass jar of pickled eggs constituted the entire food menu. The lone bartender didn't ask for money with our order, assuming as always his patrons would drink several of their favorite medicinal brews prior to hitting the gravel again. We both sat at a table, backs against the wall.

Grey Goose for me, beer for Marcus, and another change of subject.

"There's someone I'd like you to meet," Marcus said.

I remained silent.

"A woman."

"You and Mom both."

"This isn't some Southern belle Lola Wilson has vetted as soul mate material for her wandering son."

"From operator to matchmaker. There's a natural progression."

"Shut up and listen. She's from California. Her granddaddy left her the ranch adjacent to mine. PhD in something to do with chemistry. She told me, but I forgot."

I took a sip and stared out the open window. A herd of pronghorn antelope moved, grazing, a half mile distant. The rolling high plains abutted the Beartooth Range. The highest peaks, cragged, desolate, well above the tree line, stood sentinel over empty wilderness—cold and daunting.

"She's hot, you idiot," Marcus added.

"Not a prerequisite, but it helps."

"And bright. And engaging."

"She paying you for this service?"

Marcus put a booted foot on the corner of the table, drained his beer, and shook his head. "You're a moron."

"There's serious shit going down, bud."

"I'm well aware," he said.

"So let's put aside a float on the love boat until answers, or killers, come my way. *Our* way."

Boot removed from the table, he edged my way, eyes hard.

"Let's assume it *was* a bounty hunter that took Bo down. A pro. Russian. British. Maybe one of ours. It doesn't mean they have a signal on you. Or me," Marcus said.

"Maybe. Maybe not. I've got feelers out."

He raised an eyebrow. "Feelers?"

"Yeah."

"The inscrutable witch of Norfolk?" he asked.

"She's a lifeline. And, maybe, a friend."

"The word *friend* isn't part of her vocabulary."

"Information, Marcus. That *is* in her vocabulary."

He asked for more detail about my recent gig and absorbed the information, cold and calculating. He pointed out that once Russia started construction of the naval base, my role—and findings—became irrelevant. The die was cast. He glommed on to the timeline associated with my Suriname activities and Bo's death.

"That's too short a time span for the Russians to send someone to find you back in the States."

"Maybe."

"A professional hit isn't done on a moment's notice, son. I don't see the connectivity," Marcus said. "I'm leaning toward bounty hunters. No association with your Suriname activities. Well trained, for sure, but bounty hunters nonetheless."

The bartender brought us another round. A rattling pickup pulled up, and an old rancher climbed out, one side of his Stetson's brim patched with duct tape. Bowlegged, saddle years showed in his shuffle. He nodded our way upon entering and sat at the bar, gossiping with the bartender about local events.

"Her name's Irene. Irene Collins."

"You back to the girl of my dreams?"

"Early thirties. Divorced."

"Let's sit on the porch. Satellite connectivity for my laptop."

"You going to ease up?"

"Repositioning. Remember?"

Lifeline. An appropriate term for Jules at this moment. I floated blind, unsure of adversarial intents, and her information—any information—would lower the angst level. Subsurface anger and desire for revenge remained.

"I'm unsure of Irene's worldview. But she's nice," Marcus said.

"Need a pipeline to Jules."

"She seems to have made the decision to live here after a breakup with some California fellow."

I stood and told the bartender we were moving outside. Laptop retrieved from Marcus's rig, I joined him on the small porch of the bar. The wood-slat building shielded us from the wind. It blew all day, every day. Its presence only a matter of degree. From light breeze to howling, it stood as one of several weather-shared experiences for the inhabitants of the high west.

Marcus occupied an old rocker and lit a cigar, his beer on the wooden deck. He pushed his beat-up Stetson further down, and tugged his jean jacket tighter around his torso. The air cooled, a hint of winter.

I fired up the laptop, and Marcus continued the matchmaking thread.

"Did I mention she's hot?"

He puffed smoke, long legs stretched away from the rocker, and enjoyed the view. He did his Marcus thing—weighed risks, assessed immediate threats, and ascertained Fishtail and the immediate environs offered sanctuary. I didn't share the feeling.

"You weren't there, Marcus. Helluva firefight. Now he's gone. Body fed to the gators."

Marcus pulled his legs in and tilted toward me, dead serious. "Yeah. I get it. And it tears me up thinking about Bo. I loved the guy. I'm not getting over it anytime soon."

"I know. Me either."

"But I don't need the grisly guesses, and I damn sure don't appreciate conspiracy theories polluting the air here on my turf," he said.

We locked eyes. The low chatter from the old rancher and bartender filtered through the open windows, mingled with the wind moving through the prairie grass and sagebrush. Assurance from a friend, one of very few, may have been all I was looking for. Someone telling me to calm down, we'll handle it, it'll be all right. There was no shame with such desire—everyone requires affirmation, the feedback of "it will work out." I'd lived alone on the edge long enough and recognized my need. I began to crank the gut roil down a notch and opted for reasoned discussion.

"Let's say the killer, or killers, *do* come here. As part of a concerted effort from a professional network."

Marcus's eyes took a harder set, and he spoke with a low, matter-of-fact tone. "Then we kill them. Triple *S*."

Shoot, shovel, shut up. Cut and dried, and I could live with that. A semblance of definitive action, if not a real plan. But assured, final. I nodded and relaxed a bit more.

"And we've got more backup coming," Marcus said. "Although I'm not of the opinion it's needed."

"Backup?"

"Although it will be good to see him again."

"What the hell are you talking about?" I asked.

"Almost overkill on the protection side of things."

"You irritate the fire out of me sometimes. You really do."

"Juan Antonio Diego Hernandez."

"You're shittin' me. Catch?"

"Why would I deceive you?" Marcus asked.

"Because you've rambled on about movies and some woman you want me to meet and have damn near completely dismissed the possibility we've got a hot target on our backs. Catch?"

"Called him last night. After talking with you."

"Any other little tidbits you've failed to disclose? Jeez, Marcus. You really are an ass pain sometimes."

"He's driving over from the Portland area. Left this morning."

"What is that? Fourteen hours?"

"About twelve for him. He'll be at the ranch house tonight."

"Catch."

"Catch. Haven't seen him in over a year."

"You ask him to come?" I asked.

"He insisted. Once he'd found out you'd kicked the wasp nest." He puffed the cigar, self-satisfied, then rocked back, stretched his legs, and smiled. "He didn't want to fly. Bringing his own hardware."

We were all excellent shots, but Catch stood a notch above. Whatever he'd packed, it would pop a flea at five hundred yards.

"Meanwhile," Marcus continued, "we're not going to sit around full of anxiety. Tomorrow morning, fat trout. Then an afternoon grouse hunt."

"You are one sanguine SOB, you know that?"

He laughed. I sent a message to Jules, deep web. *In Montana*. An act of trust. The Clubhouse, an ally. A belief required, or the whole damn thing became too weird, too off-kilter. Firmament and friends—my current assets. With Catch tossed in the mix, a sense of protection and comradeship swept over me. I damn near cried again and wondered if there was some emotional crevasse I kept slipping into. Mental and spiritual highs and lows. This moment, at the speck of humanity called Fishtail, was a high.

We drove to his ranch house, situated on a slight rise in the middle of his five-section ranch. Thirty-two hundred acres. Marcus owned five square miles of rolling grass-covered hills and small creeks. The nearest neighbor—the much-touted Irene.

The Jules message was a marker, both geographic and operational. She'd figure it out, would know of Marcus Johnson, as he did of her.

The fine filaments of her spiderweb would tingle with the information. I kept an eye on the horizon. Big, wild country. Hunting country.

Chapter 29

Beware Chechens. An incoming message on my satellite phone. The Clubhouse. We stood on Marcus's outdoor porch, a stone fire pit throwing flames. I messaged back a simple, *Thanks.* Her help, while nebulous, required acknowledgement. And the mental blanket of doubt was cast aside with this further confirmation that Jules backed me. And a tinge of irritation toward Marcus for planting the seed. And a knotted gut as the message was absorbed.

Chechens. The Chechnya area of Russia was home to a band of people fierce and fearless. Their relationship with Russia had been more than rocky. Insurrections, terror attacks, and moves toward independence. Yet Chechens often volunteered for the Russian military's Spetsnaz. Special Forces. Operators.

Another cryptic message from the Clubhouse, and no elaboration forthcoming. But one truth stood tall. Bad news had been delivered. It was buckle-up time. I paced around Marcus's porch fire pit, scanned the horizon, rifle within reach. Logs burned, crackled, and sent sparks into the night air. Marcus chided the pacing. I'd started to reveal the Clubhouse message when a light glowed over the near horizon. I snatched my rifle from its resting place.

Headlights. They appeared on the rise leading to Marcus's home and bounced as the vehicle flew along. At a gravel curve, the SUV went into a four-wheel drift, straightened, and skidded again at breakneck speed. A war cry sounded from the open window.

We exchanged knowing smiles, and I placed the assault rifle back within handy reach.

Juan Antonio Diego Hernandez. Catch. Originally from the high desert of eastern Oregon, he now lived life among the green and rain and funkiness of Portland. His operator moniker came from his ability to catch anything that slipped through the cracks during field operations. The unexpected, the wild variables during firefights. And if any of those variables brought firepower to the party, he ensured they would catch hell.

The SUV skidded to a stop; he popped from the passenger seat and ran toward me. Never lithe, he'd put on a pound or two, wore a flannel shirt, still moved like a bear, and had added a dense beard. He reminded me of a Paul Bunyan.

Catch slammed into me, lifted me off the ground, and growled as we spun around.

"Put me down, you goofy bastard!"

Marcus laughed loud. Catch squeezed, hard.

"Your scrawny ass hardly looks any different. Gimme a kiss."

His puckered lips air-pecked my direction while I squirmed, feet dangling. Marcus and his dog Jake howled.

"Shithouse mouse, Catch. You're breaking my ribs!"

Sweet release and sound footing allowed for a more sedate return hug. Man, it was good to see him. "I get the beard. Covers the ugly."

"Wrong again, peckerwood. I've done gone lumbersexual," Catch said.

"The citizens of Portland have to be a little worried about that."

The three of us laughed, Catch and I traded a few body punches, and we found our places around the fire pit.

"It is really, really good to see you," I said.

"You too. Understand we might have a bit of a shitstorm coming."

"As per Case," Marcus said. "I'm not convinced."

"Tell me about brother Bo," Catch said.

I reviewed events. His ruddy face grew redder, blood rising, as I skimmed over Bo's murder. Marcus added a few clarifiers, pointed out the unknown unknowns.

"Everything became a lot more likely ten minutes ago," I said.

"How's that?" Marcus asked, the team leader digesting information.

"Message from the Clubhouse."

Marcus and Catch both waited. The former tossed a skeptical "Hmm" under his breath.

"Beware Chechens."

The three of us exchanged quizzical stares.

"That old woman on acid?" Catch asked. "What the shit does that mean?"

"I'd suggest we have Chechens after us," I said. "Spetsnaz. Either current or former operators."

"Screw 'em. Bring it on," Catch said.

"Unclear at best," Marcus added. "Another shot of muddy water from the Clubhouse." He stared into the big empty and processed the message. Catch drained a beer he'd retrieved from his vehicle and belched. At some point in his deliberations, Marcus opted to mitigate risk. A sop to me or real concern, hard to say.

"Daylight ops are our advantage. Nighttime, theirs," he said. Team leader, constructing the most advantageous scenarios. "It's dark. We start by getting wrapped." Armed. Prepared.

We changed into fatigues and reassembled on the firelit porch. Coyotes began yipping from nearby coulees. Jake returned barks until Marcus banished him inside.

Our weaponry consisted of two Colt 901 .308-caliber assault rifles, each with an ELCAN Specter scope wired for night vision. Mine already leaned against a porch post. Catch had brought his Remington .300 Win Mag M24 sniper rifle with a Marauder night-vision scope. Trained as an expert sniper, he now loaded a weapon system that would reach out and touch someone in the dark at well over five hundred yards. Marcus produced three HK45 pistols, semiautomatic, and three handheld radios with earbuds for communication.

"Overkill and too damn dramatic," Marcus said. "But Case isn't going to ratchet down the speculation."

"She's legit intel, Marcus," I said, reiterating my position regarding Jules.

He ignored me and continued. "Four-hour shifts. Work the perimeter. Two hundred meters out."

"I'll take the first one," Catch said. "Make it six hours. I won't sleep for a while."

Marcus nodded, added, "Everyone clear on ROE?"

Rules of engagement. Protocols for conflict.

"Hell, yes," Catch said. "Kill 'em all."

We exchanged tight nods. Whoever, whenever. Bring it on.

Catch disappeared into the night; Marcus retired inside. Jake wandered through the dog door, barked once at the deep night, strolled over, and leaned against my leg. I scratched him, his beard wet from lapping water. He pressed harder when I stopped, waited an appropriate time, gave a glance of "See you later," and ambled inside to rejoin Marcus.

I stared at the fire; white sprinkles wisped through the air. Thoughts of wild country and killer headhunters swirled. The coyote chorus picked up again, close. Social calls, interactions, bands of coyotes establishing turf. And somewhere within two hundred meters, Catch, the protector.

The yelps and whines stopped, shut down. Far in the distance, toward the Beartooth range, came a low, primitive moan, riding the wind. Wolves. A person may become inured to the yips and howls of coyotes, plaintive night music. But not the primal, deep howl of a pack of wolves. A call and response tuned to ancient fears. The sound carried, was wind-muted, and carried again across the night wilderness. Alone, not lonely. Prepared. Hunting.

Chapter 30

I radioed Catch early in the morning and relieved him. Catch's strength had always been faith in the unpredictable. Faith in the unseen, in surprises out of nowhere. And a deep conviction that violent intent would arrive when least expected. His conviction had kept us alive on more than one occasion. Together in the snow-filtered breeze and black night, we exchanged a brief chat.

"Sorry about all this," I said.

"You can file that bullshit away right now."

"Stomped an ant bed in Suriname."

"So what else is new?"

"Triggered activities. Bo. Chechens."

"You don't know that," he said.

"I do know they're coming."

"Suits me. Clean out some more bounty hunters."

We stood still and relished our friendship—comradeship—in the cold night.

"Marcus doesn't share your conviction," he said.

"I know. Wish he was right. But he's not."

He hit on the elephant in the room. "He claims you think it's Angel."

"Yeah. Signs. Feedback from the Clubhouse. My gut."

He spit, shook his head. "Angel. Chechens. Whatever. If they're coming, I'm glad I'm here. Help take out the trash."

I shifted, and the ground crunched underfoot. Icy snow, frozen pellets. Our breath showed against the blackness. Catch lived black and white, right and wrong. If Angel sat on the wrong side, Catch would have no remorse pulling the trigger. I didn't dwell there.

"How's Portland life?" I asked.

"Excellent. Found a fine woman."

"Good for you. You deserve to be happy."

"And get this. She owns a welding shop. We partner. Both the personal and business side of things."

Catch had always been good with his hands, mechanical and electrical.

"You worry? Living there?"

"Nope. My name's not on anything. Not on the business or cell phone or vehicle registration. I don't exist."

"Still."

"Yeah, still. It's getting old."

He scanned three-sixty with night-vision binoculars and continued. "Been hoping the Clubhouse would sooner or later find the source. The paymaster."

"Got another source looking. Inside the Company."

He lowered the binoculars, leaned close. "Let me know if your source hits pay dirt. You and me, we'll take a trip. Finish it."

"Done deal. You have my word. Now go hit the rack. I'll take it till dawn."

He handed me the binoculars but kept his grip. "Man, I wish I'd seen Bo. Before he went down."

"I know. He missed you, too. Said so."

"It isn't right. The world. The world without him," Catch said.

"I feel it, too. Off-kilter."

He tugged the binoculars, drew me nose-to-nose. "If they do come, with or without Angel, no mercy. None."

I returned a grim nod, bumped foreheads. He buttressed my moral waffling about Angel. No remorse, no hesitation, squeeze the trigger. Behind us another pack of coyotes yipped, moaned, and howled into the night. The night breeze emphasized winter on the horizon, biting, cold.

We stood together two hundred meters from the ranch house, inside a small coulee. Catch whacked my back and left to find sleep. I hunkered down and night-scoped the surrounding terrain. Every twenty minutes I'd change positions, move.

Three hours later, the first sign of daylight crept over the eastern horizon. My earbud crackled, and Marcus spoke. "Come in. Daylight."

I found him in the kitchen, cooking. Catch snored from the great-room couch.

"I'll accept this nighttime vigilance to a point," he said. "Three or four more days. Damn silly going through this if no one shows up."

"They're showing up, Marcus."

"Maybe." He turned the bacon and stopped fiddling with food, pressed both hands into the countertop. "You've got to leave Spookville, Case. Got to. Shadowed targets shift, grand conspiracies gamed—you have to lead a different life. Settle somewhere. And that's the end of my preaching."

"What happened to Bo damn sure wasn't in the shadows."

"You're right. All for a reward. Money. We'll handle it, if and when the time comes."

"They're coming. And I've dragged both of you into this mess."

"Basta. Enough."

Furrowed brow, hard stare. Irritated.

"You've been hiding your Italian heritage."

A headshake, a smile. "I mean it," he said. "We'll keep this going a few more days. Stand night watch. Meanwhile, we live our lives during the day."

"Meaning what?"

"Meaning there's a midge hatch on the Big Lost."

The Big Lost Creek was isolated, seldom fished, and required access through private land. Marcus's neighbors. The water level would be low, summer's snowmelt having long completed its filling renewal. Perfect for dry fly-fishing.

The river's current insect hatch—midges, a tough cold-weather bug—offered trout a fine supper. The life cycle of midge nymphs swimming for the river's surface after time spent among the rocks and aquatic vegetation made for a steady trout diet. But the hatch, the hatch. A smorgasbord of food as nymphs collected on the surface film and hatched into a flying insect. Fat trout would sip, ingest the transformed bugs before they flew away.

"Sounds good." It did. The Zen-like presentation of a tiny insect imitation, suspended on the film of the river's surface. A desultory float-by to entreat a fat trout to rise from its lair and sip from the surface.

"Afterward, sharp-tails and huns."

Sharp-tail grouse and Hungarian partridge sprinkled these rolling grasslands. Lots of walking, a good bird dog pointing coveys, and a fine, crisp fall day. It sounded better than good. The dark backdrop of a visit from professional killers hovered, but Marcus plied Montana magic. It began working.

"And to help you get your head right," he said, pausing to lift his chin toward the sleeping Catch. "Our backs are covered."

He had a point. Daylight removed the advantage from attackers. And wandering the hills and grasslands put us out of harm's way while the ranch house remained a lure. Jake sat and observed our morning ministrations, begged some bacon, and settled into his ranch-dog routine.

The bushy eyebrows and chin beard wandered about, hanging with the fellows, depositing dog toys at our feet. I'd learned from past experience that Jake didn't expect to play with the toys. They were a gift from him to a visitor. A peculiar habit, endearing.

As I called Mom and checked her situation, Jake approached Catch with a gift and nuzzled the snoring operator. Catch woke, shoved an arm under the dog, and lifted the sixty-five-pound squirming package onto his chest and belly. The dog settled, nose in Catch's beard, and snores recommenced. Marcus hummed a tune, Mom assured me things were well, and morning adopted an element of peace. I relaxed and tried hard living the moment.

Tranquility came to a screeching halt when Marcus pulled the shotguns and game bags from a closet. Preparation for a hunt. The bird-dog DNA activated. Canine synapses thrown into overdrive. The critter flew off Catch, waking him, and for the rest of the morning never left Marcus's side. He whined and cast dark brown eyes toward his owner, fearful of exclusion from the event. Marcus's commands to "Hush" and "Chill, Jake," had no effect whatsoever. Jake was a bird dog. And the boss had opened the possibility of a bird hunt. Nothing, absolutely nothing, could be finer.

Catch wandered outside, returned. "I appreciate a great outdoors piss."

"You wouldn't appreciate a high-velocity bullet nailing you in the process," I said. "Great epitaph. Died with his pecker in his hand."

"Jake isn't the only one that needs to chill," Marcus said, sending a look my way. "Come eat before it gets cold."

The dog sat and stared at the countertop while we ate, focused on the two game bags set there with their residual smell of past grouse. Catch farted, and both Marcus and I waved at the table air.

"Something crawl up there and die?" Marcus asked.

"Altitude adjustment," Catch said. "What's this talk about fishing? And a hunt?"

"Out and about," Marcus said. "Away from here."

"Like it," Catch said. "Flies to honey. The ranch house. Shoot the bastards in the back."

"Speaking of shooting," Marcus said.

"Got it. I'll walk behind while you two fish. And hunt. Cover the area. And your asses."

"And we live life," Marcus added. "Prepared, but not huddled, waiting. That's important."

I cleaned dishes after breakfast while Marcus made lunch. Jake whined, and Catch checked his rifle.

"You're a bold man," I'd commented at the sandwich creations. Large thick cuts of liverwurst, rounds of fresh onion, and gobs of mayonnaise were plastered between two slices of Italian bread.

"Be stout of heart," he said. "This is food fit for kings."

"Food for passing gas."

"A farting mule never tires," Catch added from across the room.

Marcus tossed Jake a small leftover piece of liverwurst. A Ziploc of Muenster cheese and three crisp apples joined the sandwiches in a small pack, along with a thermos of coffee and water bottles. A final kitchen cleanup, and we loaded serious armament into the Suburban, as well as the shotguns and game bags.

The tires sang a gravel song, the morning clear and fine, my gut less knotted. A good day, surrounded by fellow warriors. Friends. Brothers.

Chapter 31

Frost and frozen snow crunched underfoot as we donned waders. The distant twelve-thousand-foot craggy peaks stood white, bright with fresh snow. The air carried fresh, crisp. The high prairie had begun its dormancy—a dry and acrid and resigned smell. The morning came cold, but the sun offered promise and held its end of the bargain, warming the ground.

Marcus provided the necessary equipment. Fly rods, waders, wading boots. Catch added commentary to our morning endeavor.

"Just so I'm clear. You catch fish with a little bug imitation."

"Yep," Marcus said.

"Then toss them back in the river."

"It's called catch and release."

"It's called dumbassery. Catch a fish. Throw it back. Repeat."

"Listen to Mr. Sierra Club," I said. "They must love your progressive outlook in Portland."

"I overcome their dismay with charm. And this fine beard."

I left the vehicle several times, opened and closed ranch gates. Catch demurred involvement, explaining his backseat position best for covering our backs. Jake flung to full alert at each stop, prepared, waiting. We drove through vast swaths of private land—friends and acquaintances of Marcus—and made our way to the river.

"You talk about finding a place," Marcus said. "A place to settle. Stop all your transient living."

"So far, just talk. But I'm serious."

A herd of antelope measured our pace, cruised parallel at forty miles an hour. They neither veered nor changed speed, matched our route, taking a run on a fall morning.

"Used to hunt those as a kid," Catch said. "Tasted like sagebrush."

"Consider this day. And ignore voices from the back seat. When we head back to the ranch, think about if it gets any better."

My friend and former team leader had a point. And anchored an emotional component. I could live a long, long time seeing Marcus on a regular basis. He'd feel the same way. And this part of the world possessed a strong appeal. Wild, distant, isolated. One of the few places left where, away from the sparse fence lines, it took little effort imagining this land as it was before Lewis and Clark.

The vast Yellowstone Park was thirty miles south, and the protected bison there—ignoring mandated boundaries—wandered this area regularly. It wasn't unusual to walk over a rise and view fifteen or twenty of them grazing, grunting, rolling in a well-used stretch of bare earth. Taking a dust bath. The hills we drove through were home to antelope, mule deer, coyotes, and wolves. Elk and cougar populated the vast mountain ranges around us. The Beartooths, the Absarokas, the Gallatin Range. Big, big country. And I loved it.

But I'd spent part of a winter here as well. And for a Georgia boy, it was terminal duty. Whiteouts due to wind. Ground snow lifted, swirled, sent packing miles across the vast high prairie, obliterating visibility. Cold well below zero. Bone-chilling cold. An involuntary shiver went through me.

"Winter, my friend. Tough duty for this boy." I patted Marcus's arm and drew Jake's attention. He demanded a chin scratch as I had volunteered physical affection. "Love being here, with you. And Catch. That's a given."

"Anyone bring beer?" Catch asked. "So I can drink while you two emote."

"Again, ignore voices from the back seat," Marcus said.

"As for today, I'm not going to think about it. Just live it. Because you're right. It doesn't get any better than this."

A burr, a tiny pang, registered. I'd sent Mom and CC into hiding. They didn't mind a Grandma Wilson visit, but nonetheless, they were hiding. And I was preparing for a fishing expedition, relishing the opportunity. The possibility loomed of a call to give Mom the "all clear." But it wasn't clear, and Marcus's disregard of impending danger struck me as too simple, too assured.

We drove over a rise, and the river displayed empty for miles. The Big Lost held pools, riffles, eddies—interspersed with logjams and flat spots. Perfect trout habitat. Waders and wading boots on, fly rod rigged, Marcus struggled putting Jake back into the Suburban. The torture chambers of Torquemada's Spain must have echoed with the same sounds as the dog howled, moaned, groaned, begged, and whined—

trapped while we walked away. Prior to departure, Catch slung his rifle across his back, binoculars around his neck.

"I'll stay up top."

"Sorry you can't join us," I said, and meant it.

"Hook a fish. Toss it back. No, thanks." He took off with a bearlike gait and absorbed the terrain, calculated the possibilities. Marcus and I descended into the tight river valley.

We stood at the river's edge, watched, waited. Marcus lit a cigar. A dipper, the size of a robin, worked the rounded shore rocks. The bird dove into the water, disappeared, popped up. The sunken riverbed offered protection from the wind; the lightest of breezes caused a faint ripple across still water. Then it started.

Marcus flipped his hand through the air, grasped something unseen. He opened his hand under my nose. A tiny insect, black, mosquito-like, wavered in his palm, recovered, became airborne again.

"Midge?" I asked.

"Yeah."

A litany of aquatic insects populated these rivers. They lived, submerged, under rocks and along the bottom as a wormlike nymphs. Crawling and feeding, they provided food for trout. Survivors had a signal in their buggy little brains. A signal it was time to rise, surface. Shed the hard exoskeleton and emerge on the river's surface as a flying insect. Then their life span consisted of three or four more days. They bred, the females dropped their eggs back into the river, and the cycle started again.

Midges, mayflies, caddis flies—the list was long, with each variety hatching for certain weeks of the year. Trout home in on the hatch du jour. This was midge season.

"Griffiths Gnat?" I asked.

"That'd be a good bet."

The Griffith's Gnat fly imitated a small cluster of midges collected on the water's surface. Not a trout rib eye steak like the massive stone flies, but a tasty treat and the lone item on the seasonal menu.

A small rise, a dimple in the river's surface, indicated a feeding trout. Then another, and another. The hatch started. With midges, it could last hours. The trout dinner bell clanged loud. Marcus and I separated and fished different stretches of water.

Marcus hooked up first, as expected. I wouldn't have known it but for the loud splash of a fat rainbow trout. Hooked, it put on an initial aerial display, and tore the fly line downstream, leaped again. Spray and silver fish backlit by bright morning light. Marcus's fly line suspended in the air, a connective filament to the hooked trout. A master, calm, focused, he worked the eighteen-inch rainbow toward him, his net, and release back into the river. I watched with utmost pleasure, paused my pursuit until he'd brought it to net, and unhooked it. He gently immersed the fish back in the water, held it until it recovered and swam away. From the distance, as light twinkled from the river ripples, it appeared as interactive art, the stage unmatched.

Marcus turned downstream, wondered if I'd seen the event. I held both hands, eighteen inches apart, indicated my perspective of the size. He smiled back, shook his head, and relit his cigar. Then he held his hands three feet apart. We both laughed.

It was so unlike fishing saltwater. There, the environment— estuaries, bays, sounds—remained relatively static. The quarry— saltwater fish—dynamic. They moved, hunted. Here, the opposite. The environment moved, whirled, cascaded. The fish lay at the bottom, a pocket of calm water delivered by a rock or structure, watched, waited. A nymph rising for transformation or hatched insects still in the water's surface film elicited trout to leave their lair. A rise of primitive surety, deliberate and paced, engulfing food.

Several large fish fed near the opposite bank, swirls and dimples across the calm section as they rose and sipped clusters of midges from the surface film. A group of overhanging willows shaded, protected them. I moved, stalked, and ensured my wading boots didn't scrape or drag—sending a danger signal to the trout. Fifty feet distant, I stopped and positioned for a presentation. It would require a slop cast.

The stretch of river separating us consisted of three different ribbons of running water, each moving at its own speed. Water rushed, pushed against my waders. Twenty feet away, a large boulder offered relief from the current, a downstream pocket more sedate. Then more rushing water until, at a slight bend of the river's course, slack water, still, where the fish fed.

To fool a trout, make it believe the little cluster of feathers and thread floating by was the real deal, a dead drift made for the first critical factor. My fly had to attend the speed of the surface where they fed. These trout rose where the water slowed, calm, safe. The issue was my floating line would lie across the varying speeds of river water. Each would push the line downstream and pull the fly at an unnatural speed across the feeding zone.

The answer was a cast upstream of where they rose, a lift of the rod tip, and a pull on the fly line as the line stretched taut through the air. Create slack, or slop, in the line when it landed on the river. The current would quickly send the line downstream, but sufficient slack—if done right—allowed for my fly to float above the feeding fish at a natural pace. I would have two or three seconds before the current tightened the line slop and my tiny presentation would rocket downstream, alerting my prey of a bogus offering.

The large trout continued feeding, my focus all-consuming. Air, water, fish. And me. The universe shrunk to this pinpoint of concentrated effort on the Big Lost. One, two, three false casts, the line lengthened with each forward and back motion. It zipped through the air well upstream of the feeding fish and avoided spooking them from an overhead shadow. The final cast. A quick lift of the rod tip and light pull, the green fly line suspended, slack, frozen in the bright light. A gentle descent, slack line immediately pushed downriver. My fly kissed the surface three feet upriver from the last dimple of a rising trout and floated, sedate, drifting.

One Mississippi, two Mississippi, three . . . a swirl, a take. I lifted the rod and retrieved the line with my left hand, met resistance, and connected with the coursing vibration of a big rainbow, hooked. It skyrocketed, somersaulted through the air, crashed down, and ripped downstream. Big fish. Line screamed from my reel, the rod held high. Another leap, then another, each time spinning and flipping like a gymnast, throwing spray. No point trying to turn it, or reel it in. The almost invisible nine-foot leader connecting the fly to the fly line had a breaking point of four pounds. The ball of silver energy I'd hooked would weigh three and a half pounds, and combined with the river current would apply line-breaking pressure.

I walked, skidded downstream and followed the trout, began recovering line. Twice more it made serious runs downstream, each with less power. It eventually succumbed, and with a final rod lift it drifted into my small wooden-handled net. Twenty inches long, fat, a football. A fine fish.

I knelt in the shallows, net submerged, and pulled the tiny fly from the cragged jaws. The trout's back was dark, oily—protective camouflage from ospreys and other overhead hunters. But its sides, electric, lit, brilliant silver with a red band and dark spots intermingled. Bright, charged, alive.

The fish recovered from its battle, trapped within the net. The crunch of wading boots along the shore alerted me to Marcus, passing.

"Thought for a minute he was going to drag you to Wyoming," he said.

"A beauty."

"It's every bit of that." He passed on.

The net lowered below the recovered fish, its tail worked the water. It hung, suspended, above the rim of the small net and below the surface, assessing. Then it cruised, spent but able, and disappeared among the submerged rocks and moving water.

The day warmed, the midge hatch continued. We leapfrogged each other, fished our own private stretches and exchanged commentary as one or the other passed. Copses of aspen, nestled among the foothill creases, showed yellow. Their leaves shimmered, quaking. There were no other fishermen, this whole stretch of river isolated. A fine day—the lone cloud an occasional glimpse of Catch on the rim. Our lookout, protector.

A mile downstream, we turned and fished our way back. We each caught and released another half dozen fat trout, each a treat, vibrant, coursing with life. Before we left the river and climbed the hill for a field lunch, we paused.

"You feel Bo?" Marcus asked, out of the blue.

A small herd of mule deer watched us from a quarter mile away. A pair of golden eagles soared overhead, rode their own currents.

"Yeah. Yeah I do."

We stood still, silent, and absorbed the moment.

"Perched squatting on one of the large boulders in the middle of the river, red hair flying, smiling, watching," I added.

"Fishing with a sharpened stick. Naked."

We laughed together.

"Yeah, I feel him," I said, and paused. "With me. Joy. Wonder. Love."

A trout rose nearby and sipped midges from the surface.

"Wonder if it all works like that?" Marcus asked.

"Don't know. Hope so."

River sounds, water moving. Timeless, yet finite.

"Anyway," I said, "this is church. Here. Now. Surrounded with this glory. Why wouldn't he be with us?"

Tears welled. Marcus squeezed my shoulder, gave it a light pat, and headed up the hill. The moment flooded with real, bright and enveloping. I thought of Mom, CC. And Bo. And how lucky I was, a part of this magic moment.

Chapter 32

From our hilltop perch, we could see forever, the sky vast, grass leaning with the wind. We'd released Jake from his vehicular imprisonment, and he'd taken the opportunity to pee on a tire of the Suburban before wandering in tight circles, watchful for signs of shotguns and game bags. Catch wandered up, scanning even as he sat to join us. Marcus produced the liverwurst sandwiches, and we sat on the lee side of the Suburban.

"Rough life," Marcus said.

"Can barely stand it."

"So are you two through with your little dances-with-fish exercise?" Catch asked.

Jake smelled food and sat near Marcus and his sandwich. The breeze blew stronger above the protection of the riverbed, the knee-high grass dancing. It wasn't hard visualizing buffalo herds by the millions grazing through this area.

The raw onion slices crunched; the soft liverwurst was smooth, rich. Marcus passed me a water bottle and asked, "You miss Rae?"

Only the closest of friends could lay it out that way. He stared off at the horizon and gave me room to answer.

"Every day."

"How's that affect the dating world?"

"Comparisons. Touch of guilt."

"Not easy," he said and crunched a bite of crisp apple and cheese.

"Part of the deal."

"I know a few Portland women you'd like," Catch said. "They might even like you. If I lied enough before they met you."

"A recurring theme. Dating consultants. What is the deal with you and Marcus?"

"Your happiness. That's the deal," Catch said and wiped his beard with the sleeve of his jacket. "You were the first of us to take the plunge into a normal life. Marriage. Potlucks. Rotary Club."

"Didn't last long."

"Not the damn point," Catch continued. "It fit you. You were happy. Do it again."

"So speaks the oracle."

"Catch is right," Marcus said. "And I believe a part of your happiness, or the possibility of being happy, will come from a location change."

"And quit living on a stupid boat," Catch added.

"Didn't know Dr. Phil had two assistants. What soothing approach should I take with bounty hunters?"

"You really worried?" Catch asked. "I mean, look around. Over the last few hours, I've seen fifty pronghorns and a dozen deer. Pass the cheese and an apple."

"The point is, you don't have to travel around the world to make a buck," Marcus said. "Start there. Find a spot, get a job. Let things coalesce around normalcy."

"And maybe we should consider the current situation. Nothing normal about that." I brushed my hands clean, stood.

Catch took another bite of apple and spoke while he chewed. "Look, I may not see it, and Marcus is skeptical as hell, but you made the call. Right or wrong, you rang the bell."

"I feel it. Sense it."

"Fair enough," Catch said. "And we responded. That's the whole point. We're here for each other."

"And I can't tell you how much I appreciate it. How much it means. Whatever the possibility the bad guys are coming."

Catch stood, shook food debris from his beard. "So we going hunting, or play grab-ass with possibilities?"

Marcus and I shared a smile over Catch's worldview. Possibilities always existed. Fine. Expect the unexpected. Be prepared. Shoot first.

No human structures, no people for miles in any direction. Rolling grass hills, interspersed with coulees—draws or depressions—often brush-filled. The wild grasslands of Montana. Home to sharp-tailed grouse and Hungarian partridges. Thirty minutes later we pulled off the gravel road, middle of nowhere.

"We'll hunt two spots. Here, and one near the ranch. Both have lots of birds."

I'd learned a long time ago that "lots of birds" didn't take into account bird density. Lots of birds meant lots of country, miles of walking. It was a good thing, the day bright and clean. Striding with friends I'd been with through hell and back. A bird dog unleashed, doing what it was bred to do.

Released, Jake whined and quivered with anticipation as we strapped game bags around our waists and loaded the shotguns. Catch shouldered his sniper rifle, draped binoculars over his neck, donned sunglasses, and smiled.

"I'll hang back. Quarter mile. Work the perimeter," he said.

Nods all around and a final radio check. We'd wear earbuds, stay in contact as we spread out.

There are, regardless of breed, only two kinds of bird dogs, two types that point feathered game. The vast lion's share fell in the first category. The canine DNA took over, hardwired, and the dog hunted. With fierce intensity, all-consuming, and if trained well, it stayed somewhat within eyesight. Pure instinct, tempered with training, compelled the dog—seek, smell, find. When the scent of game birds carried close, lock. Freeze. Point. As a hunter, you find the dog, walk toward it, the birds flush, and you shoot. The cycle repeats.

A fine experience, but one of separation. The majority of high-octane pointers don't give a rat's ass if you're there or not. They hunt for themselves, hardwired. You are along for the ride. They may make fine family pets, loving, great with kids. But afield, these pointing machines are oblivious to your presence. The owner was welcome to come along. Or not. It doesn't matter with those bird dogs.

Owners often equip these high-strung and high-priced animals with shock collars and small GPS antennas. The shock collar reminds the dog to stay within a semblance of range of the hunter. The GPS used for locating the dog after it disappears over the hill, finds a covey of birds, and locks on point—in what may be the next county. Beeps, electronics, yelps when the shock collar pops. The dog becomes a tool, utilized for the experience of a bird hunt. A tool so focused and so intent, it no longer cares about the owner, the master.

Then there's the rare category of bird dog, few and far between. Dogs that hunt for you, with you. These jewels pause often, check your location, hesitate for affirmation you are together, as one. In open fields, they range within a couple hundred yards, visible, confirm you're with them.

Hunting thick brush with hindered visibility, they move tight, nearby. They ensure their partner, their teammate, is close. These hunters don't require collared electronic gizmos or harsh words of frustration as they ignore you and head off for themselves. Rare and relished, these dogs team. Partner. Hunt together. No longer a master-servant relationship. Transformed into a field partnership. Jake was one of those special types.

Now the magic moment separating the best bird dogs from the revved-up knotheads hunting for themselves. Vehicle doors slammed shut. A fine bird dog thirty feet ahead, body toward open prairie but head turned back toward its partner, teammate. Waiting for the command, quivering. The snick of a chambered shotgun round signaled the all-set. I dropped worry and concern, lived in the here.

And so Marcus delivered those wondrous words, the signal for the transformation. Issued from partner to partner, man to dog.

"Hunt 'em up."

And so we did.

Chapter 33

Jake ranged, nose windward, two hundred yards ahead. He cut swaths across our walking direction, covered wide areas, tasted the air. He cast glances at Marcus, connected. Catch followed us, dipped into coulees, ranged our flanks. We seldom spotted him. A half mile passed, and Jake became birdy, more excited, his cropped tail frantic. He froze, pointed.

"Huns."

Marcus knew his dog, and whatever birdy indications poured from of his hunting partner indicated the species of bird. Hungarian partridges. Clustered birds, gathered in coveys of ten or twenty. Imported during the 1800s, they had spread across the West.

"Don't wait," Marcus said as we marched toward a rock-still Jake. Huns often flushed far, required a quick shot. We walked past Jake, who held his point, and flicked the safety off on our shotguns. When Huns busted, flew, they often did so as a flock, at once, all of them. And far away.

I couldn't see the covey, hidden in the grass, but at twenty yards they busted. An uproar of wings, the gray-and-rust-colored birds exited the scene at full roar, headed away from us. Typical of Huns. We both picked a single bird, fought against the tendency to flock shoot, and each slapped the trigger once. Two birds fell.

At the sound of the gunshots, Jake flew past, intent on the retrieve. He brought both back for Marcus, his partner. Gray underbodies, mottled-brown back and wings, a rusty head color extending into the brown. A fine bird, about twice the size of a quail. Both destined for a pot of gumbo or stuffed and baked. Neither bird was shoved unceremoniously into the game bags around our waists, but rather admired, touched, appreciated. Then slid into the protective pockets while Jake jumped and danced around us, remnant feathers caught in his beard.

"Nice shooting" came over the earbuds. Catch.

The covey had flown a good quarter mile away, and Marcus declined pursuit. "They're liable to flush even farther next time."

So we continued, covered turf, relaxed, in concert with the dog. We dropped into a coulee, followed Jake as he climbed the other side.

The sky bright, vast, except for a thin black line at the northern horizon. A front, dark and full of ugly weather, rolled across the Great Plains toward us.

"Won't hit until late today," Marcus said as we tromped along. He'd know, and I dropped any concern about working through wind, rain, snow, and sleet on the way back.

A couple of miles passed, comfortable, anticipatory. The land rose and dipped, swells on an ocean of grass. Mountain ranges both close and a hundred miles away stood as sentinels, boundaries wild and untouched. The foreboding line of weather moved closer, stretched across the horizon, still far distant.

Jake dropped into a wide high-grass coulee and we followed. Chokecherry bushes bunched in the center of the draw, and the dog, after trotting past the bushes, slammed the brakes. Head turned, nose in the air. He reversed direction and quartered toward the thick cover, froze.

"Jake's on point," Marcus said. We had both walked past the dog, began scaling the opposite side of the coulee. "Sharp-tails."

He'd know. About twice the size of Huns, sharp-tailed grouse held better, allowed us a closer opportunity. We approached the quivering statue of a dog. Jake moved, broke point, crept forward. The covey was moving, walking or running away. We stayed behind Jake and followed his lead. Neither of us could see the birds, hidden, camouflaged.

Jake locked up again and once more moved, stalked forward, deliberate and quiet. He froze for good, a front leg suspended, static. Somewhere ahead of his nose were grouse. Ten feet. Twenty yards. Hard to say as nature had provided remarkable camouflage coloring for the sharp-tails.

We moved past Jake, cautious, and flicked our weapons' safeties off. The breeze had increased, swirled. The chokecherry bushes and tall prairie grass swayed around us, each slow step closer to a flush of wild birds.

Two, three grouse erupted from the cover, wings pounding air. Two shots, two birds, and the popcorn flush began. Another single popped from cover, and Marcus downed it. Another flushed and passed behind Marcus, negating any chance I had of a safe shot. Two more popped up at my feet. One shot and another bird for the bag. Four shots between the two of us. Four birds.

Marcus directed Jake in the general direction of each dead grouse, and the dog retrieved them, one after the other. As Marcus collected them, he handed over two for my game bag. Speckled brown with the feathers extended along the legs to the feet. Fat, healthy, beautiful birds. They would make a fine dinner.

Such moments inspire stillness and reflection. There was no urgent movement forward seeking more birds. A respite—respect for the kill and the glory of the surroundings. Another magic moment, washed by comradeship and unity with the canine teammate and appreciation for the wonders at hand and those extending to the horizon. Catch, hidden above us, again acknowledged our marksmanship.

We worked our way back toward the Suburban. Jake found another covey of Huns. They flushed at forty yards, and while Marcus and I both shouldered shotguns, neither of us fired. Too far. Too much chance of a wounded bird. A matter of discernment, appreciation for the opportunity.

The Chevy rolled through miles of undulating land, the day still bright, the storm line still distant. We would hunt a stretch of land on Marcus's ranch. A set of tight dips and rises that held sharp-tails. He mentioned the outside world again.

"Any thoughts about going after the funding source?"

It came as a bit of a surprise given Marcus's nonchalance toward the subject. He'd always back-burnered the entire bounty component of his life, unconcerned.

"Plenty," I said. "The Clubhouse is on it. Has been for a while."

"The Clubhouse," Marcus said, shaking his head.

"Yeah. And someone in the Company. An inside source."

Another headshake. "We take care of our own business," Marcus said, ending the Company train of discussion.

Miles rolled past. Jake, tired, stretched across the back seat, head on Catch's lap. Still alert, ready for more. We rolled the windows halfway, the air more brisk, our heated bodies cooling off. I poured us coffee from the stainless-steel thermos, half-full cups so the road dips and washboards wouldn't cause the liquid to spill.

"My money's on a Yemeni sheik," Catch said. "We were more than a little effective over there. Plus, they've got the dinero."

"Bo offered to go back over there. Fix the issue. Travel incognito."

"Right. Incognito. He would've blended right in," Marcus said.

We laughed, remembered, swapped Bo stories, and rolled through miles of grassland.

"Well, we know why he volunteered. Of all of us, he's the one who'd charge hell with a bucket of ice water," I said, and we nodded, fell silent.

We stopped as the road terminated at Marcus's ranch entrance, and I opened the gate. Jake bolted up, ready for round two. We drove a mile and parked, donned the game bags, loaded the shotguns. Catch again carried his sniper rifle and followed. More walking, striding, content to focus on the undulating terrain and Jake's intensity. He found another covey of sharp-tails, we each added another bird to the day's harvest, and time flowed, eased past.

"Two vehicles. North." The words crackled over the radio. Marcus and I, fifty yards apart, locked eyes and joined at the lip of a deep coulee.

Scanning north, I caught a brief flash of a mirrorlike reflection. Two vehicles, a mile and a half away. Headed down the road. The road terminating at Marcus's ranch gate.

I alerted Marcus. He shook his head, called Jake over. We sat below the rim of the coulee. Marcus retrieved an apple and slices of cheese, cut the fruit into pieces, and offered me a combination. I shook him off and fished small binoculars from the three-pocket game bag. I eased on my belly to the top of the draw and sighted the vehicles. Marcus remained below me, flat on his back, rubbing Jake's chin beard.

The SUVs stopped, a half mile distant. I increased the magnification of the binoculars.

"They stopped."

"Probably lost."

Four men got out of the trailing vehicle and stretched. One of them stood to the side and peed. Hunters, maybe, checking the terrain. No weapons were visible.

"Four guys, back vehicle," I said. "In camo."

"Hunters." The rasp of him scratching the wiry coat of Jake followed.

The passenger-side door of the leading vehicle opened, and a fifth man exited, followed by a sixth from the back seat.

"Two more from the lead vehicle."

The number had grown too large, too strange for Marcus. He commanded Jake, "Down" and paid attention, waited for more input. The six men milled about, checked the lay of the land. The driver's door opened.

I hadn't seen or heard from him in years. Angel, big as day. Buzz-cut hair, stance indomitable. He hadn't changed.

"And one William Tecumseh Pickett. Angel."

Marcus didn't comment. Instead, he extended his hand, demanded access to the binoculars. I complied.

"You two seeing what I'm seeing?" Catch asked over the radio.

"Roger that."

Marcus eyeballed the scene through the high magnification. "Son. Of. A. Bitch," he said, low and without inflection. "Son of a bitch."

Chapter 34

"Let's move!"

Marcus barked the order as he rolled from the lip of the coulee and took off at a dead run toward his vehicle, Jake at his heels. After one final glance through the binoculars, I caught up with him. Three minutes later at the Suburban, Marcus shoved Jake into the vehicle's little-used dog crate. Marcus's breath came steady, and his demeanor was grim, intent.

Angel. The sight of him flooded my memory banks, and his association with bounty hunters ratcheted up the question needle. But it didn't lower the anger, the sense of betrayal. My mental shield partway lowered—time to kill or be killed.

Fighting against a brother warrior should have brought consideration of tactical elements, not personal feelings. Know the enemy, and Angel was as dangerous as they came. But my personal thoughts and remembrances intruded.

The six other men—Chechens. Had to be. Tough fighters and hired killers. Jules's Chechens, and Angel.

Classic Russian mind-set. I'd screwed up their carefully planned Suriname ops. Russians don't carry a grudge; they act on it. The Chechens—easy dots to connect. The reward money. Bo, Marcus, me. Three million bucks. Catch would be $1 million bonus if killed. Angel's connection remained a mystery, an unknown, and intruded on my focus.

We stripped off the game bags and grabbed the Colt 901 rifles and HK45 pistols. Battle time.

"Catch, we'll park at the house. Bait. Work the coulee east of the house," Marcus said into the radio.

"Got your backs."

Catch would move farther east, behind us, and cover our flanks. He made no commentary on the enemy, on Angel. As far as Catch was concerned, Angel was a dead man walking.

Marcus stomped the accelerator. We tore across the grassland and joined the ranch road. We hit a small washboard stretch of the gravel road, rattled the vehicle. The noise would carry to the seven invaders.

"Angel," I said, letting it hang.

"Screw the whole 'find answers' noise," Marcus said. He'd glommed on to my train of thought while he focused on the battle plan. "They're not here for tea. Flip the switch, son."

He had. The Delta team leader persona had taken over Marcus, the mission clear. The enemy had arrived. Eliminate them in the most efficient manner possible.

"I'm working on it." We exchanged quick, hard stares.

He slammed the brakes, stopped inside the large attached garage, the bay doors open. The enclosure had two other regular doors: one to the house's kitchen and the other to the outdoors and barn area.

"We'll leave Jake in the crate. Move!" Like a shot, we were out the back door of the garage and kept the structure between us and the attackers' probable approach. Thirty yards behind the house stood a large barn, home for his tractors, a bulldozer, and assorted ranch implements. We ran behind it, slid down a small steep coulee that ran parallel with these buildings, north to south. Our highway.

A hundred yards later, we stopped and peeked over the edge of the ravine. Ranch house and barn on our left, the winding ranch road dead ahead—visible for half a mile before it disappeared into the rolling hills of Marcus's property.

"They'll stop when they come over the rise and see the ranch house. They'll spot the parked Suburban. Plan their attack."

I couldn't argue. We both chambered a round into the Colts. I flicked my scope to 4X magnification.

"In place," Marcus whispered over the radio.

"Got you." Catch, somewhere behind us. We waited, hidden, and watched.

Their black SUVs crept over the distant rise, stopped, backed out of sight. The dark storm line filled half the sky, roiling, ugly. The breeze had turned into gusts of wind.

"He's on the wrong side of this thing. There's a price to pay." Marcus addressed my thought process, my doubts, before the action started. He knew me as well as anyone on the planet.

"I know. But shit, Marcus. Angel?"

He stopped scoping the distant area with his rifle sight, peeking through the prairie grass at the top of the coulee, and turned toward me.

"I have to know you're on board. With the mission. Now."

We locked eyes. A man I'd fought alongside in over twenty foreign countries, odds stacked against us, bullets flying. The Delta Force team leader, unfailing, resolute, hard beyond measure when the situation called for it. He had a right to know if I was fully committed.

He addressed the Angel issue one last time. "He's no longer Angel. He's the enemy. Either we kill them, or they kill us. Black and white." His voice carried no animosity or hatred or gung-ho.

The internal warrior, vacillating, emerged from the shadows. Doubt washed away. The bloody scene in the Dismal flashed.

The switch flicked on.

I nodded back. "I'm there. Let's do this."

Satisfied, he scoped the far rise. Movement, quick and low, against the grass-covered hills. Six men, then seven, emerged from near where the road disappeared. Armed with combat weapons. The first four circled our direction, kept their profile hidden except for brief spurts, making their way toward the ranch house. The other three circled away from us, toward the other side of the house.

"Angel left," Marcus said. His voice-activated mike on the earbud carried low affirmation and a time lag. In the gathering darkness, I could see his lips move across the dozen yards separating us. His voice came a half beat after.

"Got it." Angel's distance was over four hundred yards, closing on the house. His typical flanking maneuver, seen so many times before and used with remarkable effectiveness. The two Chechens followed.

The other four continued our way, spread fifty yards apart. One of them split off, circled farther north, away from the others. Their backdoor man. Their Catch.

The remaining three were three hundred yards away. They moved, stopped, assessed the ranch house—moved again. The wind picked up, and twilight approached. The witching hour.

"I'll take these three. Case, Angel and his two. Catch, TOO." Targets of Opportunity.

"On it." Catch's voice came quiet, deadly.

"Roger that," I said. It was the right call. My position afforded a better shot at Angel's group. Four hundred yards pushed it, given the unfamiliar weapon and the gusting wind, but I'd make it a torso shot—

and wouldn't miss. Seconds passed; Marcus controlled the battle plan. Spits of snow joined the wind as daylight faded.

Angel dropped from sight, into what must have been a small coulee on the far side of the ranch house. He'd use it and stay hidden. Continue his movement toward the structures. His two Chechens followed suit. "He's burrowed. No target."

Marcus acknowledged the fluid reality. "Take my group. First on the left. At my shot."

I shifted aim and acquired the farthest left of the other three men approaching, now over two hundred yards away. I locked the crosshairs on an attacker's chest, the distance close enough for an instant kill.

My target paused, knelt, and hand-signaled his partners. They also took a knee. The three stopped moving, paused. Big mistake.

Marcus's weapon boomed, and mine followed. The recoil moved the riflescope crosshairs off the chest target but stayed with the larger picture. The body collapsed, a fine red mist suspended where the bullet hit before a gust blew it away. One of the three remained. Marcus, as expected, hit what he'd aimed for. The third man threw himself flat, hidden. The prairie grass waved, obscured, and neither of us could identify his hiding spot. The tactic didn't save him. A crack, explosive, sounded behind us. Catch. A brief flailing in the grass where the third had hidden. Catch had the elevation advantage and could spot into the blowing grass stems.

I threw my aim toward the last known spot of Angel's. No doubt Marcus did the same. Nothing. I scanned the lip of the distant coulee, followed it toward the ranch house. Still nothing. The wind blew; the dark rolling clouds dimmed the remaining light. The prairie grass leaned, stood, leaned with each gust of wind. Thirty seconds passed. Angel hunted us, and we him.

"They're headed for my house."

"Yeah."

"They'll want to finish this up close and personal. It's their best chance. Eliminate our advantage of terrain."

Bullets ripped across the top of our coulee, kicked dirt. It had its intended affect. Marcus and I both ducked from the covering fire. I popped up, attempted to acquire a target. On our left, Angel and one of the Chechens raced into the open garage door. They'd made their objective. Marcus's house. We'd come after them, close quarters fighting.

Another retort boomed behind us. "All clean, here," Catch reported. The fourth Chechen, attempting a circle maneuver, had met his match.

The third member of Angel's troops, having delivered the covering fire, dashed to join the others in the garage. He didn't make it. Marcus and I both fired. Dead before he hit the ground.

"Two left," Marcus reported. "The house."

"Roger that," Catch replied. He'd reposition, cover the structures. Cover our backs.

We both dashed along the coulee and scrambled up the side behind the large barn. The wind buffeted as we exited the coulee, sleet spitting, the day now dark. Circling to the far side, the thirty yards of open ground between us and the back door of the garage presented the most danger. An interior bedroom window afforded a perfect view of that stretch of ground. I didn't wait for Marcus's decision and hauled ass across the killing zone. Neither Angel nor the Chechen had made the bedroom. Thank God. I covered the window. Marcus sprinted and joined me.

We had no idea if they'd entered the house via the garage entrance. Or if one had entered and one remained in the garage. We stood still, listened. Waited for a telltale noise, the shift of a boot on the concrete floor of the garage, the creak of a house floorboard. Nothing. Still, we waited, sought advantage. Sleet blew against my neck, melted, ran inside of my shirt. Five minutes passed. Wind howled.

Darkness, and Marcus signaled. Circle, position at the open bay doors of the garage. The safe spot. One of us would enter through the standard door before us, enter a garage filled with uncertainty. The other would come around the corner through the garage's bay door, more protected.

A headshake, a gesture in his direction, instructing him. You circle. I'll take the danger door. Eyes locked, he'd broach no argument. Mexican standoff. Neither of us giving. He bent at the waist, mouthed a fiery, "Go!" Marcus, the leader. A disappointed headshake, a pissed look tossed his way. I went.

I turned the corner, movement slow to negate the crunch of sleet covering the ground. The long side wall of the garage afforded a view of the circular gravel drive. The Chechen who'd delivered the covering fire lay sprawled on the gravel, blood pooled.

Paused at the corner, ready, finger pressure on my rifle's trigger. Waited for the first of a three-step process. Marcus would fling open his door, stand aside, avoid immediate fire. Wait a half second. At the sound of the door, I'd step into the garage, eliminate threats. Eliminate threats while he charged through, head-on. I held his life in my hands.

The door flung open, hit a doorstop. I entered the garage, sought targets. Nothing. Marcus flew through the opening, sought as well. They'd moved into the house. Waited for us.

Silent, both rifles placed against a garage wall and pistols pulled. Tight environment combat. We eased our way toward the door leading to the interior kitchen. Listened for movement inside the house over the buffeting wind against the garage. The thin wooden door separated us from our adversaries, a chasm wide and deep. The Chechen bounty hunter and our blood brother. A brother gone bad.

Chapter 35

We stood on either side of the door to the kitchen, pistols at the ready. Sleet blew sideways across the door opening Marcus had come through. Full-on Delta mentality. Zoned. People would die in the next few minutes. My job—our job—was to make sure it wasn't us.

Marcus hand-signaled "slow open." I nodded back.

We had two choices. Burst in, guns blazing, unsure if the targets were visible. Or silently open the door, enter, assess, hunt. Marcus wanted the latter. Angel would reside at the periphery, guarding the flank. With this enclosed environment, he'd cover ingress and egress points. Protect the flanks, protect his team. A team consisting of him and the lone remaining Chechen. He'd cover the kitchen door at intervals, but the house was large. He'd move, drift, cover threats.

The Chechen, an unknown. A stone-cold killer, for sure, but tactical skills unclear. He'd killed up close, direct. I had little doubt. The question of the moment was how he would handle an enclosed-space firefight. We'd soon find out.

I turned the handle, stopped. No squeaks, no noise. Crouched, left hand overhead on the handle. I pushed it open sufficient for an inside view.

The Chechen stood at the intersection of the kitchen and great room, assault rifle shouldered. Pressed against a knotty pine support pillar. A quick glance at Marcus and a tight motion of my head toward the door indicated I had a target. I was going in. Marcus's job, one I knew he'd fulfill with absolute professionalism—follow me by a hair's breadth. Take out anything other than my prime target. I relied on him to kill Angel.

Coiled, I pushed the handle, eased the door open sufficient for a shot. The blast of wood splinters in my face sent me backward, pulling the door shut again. The crashing boom of a handgun filled the air.

Angel. Patrolling the flanks of their stand, he must have entered the great room and seen the slight movement of the door, fired offhand, protected his teammate. His forced snap shot saved my life. Angel wouldn't miss given a half second to aim.

Two more shots rang, cacophonous, and jagged small holes appeared through the wooden door. The Chechen. He'd followed Angel with two shots of his own.

I scrambled to my feet and assumed a position near the doorjamb. Marcus pressed against the other side, lifted his chin toward me. I felt my left cheek, removed two large wood shards embedded there, and nodded the "okay" back.

We thought as one. Angel would press the attack. Not a full frontal assault. He'd probe, hunt our flanks. The open garage bay door facing the front of the property. Or the back side of the house and garage.

"Case! We need to talk!"

Screw that noise. He needed killing. But Marcus nodded. Reply. Let him talk, expose his position. Occupy him while Marcus hunted.

"No, we don't, Angel. Got nothing to say to you."

"You have to know a few things. About Bo. About you."

Marcus, crouched low, eased toward the small open door leading outside.

"Don't need to know shit. Except you killed him."

"I was there to recruit him."

Angel's voice carried empty, disconnected. Wrong. He'd changed for the worse.

"Helluva recruiting strategy, asshole."

"Big Suriname assault coming. Nika sent me. Sent me to see if he'd join. Join the cause."

I remained silent. Too crazy, too messed up.

"Things went sideways quick. You know Bo. Didn't want it going down like that," he said.

"And you needed muscle to recruit him?" Crazy. He'd gone crazy.

"A fallback. I admit it. The bounty makes finding these guys easy."

Marcus peeked around the edge of the open door, worked his way outside, disappeared.

"Then why are you here? Other than being batshit crazy."

"She wants revenge."

Nika. No doubt. *Twilight Zone* stuff, Angel performing hits for a Russian spy.

"You must want to die bad. Speaking of which, shoot the Chechen, then yourself. Save us the trouble."

Three quick shots splintered the door. The Chechen understood English. Too bad for him. Marcus had made his way to a window, sought a target as the Chechen fired at me, at the door.

A single pistol pop, wind and snow muffled. A body crumpled inside; the assault rifle clattered to the ground.

"Give it up, Angel. It's over," I called. Silence.

Gusts blew weather into the garage. Snowflakes lifted, danced. Marcus's location outside—unknown. Angel, cornered. Dangerous as a cobra, prepared to strike. I called again.

"Angel. Listen to me."

Silence. Then, soft and close. "I'm listening."

I was a dead man. The low voice, behind me, at the garage bay door. He'd done his thing. Flanked me. His pistol aimed, steady. The snow swirled around him, profile visible in the night. A laser sight, held steady, created a small dot on my chest. Any movement and he'd fire. Kill me.

"She's not what you think," I said. Grasped straws, no idea where to go except Nika. Modulated my voice, calm, reassuring.

"I love her," he said. Simple statement, definitive, crazy.

"Okay." A bullet would drive into my chest any second. A roll toward the front of the parked Suburban also guaranteed a bullet, but maybe not one to the heart. A torso wound, a chance it wouldn't be fatal.

"She loves me. Said so."

Whatever Marcus's position, it was on the wrong side of the house. I was screwed.

"You had happiness, Case," he continued. "You loved. You understand."

Crazy as hell, slipped off the rails, a madman. A madman with a trigger finger squeezing my life away.

"I do understand." Couldn't lock eyes, too dark, but I stared at his night-obscured face. White snowflakes pelted his side and stuck. "It's a strange world. I get that."

Drag it out. Give Marcus a chance to find him, take action.

"No. Not strange. Pure. Pure love," he said, voice subdued, drifting.

My legs cramped, frozen in position. I'd have to dive, roll, soon. I kept my voice low, nonconfrontational.

"You're a lucky man, Angel."

Half his head blew away. An echoing boom followed. Catch. Somewhere in the night, hundreds of yards away. Howling winds, drifting snow. Used his night-vision scope. Catch. Thank God.

I stood, shaken. Called Marcus. His footsteps carried across the wooden floor of his house. He'd hunted inside. The splintered kitchen door opened. He joined me.

We stood shoulder to shoulder. Angel's body lay with the gathered snow, a dark outline against the white.

Our earbuds crackled, followed by, "It's over?"

"Yeah, Catch," Marcus replied. "Yeah. It's over. Come in."

We remained, absorbed, our former brother's body at our feet. Memories, questions, sadness. An act performed, required. Still, room for sadness.

Footfalls crunched; Catch appeared and stood at Angel's head. His beard showed white, the snow collected, rifle slung over a shoulder.

"Let's bury him," Catch said. "Over and done."

He stood as a force, a sentinel, oblivious to the weather.

"Over and done," I said. But it wasn't. The memories, the pain, and confusion would remain. As would the bounty.

"Heard your half on the radio," Catch said. "He'd gone over. Nuts. Let's bury him and be done with it."

Jake whined from his dog crate inside the Suburban.

"You're right," Marcus said. "Move on."

But none of us did. We stood, circled Angel's body. Stood in silence and wondered. At least one of us prayed.

Chapter 36

"Let's clean it up."

Over. Over and no transition or review or regrets. Marcus remained mission-focused.

Inside, he produced a gallon of bleach, a bundle of rags, and several plastic garbage bags. We wrapped the Chechen body, carried him out the front door, tossed him in the snow. Marcus shoved a rag through the window where he'd made the Chechen-killing shot.

"I'll clean. Clorox inside. You two collect the SUVs and bodies," he said.

Catch and I took flashlights and hiked to the parked SUVs. Keys were left inside both. The wind had died, snow fell, the storm front passed. Catch and I drove across the prairie and collected bodies by headlight. We spent fifteen minutes searching for the Chechen that had looped to the outside, their version of Catch.

"The son of a bitch had sighted on me," Catch said, the body shoved in the back. "He was good. I squeezed the trigger first."

"Okay."

Killing, death, empty land. Surreal and cold. So damn cold. I followed his vehicle to the west side of the ranch house and helped him toss another bounty hunter inside. Then the hitter on the snow-covered front drive—Marcus's house kill. Six. Six splayed, bloody, lifeless bodies.

The seventh remained outside the garage bay door. "I'll get him. You go inside. Help Marcus," Catch said. He moved toward our former brother.

"No. No, I'll get Angel."

He paused, understood, patted my chest as he passed and entered the front door. I approached my dead former teammate. Dragging him over the fresh sleet and snow was the easiest route. Or toss him over a shoulder, a fireman's carry. Instead, I cradled him in my arms, lifted, walked a dirge back to the SUV.

You stupid SOB. What the hell got into you? A bit of merc work, train the Suriname rebels. Okay, I could get that, sort of. Something to do. Utilize your skills. Okay. But this other crap? You stupid SOB.

Love? Money? You killed Bo, went after us because of love? Love? No freaking way. Utter madness. But the words of Jules loomed large. *People change.*

No tears. Loss and betrayal. Frustration at never knowing the answers. Senseless death. Balled up, an enigma, wrapped with pain. Culminating when I dumped him on top of the Chechens.

The slam of the car door ended it. There, it's over. I hope you knew I loved you, you dumb bastard.

We wiped, cleaned, scrubbed in silence—filled the house with the smell of bleach, deposited rags into another plastic bag. A throw rug joined the rags. Finished, the cleanup debris was tossed into one of the SUVs. Not a word exchanged since I'd carried Angel.

"Let's get warm clothes," Marcus said, turning to inspect the final product. Jake, relegated to his corner dog bed, shook his head and sneezed at the Clorox. "This will take a little while."

We donned winter wear, left the doors open, aired the place. Marcus put Jake in a bedroom and stomped toward the barn. We followed. He propped open both barn doors, flicked the light, grabbed a half-full grain sack. Climbed on his D-7 Caterpillar bulldozer. A common piece of equipment on large ranches for building roads and general dirt moving. It took it a while to fire, the engine cold. Then it roared to life and belched exhaust.

"Follow me," he called and backed the dozer out of the barn.

We did a sedate six miles an hour, drove the SUVs in the dozer's wake, my vehicle last. I'd rolled the windows down, the bleach rags too strong. Over the loud rumble of the forward dozer, music, full volume. Catch had lowered his windows, too, and serenaded us with classical music. No one for miles, pitch-black, a light snow, and a bulldozer leading the way—a weird, memorable funeral procession. Fifteen minutes later, at the base of a steep rise, we stopped.

"This will take a little while," Marcus said. "Keep the headlights on. Helps me see."

And so he began moving dirt and dug a massive grave to contain the SUVs and their contents. White stuff collected on the windshield as I stood alongside the vehicles, refusing to share space with the occupants. Catch wandered over, offered a beer from the six-pack he'd grabbed before we left for this little expedition.

"One for the books," I said, and took a swig.

"A decisive day. Progress."

"Progress?"

"Seven less after my head."

Marcus demonstrated expertise with the dozer, moved earth. He crafted a steep ramp at one end of the grave, now twelve feet deep. One tiny speck on the universe's tiny speck called Earth, occupied by three people burying any remnant of extreme violence, death, mayhem.

Thirty minutes later I followed Catch's SUV and drove down the dirt ramp to its final resting place. Before we had climbed from the hole, Marcus began filling it. The roar of the Caterpillar diesel engine filled the air. It was soon finished, smoothed over, done, and Marcus climbed down with the grain sack.

Together, we scattered pasture grass seed over the area. Sowed disguise, finality. I rode back on the dozer, standing alongside Marcus. Catch walked, humming a tune.

"Any concern over the scar that leaves on the land?" I asked.

"None. Snow-covered all winter. Springtime will sprout the grass seed. No trace of digging."

The bleach smell had dissipated, the doors and windows were closed, and a massive fire started in the fireplace. Jake ran from one to the next of us, brought us toys, was assured, and glued himself to Marcus's leg. Vigorous scratches and soothing words were applied, and Jake calmed down. Marcus stretched duct tape over the kitchen door bullet holes. It was over. Over and done. We poured stiff drinks and settled in. Marcus lit a series of lavender candles. They masked the remnant odors of bleach.

"I'm worried about you, Marcus," Catch said, watching his former team leader place the scented candles.

"I like lavender."

"When you breaking out the patchouli?"

"Shut up. I'll run to Billings and get a new door tomorrow. There's a spare windowpane somewhere in the barn," Marcus said, settling, feet on an ottoman near the fireplace.

"Just like that," I said.

"Don't start that shit," Marcus said.

I took a long sip of Grey Goose and propped open my laptop. It was over. I owed her the information.

"For someone constantly harping about getting away from your line of work, you sure do keep contact with that world," he said, certain whom I was communicating with.

Deep web accessed, I paused, uncertain what to convey to Jules. Even this hidden, deep in the bowels of hidden web traffic, it was important to remain obtuse. The fireplace logs popped, Jake curled on his dog bed near the fire, and I constructed the message.

It's over. All the Chechens and wandering son.

Cryptic enough, and Jules would understand. I hit "Send," set the laptop on the floor, and stood to make another drink. Marcus and Catch's glasses showed dregs, so I picked them up as well. Over my shoulder, mixing drinks, I started the conversation again.

"You think he really did it for love? Love for the Russian?"

"I told you not to start that shit."

Snow drifted against the great-room windows, falling heavy again. Jake groaned, shifted on his dog bed. He'd hunted hard and had then been traumatized by the firefight. I set the Scotch and soda on Marcus's side table, handed Catch his bourbon and water. Plopped in my stuffed chair, I continued.

"Well, I am going to start that shit because you and Catch and Mom and CC are all I have left in this world. It's a big damn deal when I lose someone."

"You didn't lose him. He lost himself," Marcus said.

"And why?"

He took a long sip, stared at the fire.

"Could have been love. Or money. People change."

"You sound like Jules."

"I never sound like Jules because I don't have a damn thing to do with her world. That's your hairball, son."

"Sex?" I asked.

"I doubt he was lacking," Catch said. "Wherever the hell he was living in South America."

"Sense of team? Of mission?"

"She'd have been good at pushing that line. Your Russian," Marcus said.

"Nika."

"You got a sports channel on your TV?" Catch asked. "Or strictly home-improvement TV. Maybe the Martha Stewart channel."

"You're an ass pain," Marcus said, tossing him the remote.

"I'm not the one lighting lavender candles." Catch fiddled with the device and found ESPN.

Over and done and now let's fix a few bullet holes and move on. I never understood how they did it, other than heavy compartmentalizing. The laptop beeped an incoming message. Deep web. Jules. A surprise—I didn't expect to hear back from her until tomorrow, if at all.

It's never over, dear. Glad you are well.

Chapter 37

Six inches of new snow covered the ground. Morning light reflected crystalline sparkles. Bright and fresh and masking carnage. I acknowledged the surface beauty, a hidden hell felt. A surreal greeting to the day.

Marcus left for Billings, Catch for Portland. I made a commitment. Clean the birds from yesterday, cook dinner. The grouse and Huns had stayed plenty cold since we'd bagged them.

Catch and Marcus shook hands, half hugged, and traded a few final barbs. I followed Catch outside and said goodbye.

"Let's not wait so long," I said. "I do miss you. And no commentary on the sentiment."

"Hell, I miss you, too. Come to Portland."

"Rains a lot."

"And the rainy season has started. We can hole up. Drink heavily."

"Grow mold."

"Grow beards," he said.

"Be careful, my friend."

"Be happy, my brother. Give it a shot. It's time."

The hug lasted long, his hand pat on my cheek heartfelt. I missed him before he took off, tires spitting snow, another war cry blistering the serene landscape. Juan Antonio Diego Hernandez. Blood brother.

Marcus ambled out wearing a Stetson, ranch coat, and Tony Lamas. Mr. Rancher.

"I should see him more often," he said and lifted a chin at Catch's vehicle, now sideways in a controlled drift, disappearing over the hill. "Hope to hell he stops to open the gate."

We chuckled and shook our heads.

"You know what you're doing in the kitchen?" he asked.

"Trust me."

"Always have."

Before he climbed into the vehicle, he mentioned an Irene Collins visit. To taste my fare. Irene Collins, new neighbor, Californian, scientist of some sort.

"Not necessary." Ambivalence on my part, a desire for emotional stability before social interaction. Besides, the whole matchmaker thing bugged me.

"I might like dinner conversation other than yours, moron," he said.

"Invite Miriam." With Irene coming over, I wanted Marcus's lady friend around. Another conversational contact, Miriam could offset the Irene focus.

"Already did."

He left. We never mentioned yesterday's events. Compartmentalized. Locked away. Man, I wished I could do the same.

I skinned the birds and cut meat from bone. Jake focused on the procedure, wiry eyebrows matching my movements. A large old cast-iron pot was the lone required stovetop tool.

Love? Angel had never talked of relationships. He'd always been stoic. Spartan.

A mixture of olive oil and butter, sauté the meat. Vegetables chopped. Bell pepper, celery, parsley, garlic.

Nika could have manipulated him without too much effort. She damn near did me.

A large jalapeño seeded and diced, tossed in the mixing bowl of collected ingredients.

But to kill a teammate, a brother? Something wrong, wiring messed up. I had to hang my hat, and angst, on bad wiring.

I chopped onions and tossed them in the bowl.

Angel had gone off the rails. Simple as that. Still, still—I wanted definitive answers and struggled to accept it wasn't going to happen. Move on, Case. You'll drive yourself nuts.

While the meat cooked, I placed a call. Mom answered after the second ring.

"Hey, Lola Wilson."

"Hallelujah on my end. Are you okay?"

"Fine. You can head back to Charleston."

A pause while she digested the meaning. An event, a threat, now over. She dealt with it in her own way, never pried.

"All right. You sure?" Her voice, calm and strong.

"Sure as I can get."

"CC is upset with Grandma's dogs. They haven't given Tinker Juarez the love and respect he deserves."

"I imagine." Grandma Wilson's hounds—rambunctious farm dogs—would have been less than accepting toward a new member of the pack.

"When do we see you?"

"Within the week."

"Good. Good, and I want you staying for a while. Meet the young lady I told you about."

"Tell CC I'm taking her for a trip. On the *Ace*. With Tinker Juarez."

"She'll love that."

"Me too. And you should take a break. Go connect with one of your gentlemen callers."

"Hush."

We signed off, love and affection palpable over the phone. An anchor, Mom lifted my spirits with normalcy, human relationships, family. The conversation mapped to the clean snow outside the kitchen window and conveyed a new start. Cover the past and move on.

Bird meat removed from the oil, fire lowered, I started a roux. The end goal, game-bird sauce piquante—a spiced-up version of gumbo. Flour added to the oil, a flat-edged wooden spoon stirred and scraped. After ten minutes, the flour edged light-brown, darkened. A critical roux moment between done and burned.

Time for proof that alchemy works. At the proper moment, before the roux seared, the chopped vegetables were dumped in, stirred. They melted, congealed, cooked—a thick brew of magic, transformed. A better smell could not be found. I added chicken stock, tomato sauce, a splash of wine, sautéed bird, and sliced Polish sausage for added fat and flavor. Sauce piquante, à la Case Lee. It would simmer all day, then serve over rice.

Jake and I took a walk, and the sight of last night's burial passed indistinguishable under the snow. Marcus had done an excellent job, scars smoothed. The high prairie protected its secrets without a trace.

I helped with the new door and the windowpane replacement. Smooth, working as a team, Marcus and I finished repairing the event's remnants. The simmering stew filled the house with comfort smells and overcame any lingering bleach odors. Loose ends—tied, snipped, buried.

"Early dinner, then over to the Solid for drinks and dance."

"Dance."

"Local band. They're good."

"We're going drinking and dancing?" I asked.

"You going to live in the moment? Or wallow?"

I chose the moment. It would be great seeing Miriam again. A Montana lady, she took things at face value, never pried or fished for rumor. Plus Irene Collins, fresh from California and a bad relationship. Time for focus, maintain mindfulness. And not be a jerk with the guest Marcus had invited for dinner.

She arrived in her new pickup as Marcus fired the porch fire pit. Irene was nothing short of impressive as she sauntered up, her jet-black hair in a ponytail. Not a classic beauty but arresting, different. She wore jeans, a flannel shirt, and a Carhartt fleece-lined jacket. She'd gone local.

Marcus did the introductions, she asked for a glass of red wine, and I fetched while she stood on the porch. A glance before entering the ranch house showed her warming her hands over the pit fire, a smile wide and wry. A chesty laugh at something Marcus said.

I poured wine and a Grey Goose, told myself to take it easy on the booze. Marcus moved a few logs around, then added more.

"Were you guys shooting last night?" she asked. "Thought I heard gunfire through the wind."

Well, the deal is, Irene, there *was* a little gunfire last night. Had to blow away six hired killers. Plus an old comrade. Shot them dead. Dug a hole, dropped them in. Came back and had a drink.

"We tried out a couple of new guns," Marcus said.

"At night?"

"Welcome to Montana."

They both laughed; I forced a smile. Marcus headed inside to set the table. Irene and I stood around the fire pit and chatted.

"What happened to your face?" she asked.

The kitchen door's wooden splinters had left wounds, now cleaned and—I had thought—only minor telltale signs.

"Fell down bird hunting. Steep coulee."

She bought it and moved on.

"Marcus tells me you travel a lot," she said. "Sounds mysterious." Her one-corner smile had an element of teasing.

"Independent investigator. Clients hire me to find answers, report back. Mundane stuff."

"Well, it still sounds sort of James Bondish. Independent investigator. Find answers. Man of danger and shadow." She laughed good-naturedly.

Enough about me, and a few spikes appeared along the top of my personal wall barrier. I didn't talk about my current career. Jake exited the dog door, wandered over, and sought recognition. I scratched his bushy eyebrows.

"James Bond without the tux, excitement, or glamour. So, you're a scientist?"

She sipped wine and shrugged—an indication she found her own activities mundane.

"Biological chemistry." She explained the PhD from UCLA that focused on the study of chemical processes related to living organisms. She worked for an LA pharmaceutical company who allowed her to do her research remotely. A great gig, which must have paid well. It let her dive in the netherworlds of arcane research, living wherever she wanted.

"So you're a SoCal girl?" I asked.

"Bakersfield. Working-class girl. You?"

"Coast of Georgia. Working-class guy."

"I thought I heard a slight lilt. A Southern gentleman."

"Southern, sure. Gentleman—well, I try."

A couple of more dives into her work life hit surface ice each time. She wasn't interested in discussing her research—either for professional and nondisclosure reasons or because she'd learned it led to boring conversation. A change of topic, and I peeked over her personal barriers. A few hackles displayed.

"I understand you've taken over your grandad's place. Big move. LA for the Wild West."

"Marcus must have informed you of my recent breakup. You're assuming it drove me to make the move."

"Wasn't prying."

"I've been married, divorced, and thought this last guy different. He wasn't."

Her look and physical stance projected feisty rather than bitter. Challenging instead of remorseful. I didn't recall asking for details.

"Still. Big change. And you'll experience the dubious pleasures of a Montana winter shortly." I said it with a smile. Weather as neutral ground.

"I'm looking forward to it. The isolation doesn't bother me."

Dusk moved into night. Marcus hit the porch lights, went back, and started another fire in the large great-room fireplace.

Headlights, a rattle from a road rut. Miriam's pickup rolled up and squeaked to a stop. She slid out; a cow dog followed.

"Behave, Dity. Is that you, Case? By God, you're getting more handsome by the month."

We hugged and swapped brief tales. Jake bounded from the dog door and confronted Dity. They'd met before.

"Dity, I mean it," Miriam said, her full-force intent sufficient to curb the cow dog's aggressive nature. "Irene, don't you look good. Has Marcus been telling you more lies about ranching?"

"A few." We laughed; Jake and Dity cut inside to seek handouts. Miriam soon followed. "If he's setting the table, we're liable to end up with a combination of chopsticks and ladles."

It was good seeing her again, honest and salty and sincere. The real deal.

Irene and I huddled over the fire pit. Serious cold had arrived.

"So what's your social situation?" she asked. No buildup, no circling. A quid pro quo. She'd revealed enough. My turn.

"A mom and kid sister. No partner."

"Marcus said something about you living on the East Coast."

"Live on a boat. Ply the Intracoastal Waterway between Virginia and Florida. Alone."

She digested the information. There were a lot of ways to look at my situation, one of which was loner nutcase. I added, "I'll settle at some point."

"Are you gay?" she asked.

"I need to learn to ask that."

"What?"

"Nope. Not gay. Single."

She sipped and assessed me over the wineglass rim.

"You have the rugged good looks thing working. So what's the issue?"

"No issue." I brushed the truth as this had gone deep way too fast. "I'm widowed." It was tossed on the table as a sign of previous stability, normalcy. And because it meant something. Meant something to me, a verbal acknowledgement of fierce love.

"Sorry."

"It was a while ago."

She took a deep draft of wine, and commentary commenced as she stared into the outdoor fire. Logs popped, crackled. Coyotes yipped from a nearby gully. Rocky shoals appeared on the conversational front.

"I'm not heading into the 'You're clearly running from something' routine. But it isn't a lifestyle that indicates emotional maturity, widowed or not. Just saying."

Yeah, just saying. And drawing conclusions without knowing a damn thing about me. The real me. It irritated.

"A person might want to know the larger picture before slapping labels," I said.

She looked up from the fire, a look of observation, clinical, clear in the firelight. Jake had returned and leaned against me. Dity sat away, sought no affection. I scratched Jake's beard, and he drifted into dog heaven.

"So off you go on mysterious jobs in mysterious places under the direction of mysterious clients," she said. "Then return and wander up and down the East Coast. On a boat. Alone."

Well, it's the whole deal about the $1 million bounty for my head, Irene. A moving target is harder to hit.

"It's not a bad life."

"No girlfriend."

"Didn't realize it was a black mark on my character."

"*Black mark* is a bit harsh. But I can only circle back to the emotional-maturity facet. Just an observation."

You should have observed me last night, Irene, and drawn a few clinical conclusions from that little event.

Marcus's appearance halted our conversation.

"Gorgeous night. Might get a dusting of snow," he said. "Come eat."

Seldom do my social interactions go off the rails with such rapidity. Irene was bright as hell, with striking looks and an initially pleasant demeanor. Then the clinical assessments. Maybe an affectation from her job. Clinical. Or maybe an in-your-face personal assessment delivered from past burned relationships. Either way, it grated.

I followed Irene and Marcus, halted, stared northeast. Out there, buried, forgotten. Cold, cold ground.

Marcus held the door for Irene and waited. When I started toward him, we locked eyes and stayed locked as I passed. I stopped when his hand pressed my chest.

"Push it behind you," he whispered. "Now."

I returned a nod, acknowledgement, resignation. A fire log popped; Miriam called us in.

Cold, cold ground.

Chapter 38

We settled at the great-room table; the fireplace flames threw heat, and we enjoyed the meal. I switched to red wine and stopped reminding myself to take it easy.

Marcus led the conversation and discussed cattle with Irene. Management, pasture rotation, hay procurement, getting through the winter.

"You'll want a good ax. Your grandad probably had one in the barn," Marcus said.

"For firewood?" Irene asked.

"Yes, but also for chopping the ice on the water tanks for the cattle. Even with solar heaters, it'll freeze solid."

"I'll do that. Three water tanks on the place."

"Twice a day. They're tough critters, but there's an element of babysitting you'll have to do during winter."

Irene nodded, without a trace of resentment or irritation at Marcus's instructions. This is how it's done. Plain and simple. She absorbed the information. Clinical. Checked a box. Moved on.

The conversation drifted through Billings grocery trips, new tires, good dogs, movies.

"Did he tell you about the movie we saw?" Miriam asked. "A good one. Real tearjerker. Marcus fell asleep."

"Next time let's drive spikes into my eyeballs for entertainment."

"Every time you pick one, it's a bullets-flying, women-swooning, hero-could-use-a-bath movie."

"Yes, but at least they're in color."

We laughed, teased, talked mundane part-of-life things. Good stuff—real, comforting.

Marcus sent us back outside with two brandies while he and Miriam cleared the table and washed dishes. My old friend played matchmaker, corralled Irene and I together. If it was obvious to me, Miss Clinician would pick up on it as well.

The porch fire pit contained red coals and low flames, so I added three midsize logs. Flames lifted and cast warmth. Irene and I had both put our jackets back on. I'd added a black fleece watch cap.

"Great meal," Irene said. "Good conversation, good company. You're still upset about our discussion earlier."

Irene Collins damn sure went straight to the point. No guesses about what she thought.

"Let's just say we disagree on your assessment. Of me."

She shrugged, took a nose hit from the brandy snifter, and sipped. "I wasn't trying to belittle you. Or be mean."

"Okay."

She flashed a smile, good nature expressed with the delivery. "You're not pouting, are you?"

Man, she could push buttons. Pouting? No. More of a disconnect, a lack of mutual understanding.

"Maybe a little."

She laughed. "This whole woman–man thing has a lot of variables. I'm certainly no expert. But each time is a learning experience. I do try to learn. Absorb. Figure it out."

"Not easy, for sure."

"No. Not easy."

Jake wandered out the dog door, having begged what he could from Marcus. He stood, barked once at the deep night, and strolled over. Dity joined us and parked ten feet away.

"Is what you do dangerous?" she asked and lifted a booted toe to scratch Jake's hindquarter.

"No, not really." My butt wound began to ache. Too much activity the last twenty-four hours. But the stitches held.

"Marcus said you two were soldiers. Army."

Army would have been all he'd said about it. Delta Force, technically, didn't exist. A band of warriors, better trained than any, and the worst-kept secret on the planet. But Marcus wouldn't have gone there. Telling someone—anyone—you were former Delta cast you into the "Dude's a stone-cold killer" category with the general public. We were a helluva lot more than that, but the easy road lay in the more general term *army*. If pressed by a current or former military individual, we'd further elaborate and state *airborne*, the army's elite parachute troops. Much of Delta Force's personnel came from airborne, and it made for good cover.

"True enough. Several years ago."

"Did you kill people?" she asked with a flat voice, a clinical inquiry.

Should have been here last night, Irene. Plenty of killing going down.

"Weird question." Seldom did the question come so fast, so blunt. Most often it was couched in terms like "Did you see action?" or "Were you in any firefights?" Or questions about combat experience. But diving to the heart of the matter, killing, seldom pierced a casual conversation.

"Not so weird," she said.

"You going to finish that?" My brandy had disappeared. She poured hers into my snifter with a sure and easy move.

"Thanks," I continued. "I don't talk about it. Killing. So how many cattle do you have on your place?"

"How'd you kill them? Long rifle shot? Close up?"

Clinical questions. Not a trace of macabre fascination. Information for her relationship data banks.

"Let's park that subject. Why don't you tell me about LA life? Working in the corporate world. Bright lights, big city." A single gulp downed her brandy.

"Traffic. Organizational secrets. Who is developing what. The next cancer treatment. Cures for very specific diseases."

Jake stopped his dream lean and wandered over to an old folded blanket near the dog door, circled twice, and plopped down. Dity joined him.

"Sounds pretty cool. Smart people."

"My ex-husband found it irritating I couldn't talk about what I did at work."

"I can see where that'd be tough."

"Like asking you if you'd killed."

"A bit different."

"The last guy didn't like my long hours," she said. "His excuse for cheating. I was always at work."

The proverbial ten-foot pole appeared, and I shifted subjects. "Well, it's nice you can work remotely and still keep the bosses happy."

"It's a specialized field. Lots of research. Research feeding the lab work."

"Good for you." I meant it.

"There's too much killing in the world. That's why I asked. I don't know what drives it. Psychosis. Culture. Manifestations of what we call evil. I don't know."

Thin ice, but an interesting topic. I shuffled onto the winter lake. "At the detail level, the individual level, there are really nasty people in the world. Evil people. People that should be removed."

"I thought you were regular army. Jumping out of planes."

Damn, she was sharp. Regular military personnel aren't in the "go terminate a couple of select bad guys" business.

"Just thinking out loud."

"Hmm."

She didn't buy it. Back to terra firma. "So what do you do for fun?"

"Read. I like biographies and historical novels. Take long walks. This country is perfect for hiking."

"It is. Be aware of grizzlies." If you hiked the Beartooths or Absarokas, either potent pepper spray or a more potent sidearm was well advised. A lot of folks hiked with a bear bell clanging off their packs as they strode to warn bears away. Not my preference. Too much noise.

"So I've heard. You and Marcus were talking fly-fishing. I may give it a try. It looks very cool."

"Great sport." No elaboration was needed. Either you did it and dove into the endeavor, or you didn't. It could be a frustrating learning curve.

Miriam and Marcus put the dogs inside, and we bundled into Marcus's Suburban, ventured forth to the social center of this four-hundred-square-mile area.

The band played country standards; we danced the two-step. Marcus and I swapped partners every third dance, and the other thirty or so patrons crowded the small dance floor. Each pass of the potbellied stove brought a wave of wood-fired heat, and the touch of Irene felt fine. A good time—laughter, conversation, drinks. Grey Goose flowed.

When the band busted into a reel, the dancers spun, a whirlwind of Levis, boots, and let 'er rip. Irene and I joined, spinning, building momentum.

Eyes closed, an overwhelming desire flooded me. Spin out of here, through the wall, soar. Fly over the grasslands, the mountains. Soar into the atmosphere where sky and light and lightning lived. Spin, release, escape. Snatches of memories. Rae in shorts and halter top, bright, alive, radiant. Spin. Twirl off the bad things, the ugliness. Fly and depart and leave it behind. Wash in joy and happiness. Bring Mom and CC and even Tinker Juarez. Spin and twist my way out of blood and death. Holding hands with Rae, walking on the beach. Fly away from cold, cold bodies. Into the light, the warmth of love past, unbounded. Toward a place where unbridled joy reigned. Depart the great tumbler of life, rolling, changing. Fling, fling myself away from it, float, relax.

And bring back my wife.

Chapter 39

The Raleigh flight departed early afternoon. Marcus and Miriam prepared breakfast. My former team leader challenged me to eat and keep it down. Yeah, a bit of a rough night. But this day, better. Going home.

"So you'll head back," Marcus said. "See your mom and CC."

"That's the plan."

"Cruise on the *Ace*."

"Amen."

"Hide until the next catastrophe."

"You're getting snarky in your old age."

He lit a cigar and inspected the burning tip.

"You remember the invite?"

He meant move to Montana. Live there.

"I appreciate it. You know I do."

"But?"

"But winter's coming. I'm a bit of a wuss in that regard."

"You'd survive. Look who's coming."

He lifted his chin, indicated Irene's pickup rolling toward the ranch house.

"You say goodbye to her. We're leaving soon." He ambled back inside.

She slid from the pickup, smiled.

"I had a great time last night," Irene said. She kept her hands in her coat pockets, the day cold.

"Me too."

"How much do you remember?" Delivered with a laugh.

"Most of it. The important stuff."

"You're an interesting guy, Case."

"Not from my point of view." I was a mess. But last night had had a cathartic affect. Demons were halfway purged. Back on stable ground.

"That's part of what makes you interesting."

"Well, I've enjoyed spending time with you."

She laughed.

"What's funny?"

"You enjoyed time with me."

"Yeah."

"Even though I irritate you to no end."

"Yeah. I suppose. Your style would take getting used to."

"You too."

"No argument there."

A friendly hug, a wry smile, and she climbed into her pickup. I followed her to the truck's door, and she cracked the window.

"Well, I wanted to drop in and say goodbye."

"Glad you did."

"Am I going to see you again anytime soon?"

"It'll be after winter."

"I thought you were a tough guy."

"Not that tough."

"You've got my number. Call anytime."

Miriam's goodbye had more tight hugs and an ass-chewing about the rarity of my visits. I assured her of a return when three layers of clothing weren't required.

The Billings drive with Marcus settled into a comfortable silence. Fresh snow, now melting. The low sun of fall, shadows long. Marcus played country music and hummed.

"So I'm going to talk about the whole deal," I said. "Even though it pisses you off."

He turned up the music. I turned it off.

"I knew it," he said, shaking his head. "Absolutely knew it. You have to mull all this crap over."

"They didn't have a problem finding you, Marcus."

"So?"

"So I want to talk about it."

No response.

"You've got to be careful," I said. "Until we find the funding source. The sponsor."

"I'm careful."

"No, you're not."

"Meaning what?"

"Meaning you hop over to Billings or Livingston without any concern. It doesn't ever register with you."

"I'm armed. Always."

"Yeah, but you'd be armed regardless. Not what I'm talking about."

He smiled and added several backhand whacks to my belly.

"I'll be fine. Chill."

There was no point elaborating or warning or spewing precautions. He'd live as he always did. Open. Himself.

At the airport, I climbed out, and the butt wound said hello. I grabbed my rucksack and leaned across the seat.

"So why don't you come visit me?" I asked. "Warmth. Sunshine."

"I have cattle."

"You have a weird desire to suffer through winter."

"I won't see you till spring?"

"Unless you want to thaw out."

He stared through the windshield, put the Suburban in Drive. "Call me. At least we can talk."

A long handshake across the seat, sad smiles. "Yeah. Yeah, we can at least do that."

Alone at the Billings airport. The drain of departure, leaving friends. Catch would be home in the Portland drizzle, living full-frontal. Marcus humming a country tune, tires whining, the miles eaten as he headed for home.

And home was my final destination for the day. The Raleigh flight landed at midnight. I'd be on the *Ace* at two a.m. I dozed during the flights, slept off the hangover, and dreamed of dead silence, the night calm, cold. Far distant from the bowels of hidden wildness, wolves. First one, then three, then the whole pack. Primitive, unyielding, announcing their presence, their turf, their warning.

Chapter 40

Tinker Juarez stood sentinel, the new figurehead perched at the prow of the *Ace of Spades*. CC joined me in the small wheelhouse and commented on passing attractions.

"Another one!" She pointed, always to ensure I captured the same sight. Hooded mergansers, the males with a hooded crest of puffed-up white. Male and female dove at intervals, hunted fish. We eased through coastal estuaries and along winding rivers, meandered toward Beaufort, South Carolina.

"I see it."

She smiled. I did the same, mutual confirmation of the observed wonder.

"Will we see more dolphins?"

"Probably on the way back."

"But not now?"

"Not now."

She ruminated on that fact.

"But pralines in Beaufort, CC. Pecan pralines. A couple of hours away."

She smiled again. Another upcoming wonder.

It had been four days of pleasant cruising to reach Charleston, Mom, and CC. Past Swansboro and Sneed's Ferry. Wilmington, Bald Head Island, Myrtle Beach. Across the Santee and into Charleston Bay. Cooperative weather, still warm. The *Ace*—as always—plowed ahead. I pulled over at night, tied off on riverbanks. Relaxed, reset the internal gyroscope.

Mom fed me like I'd been denied valid sustenance since our last visit. CC and I took walks. Then off with CC for a week. It was my pleasure and gave Mom a break. Off for Beaufort, taking our time. A two-day trip stretched to three. The Ditch held wonders galore, and we'd pull over every few hours, let Tinker Juarez do his business, and stretch our legs. The snow of Montana far behind and the fall of South Carolina warmed the bones. T-shirt and flip-flop weather. CC and I shared boat routines. Made cheese, fresh tomato, and mayo sandwiches. Absorbed the proximity to each other and the immediate world.

"I miss you, Case."

"I miss you, too, my love."

"Maybe Tinker Juarez misses you."

"You think?"

She laughed at the absurdity of my question. "He doesn't tell me *everything*, Case!"

My laughter washed away the outside world. Here and now, with CC, the salt marshes and moss-draped live oaks, the occasional house alongside the Ditch. The occupants waved, and CC laughed, waved back. It couldn't go on forever, but it would go on for a while. And it was enough, now.

The Stono River to the Wadmalaw River, through bays and estuaries, cruising, laughter and smiles. CC loved fishing, and I'd throw a cast net for minnows, bait her hook as we anchored at a fishy spot. The bright white-and-red bobber held her attention for long spells, and her reaction when a fish struck, pulling the bobber under, was priceless. Excitement, squeals, expansive wonder as she pulled the aquatic creature onto the deck.

They'd be dinner when traveling alone. With CC, each was thrown back. No death, no killing. She'd name each one at departure, ensured a hearty goodbye when Trig or Henry or Maria was tossed for a splash back in the river.

I'd tell her stories at night. Kings and queens and princesses. Giant forests and beds of ferns. Sailing ships and strange lands.

"A good one, Case," she'd say when I finished. The cool of the evening covered us while she nested on the recliner, blanket-wrapped. "Did it really happen?"

"Did it happen in your mind?"

"It did. A good story."

Tinker Juarez had his own deck bed, a pile of old towels. Towels moved next to CC's bed when time for sleep. And she'd ask each morning, before rising, "How is Tinker Juarez?" He'd reply with a tail wag and lick her face. Morning routine, brought from her home and carried onto the *Ace of Spades*.

We made a side trip to Hunting Island, walked the beach, found seashells. Then Shackleford Banks, more beach, more shells, no people, and wild horses. The horses, descendants of Spanish mustangs from early explorers, captivated CC. I kept Tinker Juarez leashed while she wandered into the salt grass, stood still. A few mares wandered off from the herd and approached. Wary, a thirty-yard comfort zone prevailed between human and horse. But the mind's eye capture as CC stood still, mustangs with ears perked checking her—absolute magic. Her hair and the mustangs' manes blew, bay water cast diamonds of light as the *Ace* lay at anchor. When she turned, caught my eye, the total and all-encompassing wonder on her face drove an arrow of poignancy into my heart. It didn't get any better. Memories squeezed, locked away. The future a thing, an object, in the mist, ahead. Both past and future removed, cast aside for the now. A connection sought with a higher power reached, radiated. It anchored, filled me. I was home.

Chapter 41

Beaufort, South Carolina. Founded 1711. Now offering ice cream. And pralines for later, on the *Ace*. A gorgeous old town, oak trees dripping with Spanish moss. A walking town.

CC focused on the ice cream, absorbed with taste and texture. Tinker Juarez at her feet, focused on her treat. She insisted I taste hers, and her mine. A comparison, and insightful flavor comments followed.

Time floated, suspended. An adjustment, an accommodation of the Glock tucked in the back of my jeans—hidden under the tail of my shirt—the sole bridge to the rest of the world.

CC licked her upper lip, shared stares with her dog. Questioned a look my way.

"Maybe the last of the cone. He'd like that," I said.

Issue resolved, she focused again on the frozen treat. Fall and few tourists, middle of the week. A passerby stopped and scratched Tinker Juarez. The sun was bright and the breeze moderate. Beaufort was our turnaround spot. Three or so days, and she'd be back with Mom. I missed her, even as she sat next to me.

"Can we go see names?" she asked, the tip of her cone held toward the dog. Tinker took it gently, tugged it from her grasp. She'd meant a cemetery. Gravestones. How the fascination manifested from her past, unknown. Mom and I speculated it was years before, at Dad's funeral. It had been explained that Dad was in heaven. This was just his body. And funerals were to celebrate a person's life, now departed for a better place. The body, the grave, the headstone reminded us of them so we wouldn't forget.

CC could read. Slowly, she'd sound out the words. And wander among the headstones and obelisks and statues, stopping without pattern, speaking a name. And saying goodbye. And stating, "Enjoy heaven." Heartbreaking, but an exercise deemed harmless as the years passed. Mom didn't take her often, but trips with me afforded fresh opportunities.

A horse-drawn carriage stood nearby, waiting for a fare. A diversion, one that might take her away from seeing names.

"How about a carriage ride?" I asked, pointing to the waiting conveyance. Her eyes lit up.

"Can Tinker Juarez come?"

"Let's go see."

An extra twenty made it happen. With a slap of reins, we took a sedate ride through the small area of old-town Beaufort. We dodged hanging moss, waved at passersby. The driver's historic commentary contained the word *Revolutionary*—as in the Revolutionary War—as we passed historic sites. It was an opportunity to tickle her each time. She'd squirm and laugh as I repeated the word. He'd say it again, we'd repeat the tickling, until she'd wait for the word and begin howling before I touched her. The driver caught on, and—if it had been too long between historic references—would point along a street and say, "Revolutionary!" Tinker Juarez, excited, joined at each reference, barking.

"Case, Case! Such a good day!"

"A fine day, my love."

We passed the old Saint Helena's Anglican Church, a tall wall hiding its peaceful graveyard. But one of two cemetery entrances appeared, and CC blurted out, "Names!"

I asked the driver to stop.

"Are you sure, CC?"

"Yes. Yes, let's look. Please, Case. Please."

I paid the driver and helped CC read the historic marker between the old church and the brick graveyard walls. *Established in 1712. The church was used by the British to stable horses during the Revolution and used as a hospital in the Civil War. Among those buried in the churchyard are two British officers and three American Generals.*

"Let's go!" She tugged my hand, pulled me toward a wall opening, the wrought-iron gate open. I couldn't resist her enthusiasm, fascination, and had gone through such exercises before.

"We have to leave Tinker Juarez outside the cemetery."

"No."

"I'll tie his leash right here. At the gate."

"No." She shook her head, stared at the ground.

"He might pee on the gravestones. On the names."

She considered the possibility.

"That would be bad."

"That would be bad. But he's fine here. He'll wait."

Tinker wasn't pleased but settled on the cool gravel at the small entrance. The cemetery stood empty, quiet, with massive oaks thick throughout. Spanish moss hung, moved with the light breeze. Small stone walls, thigh-high, segregated sections of the graveyard. Ferns and moss had taken root along the tops of the small barrier walls. Other trees grew among the laid to rest. Palms, magnolias, redbuds. A maze of delineations, thick trees, old graves, and peaceful silence.

More than a thousand headstones. The stonework aged, watermarked. The etched names faded by time and weather. Gravel paths meandered throughout. Stone benches, rest for the living. The high brick perimeter wall isolated us, and deep shade under the canopy of trees cast subdued light. CC wandered, stopped, struggled to read a name, moved on.

"Ge . . ."

"Gebhart."

"No, Case! I can read."

"I know. Sorry."

I trailed her and confirmed pronunciations.

"So we can remember them," she said.

"That's right."

"But they're really in heaven."

"That's right."

She'd smile, nod, wander.

I paused at a collection of headstones from the 1700s, surrounded by another short stone wall. Were they remembered? Hard to say. Generations passed, the fog of time obscured, lineage forgotten.

I searched for CC, somewhere nearby. Past an old oak, along another short stone wall. Followed the path. A sense of something amiss filled me. Real and present danger. I turned a corner and bent my arm behind my back. Slid a hand over the Glock's grip.

They sat together on a low bench, seven paces distant. Nika held her pistol at my sister's back, her other hand locked on CC's arm. Too shocked to speak, CC radiated fear, horror. Her body expression cried for me to take her, save her. Nika used her as a shield, an opportunity, prior to killing.

"How appropriate for it to end at a graveyard."

"Let her go."

"You went too deep. Over your head."

Harsh exhales blew from CC. She sat at a lean, toward me, ready to propel herself in my direction. Nika's lock on her upper arm anchored the scene, offered no opportunity for immediate action, for the chance to do *something*.

"Let her go. This is about you and me."

"No, Case. This is about you. I'm merely the tool. The one who lowers the curtain."

Options, options—nothing. She'd kill both of us. No regrets, no remorse. A quick move, a rush toward them, would force her hand. Fire a shot. I'd take a bullet, maybe two, but the Glock would speak back. Kill her. Leaving CC. CC with two wounded, dying bodies.

"Think of how different it could have been." She smiled. Actually *smiled*.

"Walk away, Nika. It's over. I won't pursue." A lie. I'd pursue her to the gates of hell.

"Yes. Yes, it's over."

A breeze moved hanging moss behind them; a mockingbird chortled overhead. CC's look of desperation intensified, her exhales louder, explosive. She strained harder against the Russian's clench. Nika's eyes changed, the gauzed gaze of a killer pulling the trigger. I coiled to charge.

A red mist from the back of her head, haloed, the forehead exit hole dead center. The spit of a silencer pistol. And Nika leaned forward, collapsed. CC shot toward me, released. Glock pulled, I glanced for the shooter, absorbed CC's momentum, ensured she didn't look back. We ran, a protective arm around my sister. I cast frenzied searches for the other party.

We left through the other cemetery gate and paused. I pressed us against the tall wall, protection, and stole peeks inside. Nothing. No movement, no shooter.

"I don't like her." CC had quit panicking, moved forward, defined the moment. "I don't like her, Case."

Speckles of blood dotted her neck. I licked a handkerchief and wiped them away.

"You'll never see her again. Ever. I promise."

She hadn't seen Nika killed. Only release, movement, get away. Thank God.

We walked fast, the Glock in a front pants pocket. My hand still gripped the weapon. No clue who did it, or why. Government agent, another killer sent from a global player. It didn't matter. We were getting the hell out of here.

"Tinker Juarez!"

"Yes. We're getting him now."

Running would bring unwanted attention, even though the church grounds remained empty. Move. Move and don't panic CC. Move and retrieve the dog and get to the *Ace of Spades*.

"Tinker Juarez!"

"I know, my love. We're going there now." Around a high-walled corner adjacent to the old church, the next corner close by. CC's mind had left the event, focused on her four-legged companion. One more turn, the other gate a short distance, untie the dog. Move fast. Leave. Get to the *Ace*. Wheelhouse bulletproof windows. Get there, move, move.

Momentum carried us around the final turn, then a dead stop. Fallen leaves lifted, shifted in the breeze at the scene before us. CC pointed, giggled.

Tinker Juarez, tail wagging, pushed his head against the forehead of a squatting man who growled pitch for playful pitch with the dog. A game of billy goat, chins down, shoving, raucous, head against head. It was hard to discern Tinker Juarez's face as the wild red hair of the squatting man obscured the view.

Bo. Bo Dickerson, alive, in a head-butting battle with a dog. Outside the cemetery walls of the Saint Augustine Church in Beaufort, South Carolina. Mouth open, I was too stunned to move. Bo turned his face in our direction, forehead still in playful combat, smiled and winked. The grip of a pistol showed above the back of his jeans waistline, the long barrel and silencer outlined against his butt.

"He's funny!" CC said. She tugged me toward the two.

He stood, head cocked, arms outstretched.

"We're going to hug, goober boy. But don't squeeze too hard. Tender mercies, my brother. Be tender."

Hug we did, the medical wrappings around his midsection and left shoulder felt under his shirt. A sob, short, loud. Bo pressed my face against his neck, muffled any subsequent explosions of emotion. A gentle rock back and forth. Unreal. Unreal and lifesaving and too joyful to absorb.

CC untied the dog, and Bo addressed her. "I'm Bo."

"Case likes you."

"I like Case."

"I'm CC."

"I know. Case has told me about you. But he didn't tell me you were as beautiful as a princess on a mountaintop."

She laughed. Tinker Juarez stood on his hind legs, tried licking her face. Bo's shirt collar wiped tears.

He pushed me away, held my shoulders. "We gotta boogie. Depart. Pronto."

"How? How did you . . . ?"

He interrupted me. "Later. Let's go. Now."

We did. Bo grabbed his rucksack from the sidewalk, and the four of us, quick pace, moved toward water. Three blocks to the waterfront park, the *Ace* nestled among sailboats and cruisers.

A short mile later, we motored into the cuts and sloughs of the Harbor River, wove our way north. CC sat in the foredeck lounger, eating pralines. Tinker Juarez stood sentinel at the tip of the bow, nose to the wind.

Bo entered the wheelhouse. "It spins and it tumbles, does it not?"

"Life?"

"What else, my cretinous Georgia peach?" he asked. "What else?"

Chapter 42

Rhythms of water, tides. Shorelines passed. We took our time, no rush back to Charleston. Stops to walk, stretch our legs. Bo hung out in a hammock he'd purchased somewhere, napped, recovered.

We caught up after our Beaufort departure. I pressed for clarity, answers.

"Let's begin with the dead body we left behind."

"A Russian. With her gun at her side."

"That's the one."

We spoke in low tones, the wheelhouse door and windows open. CC nibbled her pralines, watched wonders drift past.

"It'll keep the local constabulary plenty busy. Intrigue. Mystery."

"I don't know, Bo."

"They'll figure a Russian mafia hit. I like CC. Her world abounds with joy."

"And we wash our hands. Cruise away."

"Already happened, old son. It lies behind us."

"A dead Russian lies behind us."

"The question is, what's before us? There lies the true intrigue. What's for supper?"

The Beaufort incident. Disappearing in our wake.

"Grilled pork chops. Tell me about the infamous Battle of the Dismal."

"Soon enough. This magnificent specimen before you is at less than full strength. I require rest."

And so he hung his hammock on the foredeck, under the tarp, next to CC and the lounger. They chatted, soft, Tinker curled at CC's feet. Bo drifted off, mouth open.

Dusk found us pulled up in a slough off the South Edisto River, alone and isolated. CC took Tinker for a shore romp, always within close distance of the *Ace*. New rule. The two-burner grill fired, pork chops and veggies prepared, a drink poured.

"The Dismal battle," I said. "I knew you were killed. Too much of your blood. Knew it."

"You truly dislike mystery, don't you?"

"Don't start."

He fished around his rucksack, produced a pipe and some weed, sat sideways across his hammock.

"I'll burn through this while CC is on shore."

"Bo."

"Dog on a bone, brother. You won't let it go."

"Bo."

A lighter fired, he took a deep hit, held it, exhaled through his nostrils. "Knew they were coming, of course. My cameras."

"And?"

"So I sashayed out for observation."

"How do you sashay in a swamp?"

"A challenge, admittedly."

"I bet."

"Observed Angel and his little party. When they, or rather Angel, cut the lines to my preventative measures, it struck me as less than hospitable. Truly."

His trip wires. It was a Delta member move, cutting them. An invasive move.

"You talk with him before it went down?"

"A bit. While he hid and his henchmen established an offensive perimeter."

"And?"

"And it's good. Good to see you, goober. Here on the *Ace*. Feels positive, fresh."

"Bo."

He took another hit, lifted his chin toward the pork chops. They required flipping. CC laughed from the shore. Tinker barked. I turned the meat, stirred the sautéing vegetables, sipped Grey Goose, and smiled. A bucolic scene, quiet.

"You wish gory details." His foot pushed off the deck, swung the hammock. The day's warmth began departing. I went belowdecks and brought back old blankets for the four of us.

"I saw remnants of the gore. Tell me what the hell happened."

"He prattled on about helping him. South America. Join the revolution. Now there, sadly, is an underused word. *Prattled*." He twisted, groaned from the pain, called to CC. "Where's your goat?"

She stopped and tilted her head. "Goat?"

"Your goat. Tinker Juarez."

She laughed and laughed. "He's not a goat!"

"Are you sure?"

More laughter, a declarative statement launched. "I like you, Bo."

"I like you, CC."

"He's not a goat!"

"Maybe you'd better ask *him.*"

She laughed again, found a stick, and threw it for Tinker. Bo eased back around.

"Lead flew. I got popped. The side and shoulder."

"And?"

"And I crawled into the water, planned on circling. Take out Angel."

"But you were too shot up."

"A development I quickly ascertained."

"I bet."

"I crawled to another island. Stripped to my skivvies, used my clothes to stanch the bleeding. Traveled that night, swam the Ditch, made my way to the old farmhouse. And the old pickup."

"So now you're at your farmhouse. Bleeding like a stuck pig."

"Got a South Mills veterinarian to stitch me up."

"A vet."

"Told him I'd die if he didn't take action. Probably true."

"A veterinarian."

"Former 82nd Airborne. He didn't ask too many questions. He understood, my brother. Understood."

"How you doing now?"

"No vitals struck. Lost a lot of blood."

"Not what I asked."

"My animal physician—and we could unpack that designation—even gave me pills. Antibiotics. Pain. All good."

"Back to how you're doing now."

"It hurts. But I can move. However, my break-dancing career is on hold."

CC and Tinker scrambled up the short gangplank. The pork chops sizzled, supper ready. We ate under the stars. CC regaled us with what she'd recently experienced with Tinker. Conversation flowed, laughter genuine, love permeating. I cleaned dishes and insisted Bo relax on the hammock. CC and Tinker put to bed belowdecks. I made the day's final Grey Goose and settled near Bo.

"The Russian," I started.

"She who no longer walks among us?"

"One and the same. How'd you find her? Or find me?"

He lit another bowl of weed, wrapped a blanket around his shoulders, and adjusted, with evident pain, in his hammock.

"Found you easy enough. You're not the sly bumpkin you make yourself out to be."

"Do tell."

"Rested at the vet's place a couple of days. Then back to the Dismal. The *Ace*, strangely enough, was gone. Disappeared." Another hit of weed with obvious discomfort during the inhale. "Considered a tear in the fabric of time and space."

"Of course. Always a possibility." Man, I missed him.

"But dismissed it for the far more probable scenario of a lonely man captaining his yacht down the Ditch."

"We just missed each other."

"Ships passing in the night," he said.

The Earth had settled back on its axis. Bo conversed, projected, and all was right.

"And then?" I asked.

"The aforementioned conveyance. My pickup. Headed south."

"Why south?"

"You'd head in the direction of home. Family."

"Maybe I didn't want to backtrack."

"Maybe you told yourself that."

Tinker groaned as he shifted on his bed of blankets belowdecks. CC woke and asked if he was happy. I padded to the top of the short flight of stairs and spoke softly. "Everything's okay, CC."

"I know. Good night."

"Love you."

"You too."

The *Ace* shifted as I made my way back to the lounger. Frogs called, stars filled the sky. A couple of pralines remained. We shared. Pecan pralines—fine and sweet.

"So you found me," I said.

"No. You suppose a predestined path plays with all this? Etched in cosmic stone while we pretend it's free will?"

"What do you mean, no?"

"Cosmic stone. Not a bad name for a rock band."

"Bo."

"Found this tub. The *Ace*. New Bern. The proprietor of the little docking area said you'd left a note. Back soon. So I waited."

"Then followed me. Why?"

"To cover your back, dumbass. Angel still roamed."

To cover my back. Shot to hell, his boat burned, with minimal possessions. And one focus. Cover my back.

"Know what you're thinking," he said. "You'd do the same for me."

And I would. Bo, Marcus, Catch. Anytime, anywhere.

"And what did you surmise from observing Case Lee, Esquire?"

"Tedious. Your chosen lifestyle. Glad you picked up CC. It adds brightness. Color."

"Sorry I bored you."

"I also picked up the trail of your Russian amore. As you departed Charleston."

"Nika was in Charleston?"

"Quick as a drugged sloth, you are."

Bad, bad news. If she could do it, others could. But she had the whole clandestine services of Russia behind her. Not a likely support mechanism for a plain-vanilla headhunter.

"She tracked you. I tracked her. And kept an eye out for Angel. I'm keeping this simple for you. How's Marcus?"

"How'd you know I'd gone to Montana?"

"I'm begging here. Fire a few synapses, Mr. Lee."

Well, he had a point. Thinking Bo dead, sending Mom into hiding. Where else would I have gone?

"You could have called me. Or did you enjoy having my heart ripped out."

A major bone of contention. He could have called, shown at one of my stops. Or warned me Angel might head for Montana. It irritated.

"I hunted. Angel, remember? On your trail. I didn't want you breaking your tedious patterns. Speaking of which, he's still around."

"No, Bo. No, he's not. But you could have announced your presence."

"He's not?"

"And CC's life was just on the line."

"A failing on my part. Didn't see that coming. Sorry."

"She's the one person on this planet not in the mix. Uninvolved."

"I know. I tailed the Russian to the graveyard but couldn't move fast enough to cut her off. Sorry, old son. I mean it."

My anger at CC's place in all this dissipated. Bo was Bo, and he clearly had not intended for the final act to play out the way it did. But emotions whirled, and I was going to have my say.

"Back to my feelings, my heart. Shitty thing to do."

"Keeping low moved your Russian friend into a pattern. Your pattern, her pattern. This Oklahoma lad at the tail end."

"Still sucks."

He shifted, cautious. Eased into a better position. "My apologies. But the righteous path, the sure way, led elsewhere."

"Why not shoot her and be done with it earlier?"

"Wasn't sure of her intent. Had an inkling, strong, but wasn't sure. What happened to Angel?"

"It tore me up thinking you were dead."

"Understood. Sorry. Now Angel."

My turn, and I plodded through the whole Montana affair. He didn't interrupt once, listened, eyes closed. Between sips of Grey Goose, I revealed details.

"Love?" Bo asked.

"It's what he said." Angel's sick rationale.

We sat in silence. A ship's horn sounded, miles away.

"I like the bulldozer bit."

"I didn't like any of it."

"And Catch has always been a helluva shot."

"Let's not critique the event, okay?"

He groaned again, shifted. I found another blanket and laid it across him. He'd settled for the night. I rested a hand on his ankle, squeezed. "Thank you, Bo. Thanks for covering me. For taking care of the Russian."

He wiggled the ankle I grasped.

"Thought maybe I'd see light, or a tunnel, or wash with universal warmth."

"At the veterinarian's?"

"Yeah. Nothing like that. But not lonely. I wasn't alone. Felt it. I've thought a lot about that."

"I think a lot about it, too."

"Going to sleep. *Vaya con Dios*, Case."

"You too, my brother. You too."

Epilogue

Winter, full force. At least full enough for south coastal Georgia. Sweater weather, the days short. I holed up, moored at small towns, and moved every few days. Ridgeville, Hickory Bluff, Jekyll Island. Good days, uneventful, although I remained armed and alert.

Executive Decisions emailed and offered a new gig. Something to do with the sapphire trade in Southeast Asia. Claim jumpers, theft, murder. I declined.

Bo stayed in Charleston a few days. Mom did her best and tried placing him on some variant—the Bo variant—of the straight and narrow. To no avail.

"Ma'am, I just don't clean up all that well," he'd told her. Mom sighed agreement.

He called Marcus, a conversation filled with joy and, at the end, critique from Montana. Bo countered with philosophical positions based on parts unknown. Ten to one Marcus made himself a drink after the call.

When he called Catch, it had been short and sweet and unexpected.

"Very good," he'd told me. "Pacific Northwest."

"You're heading Catch's way?"

"*Señor* Hernandez. Conquistador strain. Nestled in the dripping conifers of Portland."

"Should I alert the state of Oregon?"

"You should celebrate, my friend. A new adventure awaits."

I had a glass of wine with Mom's female selection for me. A nice woman, kind, but no sparks flew from either side. I did commit to a more social existence. Reached out, called people. Chatted.

Special Agent Abbie Rice. The phone atmosphere was relaxed, easy. She bugged me again about partnership. I bugged her about finding the bagman for the bounties. Good-natured, and I expressed an interest in sharing wine with her and her partner next time I visited the DC area.

Irene Collins. A simple chat, noncommittal on both sides. Pleasant, no grating interludes. I promised to keep in touch.

Oh, and Jules. Sent her a note. *Redheaded stranger alive and well. Staying low for a while.*

She didn't reply.

Bo had departed; time for the pain of goodbyes with Mom and CC. Mom claimed complete befuddlement at my rejection of her matchmaking choice.

"No rejection, Lola Wilson. Just no fire."

"You can build a fire, son of mine."

Mom and CC joined me at the dock. The *Ace* idled, untied. A big hug and kiss for Mom, and I promised a near-future return trip. Then CC. She always cried. My heart always ripped.

"You remember the one big thing, CC?"

She looked up from the hug and cast a small smile. The offshore breeze ruffled her hair, flyaways stuck to her tears.

"You love me. More than the sun."

"And?"

"More than the moon."

"And?"

"And more than the stars! That's a lot!"

"And always will, my love. I always will."

Thank you for reading *The Suriname Job*!

I hope you enjoyed the experience, and thank you for joining me on the trip.

If you would like to get updates and insights on the next Case Lee adventure, please join my newsletter list by simply pasting the below link into your browser.

http://eepurl.com/cWP0iz

And I need to ask a favor. If you are so inclined, I'd love a review of *The Suriname Job* on Amazon.com. Whether you relished it or it put you to sleep, I would appreciate your feedback. Reviews mean a lot to potential new readers.

If you enjoyed *The Suriname Job*, please check out Case Lee's second adventure—***The New Guinea Job**.*

Also, be sure to check out the books in my good-versus-evil Challenged World series. Come celebrate remarkable characters who band together to confront dark supernatural forces.

***The Unknown Element**

Pretty Little Creatures

Gather the Seekers.*

Again, thank you so much for dedicating the time to spend with me and Case in *The New Guinea Job*. Here's hoping you and yours are doing well. And remember, we're all in this together.

Sincerely,

Vince Milam

Made in the USA
Columbia, SC
16 September 2022

67387023R00148